THE CAT SITTER'S
WHISKERS

This Large Print Book carries the
Seal of Approval of N.A.V.H.

A DIXIE HEMINGWAY MYSTERY

THE CAT SITTER'S WHISKERS

BLAIZE AND JOHN CLEMENT

THORNDIKE PRESS
A part of Gale, Cengage Learning

GALE
CENGAGE Learning·

Farmington Hills, Mich • San Francisco • New York • Waterville, Maine
Meriden, Conn • Mason, Ohio • Chicago

GALE
CENGAGE Learning®

Copyright © 2015 by Blaize and John Clement.
Thorndike Press, a part of Gale, Cengage Learning.

ALL RIGHTS RESERVED
This is a work of fiction. All of the characters, organizations, and events portrayed in this novel are either products of the authors' imaginations or are used fictitiously.
Thorndike Press® Large Print Mystery.
The text of this Large Print edition is unabridged.
Other aspects of the book may vary from the original edition.
Set in 16 pt. Plantin.

LIBRARY OF CONGRESS CATALOGING-IN-PUBLICATION DATA

Clement, Blaize.
    The cat sitter's whiskers / by Blaize and John Clement. — Large print edition.
        pages cm. — (Thorndike Press large print mystery)
    ISBN 978-1-4104-7995-2 (hardcover) — ISBN 1-4104-7995-1 (hardcover)
    1. Hemingway, Dixie (Fictitious character)—Fiction. 2. Women detectives—Florida—Fiction. 3. Pet sitting—Fiction. 4. Siesta Key (Fla.)—Fiction. 5. Large type books. I. Clement, John, 1962– II. Title.
PS3603.L463C45 2015b
813'.6—dc23   2015016239

Published in 2015 by arrangement with St. Martin's Press, LLC

Printed in Mexico
1 2 3 4 5 6 7 19 18 17 16 15

For Blaize . . . you'll always have the last word.

ACKNOWLEDGMENTS

As always, thanks go to my beloved friends and family; to my editor, Marcia Markland, for her vision; to Dana Beck, Hellyn Sher, and David Urrutia for their encouragement and feedback; to Elizabeth Cuthrell and Steven Tuttleman for their support; to Sharon Salzburg, Dr. Anna Owren Fayne, and the men and women of the Sarasota Sheriff's Department for helping me get my facts straight; to the team that keeps me in line: Kat Brzozowski and Quressa Robinson at St. Martin's Press, and Al Zuckerman at Writer's House; and finally to my amazing and generous readers and fans, who have welcomed me into Dixie's world with open hearts.

The ache for home lives in all of us,
the safe place
where we can go as we are
and not be questioned.
— Maya Angelou

1

It was a little after 5:00 on Monday morning when I pulled my bike out and brushed off the dewy cobwebs that had appeared between the spokes overnight. The sky was coal-black except for the vaguest hint of pale pink breaking at the horizon to the east. I knew once the sun got herself situated it would be hot as blue blazes, but for now there was a cool breeze riding in on the waves from the ocean, so I zipped up my hoodie before I rolled across the courtyard.

It was still pretty dark and there was a blanket of fog covering everything. Anybody else would've needed a bike light — the driveway twists and turns through the jungle that separates my place from the main road — but I've been riding up and down this narrow lane since I was a little girl. I know it like the back of my hand. Plus, my bike light burned out two years ago.

The crunching sound the bike's wheels made in the crushed shell sent the yellow parakeets in the treetops bouncing around like kernels of corn on a hot skillet. I mouthed a silent, *sorry,* for waking them up so early.

I'm Dixie Hemingway, no relation to you-know-who (as far as I know). I'm a cat sitter. I live on Siesta Key, a sliver of sand that hugs the shoreline of Sarasota, Florida, about midway down the state on the Gulf side. On a map, our little island looks like a prehistoric heron — a slender, feathered dinosaur with long, graceful legs hanging south and a scraggly neck stretching north, with Bay Island as its beak pointing east toward the mainland. I like to imagine it's a faithful sentry, keeping an eye on Sarasota and all its suburbs, guarding it from angry sea dragons and marauding pirates (or at the very least absorbing blows from the occasional hurricane).

I mostly take care of cats, but I do have a few dog clients here and there. In fact, I'll pretty much take care of anything — hamsters, lizards, parrots, iguanas, rabbits . . . but not snakes. If I get a call from somebody with a snake that needs looking after, I politely decline and refer them to someone else. First of all, I hate snakes.

Second of all, I hate snakes.

Yes, I know we're all God's creatures and everything, but I'm not sure God was thinking straight when she came up with the idea of a fanged, slithering cylinder of scale-encrusted muscle that goes around swallowing whole animals alive. Just the thought of it makes me want to jump up on a chair and stay there for the rest of my life.

At the end of the driveway I looked both ways — mostly out of habit. At this hour, Midnight Pass is pretty much deserted except for maybe a few early-bird scrub lizards skittering back and forth in search of breakfast, hoping to get a head start on their less ambitious friends. The fog was moving along the road, and as I rolled to a stop little wisps of it curled up around me like baby ghosts.

I took a moment to breathe in the cool, salty air, imagining it filling my entire body all the way down to my toes. This is my favorite time of day, when there's not a soul in sight and all the world is mine. I'm not really the type to wake up and loll around in bed half the day reading magazines and eating donuts . . . well, actually that's exactly the type I am, but I'd go broke in two seconds flat if I let myself do that, so I always get up early. It's the only way I can

13

manage to fit all my clients in.

I was just about to lean on the pedals and take off into town when something stopped me. I inched the bike out into the road and peered down toward the end of the island, waiting for my eyes to adjust to the darkness. At first all I could see was the faded lines on the asphalt disappearing into the mist, but then something dark floated into my vision on the right.

There, at some indiscernible distance — it could have been a hundred feet, it could have been twenty inches — was a looming, motionless field of darkness, just slightly darker than the black shadows around it. My heart started racing. I didn't know exactly what it was, but I knew one thing for certain: it wasn't supposed to be there.

Slowly, I let my backpack slide off my shoulders and zipped it open with trembling hands. I whispered, "Stop shaking, you idiot. It's probably just a . . ." But I couldn't come up with anything good.

A few weeks earlier, a woman outside Sarasota had opened her back door to find a six-hundred-pound black bear helping himself to the bird feeders on her patio. The first thing she'd done was scream bloody murder. Then she slammed the door and called animal control while the bear lumbered off into the woods.

He hadn't been seen since.

As I fumbled around in my backpack for a flashlight, I reminded myself that a bear would have to walk over one of the two bridges to get to the island, either that or swim clear across the bay, both of which seemed pretty unlikely. Just as my fingers closed around the cold metal of my flashlight, the entire road beyond the dark shape filled with white light, and a moment later two glowing orbs of red appeared at its center.

Well, I thought, *it's finally happening. They've come to take me to their mother planet.*

I'd read about it. Innocent country folk sucked out of a cornfield and flown to a research lab in another galaxy, where they're probed and prodded by slimy, mute aliens with eyes big as bowling balls. Then they're flown home and released back to the field they disappeared from, with their memories erased and nothing to show for their journey except some sore spots in various embarrassing places on their bodies.

As I saw myself being interviewed by Oprah and describing my vivid memories of being a human guinea pig in space, I heard the sound of an engine start up and rumble softly.

The black shape was a car, a dark brown four-door sedan parked on the side of the road about fifty feet past my driveway. I dropped the flashlight down in the side pocket of my cargo shorts and let out a sigh of relief . . . with maybe just a smidgen of disappointment mixed in.

At this end of the island most of the houses are the kind you only get to see in movies or on old reruns of *Lifestyles of the Filthy Rich and Annoyingly Fabulous.* They're hidden behind manicured hedges and meticulously kept gardens, which of course you can't see because *those* are hidden behind big iron gates and stucco walls painted shell-coral or lemon-yellow and overflowing with masses of flowering bougainvillea. The walls are mostly a security measure — sometimes there's even a coil of razor ribbon hidden beneath those innocent-looking vines — but they also serve a more practical purpose: keeping the riffraff like me from being able to stand around and gawk and upload pictures to Twitter and Facebook.

In other words, it's not the kind of neighborhood where people park their cars on the street. They house them in garages

16

bigger and nicer than my whole apartment. Hell, some of their *cars* are bigger and nicer than my whole apartment, so I knew there was only one person who could have been parked on the side of the road this early in the morning: Levi Radcliff, the paperboy.

Well, *boy* isn't exactly the right word.

Levi's about thirty-five, the same age as me. We went to high school and junior high together, but I still call him the paperboy because he's been delivering the *Herald-Tribune* for about as long as I can remember. He couldn't have been much older than twelve when he started.

He was a big shot in high school — good-looking, blond, star of the baseball team. After we graduated there was talk of sports scholarships and professional recruiters, but nothing ever came of it. I'd heard rumors of drinking getting in the way, but I never really found out what happened. He'd started spending a lot of time hanging out with friends and surfing, and I figured he'd just decided a life at the beach was good enough.

And anyway, people's dreams don't always pan out. Believe me. I know.

I guess I should mention that Levi was the first boy I ever kissed. Yep . . . it sounds like a big deal, and in a way I guess it was, but it wasn't like we had some big hot and heavy romance. It was ninth grade, after all. I guess we were old enough to know what we were doing, and yet still young enough to have absolutely no clue. It happened in Hallway B in the old Sarasota High building, just outside Mrs. White's history class.

We were playing "Who Am I?" a game that Mrs. White claimed to have invented herself, where two people were sent out of the classroom, one boy and one girl, and then the class chose two prominent figures from history. The two kids were called back in, and then they each took turns asking the class questions about their secret identity. Whoever guessed right first was the winner.

There was only one rule. While you waited in the hallway and the class chose your identity, you were supposed to stand with your back against the lockers so you couldn't hear, but of course we always cheated. I was on my hands and knees with my right ear pressed against the door, and Levi was crouched down just in front of me, cupping his left ear against the gap of the doorjamb. I can still feel the giddy rush of adrenaline at the prospect of getting caught, and of course we couldn't really hear a thing because all the kids were talking at once, and then the next thing I knew Levi leaned forward and kissed me — not on the cheek or forehead or anything like that. Right on the lips. And I didn't move, I just stayed there, perfectly still, with my lips slightly puckered. His eyes were closed, but mine were wide open, like a deer in the headlights.

I remember thinking it was a little rude of him not to ask first, like he didn't even care one bit if I wanted to be kissed or not, but I was so overcome with the excitement of it all that I didn't dwell on it. At the clicking sound of Mrs. White's high heels approaching, we both leapt up and threw ourselves against the lockers, just in time for Mrs. White to swing the door open and call us back in.

I was in such shock that I could barely concentrate, and I don't remember which of us won, just that it turned out I was Rosa Parks and Levi was Amerigo Vespucci. After class, Levi must have bragged to his friends about what had happened, because by the time the school bell rang at the end of the day we were officially a couple.

Everybody was talking about it — well . . . everybody except me and Levi. We just continued on as if nothing had happened, and within a few weeks the whole thing was forgotten.

Of course, I should have recognized his

car — a lovingly restored Buick LeSabre convertible that he'd bought senior year with money he'd saved from his paper route — but it was too dark and foggy. I hoisted my backpack over my shoulder and waited. He'd probably pulled over to look at his delivery list or make a quick phone call, but I noticed the engine was making a funny hiccuping noise every once in a while — as if it might stall any minute — so I figured I'd better check on him just in case he was having car trouble.

I wheeled my bike around, but when I got about even with the back bumper he pulled forward and headed off down the Key, leaving me in a cloud of sooty exhaust.

So much for being a good Samaritan.

I pulled my phone out to check the time. It was already 5:15.

In the dead of summer, when it feels like the Florida sun has a personal beef with you, a lot of full-time residents hop on a plane and escape to cooler climates for as long as their bank accounts allow, but since most pets, especially those of the feline persuasion, aren't exactly thrilled with the idea of air travel, that means it's usually the busiest time of year for me. I knew if I didn't get a move on I'd never stay on schedule, plus I figured if Levi was having

20

car trouble he certainly didn't need me. He was a big boy and could take care of himself.

The parakeets had quieted down again, but I knew any minute there'd be a chorus of birds announcing the new day. For now, though, they were probably still snoozing away in their leafy beds.

Looking back, if I'd known what was right around the corner I would have gone back to bed myself. In fact, if I'd known what was coming my way I'd have gladly hopped aboard a spaceship, flown clear across the universe, and submitted myself to any and all experiments those slimy aliens could come up with.

But that's not what I did. Instead, I slipped my phone down in my back pocket, stood up on the pedals, and headed out for a brand-new day.

2

I hate the word *widow*. It makes me think of black spiders or gaunt-faced spinsters wasting away in a decrepit old shack down by the river, but I might as well tell you right off the bat that I am one. My husband Todd and my daughter Christy were both killed in a freak car accident about five years ago. I could tell you the exact number of months, weeks, days and hours that have passed since then, but I know I'd come off a little "tetched," as my grandmother used to say, so let's just pretend the numbers are getting mushy around the edges.

Christy was three years old. You'd think my memory would be frozen, that I'd still see her as the same scrawny, independent, headstrong little girl she was on the day she died. But no. In my mind, she's almost nine now. She has a burgeoning collection of silver dollars — one for every baby tooth she's lost — and any day now she'll put in a request for her own smartphone. We have words like *widow* and *orphan* to describe people who've lost loved ones, but there's no word for a mother who's lost a child.

That's because it never stops.

Up until the day my world shattered, five years, blah-blah months, so-and-so days, and whatchamacallit hours ago, I was a deputy with the Sarasota Sheriff's Department. I was good at my job. *Real* good. I traveled the streets in my patrol cruiser, my mirrored sunglasses perched on my nose, my department-issued SIG Sauer 9mm handgun tucked securely in my side holster. Protecting children, catching criminals, rescuing tree-bound kittens . . . you know the type. Just another blond badass, making the world a better place.

But the day Todd and Christy died, a little switch flipped in my head — a *crazy* switch. I'll spare you the details, but let's just say all parties involved agreed it would be best if I took a little break from law enforcement. This is Florida. There are enough maniacs walking around with guns as it is.

After wallowing in my own wacko for about a year, I finally managed to stand upright and fraternize with the human race again. I have Michael, my older brother, to thank for that. He'd always taken care of me, even when we were little kids, but that whole year he barely left my side. I remember watching his hands as he laid out lunch for me and set the tray down on my bed. I remember him gently waving a spoon-ful of homemade soup under my nose and whispering, "Mmmm, soup!" as if I were a brain-addled infant barely capable of feed-ing myself . . . which basically is what I was.

I don't know what I would have done without him.

The sky had lightened by the time I biked into the village, enough that all the leaves were glittering with dew. There'd only been one other car on the road the whole way into town, but it had stayed back at least half a mile, not going much faster than I was, which meant it was probably Levi. I knew he started his route on the south end of the Key and worked his way up.

I didn't have much farther to go, just a couple more blocks and left on Island Circle Road to my first client of the day: Barney Feldman, an eight-year-old Maine Coon. Mr. Feldman (only his closest friends call him Barney) lords over the two thousand square feet of his domain like a pirate guarding a treasure ship, which makes sense when you consider that Maine Coons are believed to have descended from cats that traveled around the world on Viking ships in the eleventh century.

He lives with his owners, Buster and Linda Keller, in a decidedly nondescript three-bedroom ranch house. It's all white stucco, with a simple lean-to carport off the right side and a poured concrete driveway in front, cracked and buckling in its old age. If you didn't know better, you'd assume it was just an old tear-down waiting for somebody to snatch it up for a few thousand dollars and put a proper house in its place. But this is Siesta Key, and the beach is only a two-minute walk away. The Kellers bought their home ten years ago for roughly half a million dollars. There's no telling what it's worth today.

As I rolled up the driveway, I didn't think Levi had beat me there, but I glanced around for the newspaper just in case. Then I remembered Mrs. Keller saying that, like a lot of people, they got all their news online now, which was bad for the *Herald-Tribune* but great for me, since it meant I wouldn't have to worry about collecting the newspapers while they were away.

I propped the bike up next to the front door and fished around in my backpack for my chatelaine, the big brass ring I keep all my keys on. It seems like every client I've ever had wants me to keep a key to their home just in case there's an emergency. I've never sat down and done an official count, but there must be at least a couple hundred keys on it, if not more. It's about as heavy as a bucket of clams. At first it was hard to keep track of them all, but eventually I worked out a system. Each key is individually numbered with a permanent marker, and then I have a list that matches each key to its owner, which I keep in the same notebook where I write down all my alarm codes and pet instructions.

There was a time when I carried that notebook around with me, but after a while it just seemed too risky. If the wrong person got their hands on both my chatelaine and my notes, they could make off with half the valuables on this island, so I keep it hidden in my apartment for now. I'd tell you where, but then you'd be suspect number one if it ever went missing, so let's just say it's in a safe place.

As I was unlocking the door, I thought I heard a car in the street behind me, but by the time I had the door open and looked back, it was gone. I punched in the code for the alarm system, dropped my stuff on the white leather bench next to the front door, and knelt down to untie my sneakers.

The Kellers have a strict no-shoes policy, which I thought was kind of silly until I saw the inside of their house. You wouldn't think a place so drab and boring on the outside could be so elegantly stunning on the inside, but it is. The furniture is all sleek and modern and covered in soothing shades of sand and fawn and bird's-egg-blue, with bleached hardwood floors buffed to a shiny gloss and walls painted a soft milky gray. It's like walking through the dunes at dusk.

As I kicked my sneakers off, hopping around on one foot and then the other, I noticed there was a small box on the floor, tucked back under the bench at the far end. It had a white address label on top, but no postage, and there were some red FRAGILE stickers on both ends. I made a mental note to ask Mrs. Keller if she'd meant to mail it. I knew they'd been in a rush when they left the night before because she'd called to apologize for leaving the house in such a mess.

Of course, for Mrs. Keller, *mess* probably just meant a couple of unwashed coffee cups in the sink.

"Mr. Feldman?"

I didn't exactly expect him to come running. Dogs like to greet you at the door and dance around your feet, bouncing this way and that while they tell you how *absolutely* fabulous you are, how *absolutely* overwhelmed with excitement they are, and how they *absolutely* adore you. Cats are a little different. They're glad you've arrived, but they're certainly not about to embarrass themselves with such demeaning displays of subservience.

Instead, they'll allow you to give them a few good scritches between the ears while they stretch themselves into a scary-cat shape, and then maybe they'll circle around your legs, purring loudly to let you know that you are indeed loved. I smiled to myself. Barney has his own particular way of greeting visitors. As I pulled my socks up around my ankles, I gave a little nod to the room.

"Good morning, everybody."

That wasn't meant for Barney. That was my customary greeting for what was hanging on the walls all around me — Mrs. Keller's passion, or, as Mr. Keller refers to it, his "financial ruin."

Masks. All kinds of masks. Big masks. Small masks. Wooden masks from India, sequined masks from New Orleans, feathered masks from Siberia, healing masks, ceremonial masks, tribal masks, voodoo masks, and dozens of other masks from parts of the world I've never even heard of.

They're all artfully arranged on the walls in every room of the house, including the laundry room, the hallways, the bathrooms — even the walk-in closet off the master bedroom. Some of them are quite simple, like the stone masks with blank oval mouths frozen in a perpetual *OH!* like a shocked smiley face. Others are more fancy affairs, with seashells for teeth and marbles for eyes, and headdresses adorned with brightly colored feathers and painted beads.

Mrs. Keller's latest addition was a big wooden mask from the Himalayas, hanging dead center in the middle of the wall facing the front door. I remembered how her voice had dropped to a conspiratorial whisper when she told me where she'd found it — in a "charming little gallery" on the outskirts of Tampa. She'd said the owner of the shop had had no idea how rare it was, and that it was probably worth a small fortune.

It was a man's face, intricately carved out of wood and painted with bright splashes of red, green, and banana-yellow, with gnashing teeth, arched eyebrows, and a string of tiny bleached-white bird skulls perched on the top of its head like a crown. Mrs. Keller said it was from a region in Tibet called

Aroomy Choo Pinky, or something like that, but I just called him "Dick Cheney."

The expression on his face was either a mischievous grin or a gruesome snarl, depending on the angle, and his sinister eyes seemed to follow me around the room, watching my every move.

I tipped my chin in his direction. "Hey, Mr. Cheney. How's it hangin'?"

He didn't answer.

Mrs. Keller had told me that when her husband found out how much she had paid for Dick Cheney, he nearly had a nervous breakdown. He accused her of systematically wasting away their retirement fund, and if she didn't get ahold of herself they'd end up living in an old refrigerator box down on the beach. To make up with him, she'd made a solemn promise: no more masks, which, I have to say, I was a little sorry to hear.

You'd think it would have been kind of creepy walking around with all those soulless faces staring out from the walls, but over time they've grown on me. Every time I take care of Mr. Feldman, I look forward to seeing Mrs. Keller's latest purchase. Each mask is stunning and beautiful in its own peculiar way, and I can see why she loves them so much. I'm not sure I could live with them 24/7, but they're wonderful to visit every once in a while.

I padded into the kitchen to get Barney Feldman's breakfast ready, taking care to steer clear of the credenza in the hallway just in case he was hiding underneath it. Maine Coons are known for their sweet disposition, but Mr. Feldman is not your typical Maine Coon. Don't get me wrong, he's an angel most of the time, but just like those Vikings his ancestors used to hang out with, he's got a mischievous streak of savagery in him.

Occasionally he likes to set up camp under the furniture and take sharp-clawed swipes at innocent passersby, which was why I had pulled my socks up, naively hopeful that they'd protect my ankles. The six-inch space under the hall credenza isn't exactly Barney's favorite staging ground, but I wasn't taking any chances. As I went by, I hugged the wall.

In the kitchen, I cleaned out his water bowl and filled it with fresh water, and as soon as he heard the silverware drawer open and the clunk of the can opener on the countertop, he came running in with a couple of chirps, as innocent as can be, and greeted me with an excited, *"Thrrrrrip!"*

I said, "Oh, Mr. Feldman! What a

31

coweenky-dink. I was just about to serve your breakfast."

He trotted over and rubbed his cheek against my ankles, pointing his tail straight up like an exclamation point and wriggling it in anticipation. He's long and muscular, with thick chocolate fur soft as velvet and ticked with undulating bands of cream and gold. All four of his paws are dipped in pure black, and his wise old-soul eyes sparkle like pointcut aquamarines.

"We've got a special treat on the menu today, just so you know."

I mixed a couple of spoonfuls of tuna in the bowl with his allotted breakfast portion of kibble — about half a cup — and then laid it down on his plastic-coated place mat at the foot of the dishwasher. The place mat is there because Barney Feldman is not a tidy eater. He likes to pull pieces of food out and line them up on the floor around his dish like trophies from a hunting expedition. Then he pounces on them one by one, making a complete mess of everything in the process.

I figured while he ate I'd take a spin around the house just to make sure nothing was out of order. I always do an inspection of all my clients' houses, even if I'm just taking care of a bowl of goldfish. You never know what you might find: a leak in the roof or a houseplant that needs a little TLC. Plus, with cats there's always the very real possibility that they might have woken up in the middle of the night with the best idea *ever,* like applying a fringed edge to the arms of your favorite love seat, or maybe peeing in the middle of your pillow so you'll always have a memento of your time away. Barney Feldman is usually on his best behavior, though, so I wasn't expecting any surprises.

When I got back to the kitchen, he was nowhere in sight, but he'd eaten every bit of his breakfast. I took his bowl and place mat over to the sink and scrubbed them both with a soapy sponge, then I went back over to the antique cupboard and pulled open one of its heavy wooden drawers. Inside was a bundle of plastic grocery bags wrapped in a rubber band. As I loosened one of the bags, there were some lightning-fast paw swipes at the space where my feet should have been.

I said, "Nice try."

I pictured him wearing a horned Viking helmet and swinging his paws back and forth like two battleaxes, but I was standing a good three feet away and stretching my arms out to reach the drawer, so my ankles were safe.

I dropped the tuna lid down in the bag and wrapped it up. The Kellers wouldn't be home for a week, so I didn't want to leave anything smelly in the garbage under the sink. The laundry room is just off the kitchen, and beyond that is a short hallway leading out to the carport where the garbage cans are kept. The side door locks automatically with a spring that pulls it shut, so I always prop it open with an old tin flower bucket that the Kellers keep nearby for umbrellas.

It's not the best system in the world, mainly because given half a chance Barney will sprint out any open door as if his life depends on it, but also because the flower bucket is pretty top-heavy. It can easily tip over from the weight of the door, and then, *click* . . . you're locked out. I found that out the hard way, so I always leave the front door unlocked when I come in, just in case.

I propped the door open and padded over to the garbage cans, which are enclosed in a cedar-paneled bin to fend off marauding raccoons. Keeping an eye on the door just in case Barney tried to escape, I lifted up the door on top of the bin, dropped the bag down in the garbage, and then hustled back inside, sliding the flower bucket back in place with my foot as the door pulled itself closed.

When I turned around to head back into the kitchen, I came face-to-face with none other than Dick Cheney.

The first thing I thought was, *Hey, you're not supposed to be here.* But then I noticed something different. He seemed to have arms and legs. He wore a long-sleeved black sweatshirt and dark track pants. My lips formed into a *W* with the intention of saying, *What the f . . . ?* But I never got that far. It was like watching a movie projected onto a screen right in front of me.

He raised one of his arms up over his crown of tiny bird skulls, and I saw he was holding something about the size of a softball in his black-gloved fist. It was a white stone figurine, like a Buddha, except naked, with voluminous breasts and a bald head as smooth as a river stone. It hovered in the air for a moment, and then, as if in slow motion, came down right on top of my head.

Just before it hit me, I noticed its little naked feet. The toes were painted bright crimson red.

After that, the movie screen went completely dark.

3

I could hear a faint ringing in the distance, sort of like a church bell, and the first thing I saw was Barney Feldman's big fluffy face looming over me. I was lying flat on my stomach with my head turned to the side and my cheek smashed into the floor, and Barney was gazing at me with a slightly worried expression. He seemed to be saying, *It's a good thing you woke up because I have no idea how to use the phone.*

My whole head was throbbing, and when I tried to roll over to my side a blistering pain went bouncing through my skull and right down my spine, all the way to the soles of my feet. I let out a low moan, which apparently Barney took to mean everything was fine now, because he licked one black paw and drew it daintily across his long whiskers.

I did a quick inventory up and down my body. My clothes were on, which is always a

36

good thing, and I didn't see blood anywhere, which is also a good thing, and except for the throbbing pain in my head and a vague ringing in my ears everything seemed okay.

I rolled over on my back and then slowly sat up on my elbows, trying as hard as I could to ignore the pain as I waited for my blurry eyes to focus. There was a shaft of sunlight streaming in through the window illuminating tiny specks of dust floating in the air, and I tried to decipher by the sun's angle what time it was . . . until I remembered my cell phone in my back pocket. I pulled it out and looked at the screen.

It was 6:30, which meant I must have been out cold for at least a half hour. I was about to close the phone and lay it on the floor next to me when I noticed something else on the screen. There was one missed call and a new voice mail: It was from Mrs. Keller.

I almost laughed out loud at the irony of it. While I was lying there knocked out cold on the floor of her laundry room, she had left a message. I wondered if she'd called to ask me to mail that box in the foyer, or maybe to warn me about statue-wielding, mask-wearing degenerates sneaking around inside her house looking for unsuspecting cat sitters.

I had a view through the laundry room into the kitchen, which opened up into the living room beyond, and at first everything seemed perfectly normal, but then the gauzy curtains behind the couch billowed out slightly and I realized with a jolt that the folding glass doors leading to the back garden were standing wide open. In front of the couch was a marble-topped coffee table, and when I saw what was sitting on top of it, I froze.

There were two tapered candles. One red, the other black, and they were both lit. Their yellow-white flames were flickering gently in the breeze from the open doors.

I flipped my phone open and punched in the numbers as fast as I could.

"911. What is your emergency?"

I whispered, "This is Dixie Hemingway, I have a code 11-99. Somebody just hit me over the head with a statue and I think it's possible they're still in the house."

The operator's voice was thin and nasal. He said, "They hit you with a statue?"

"Yeah, a little statue made of stone or marble or something."

"Are you bleeding?"

"No, but it knocked me out and I just

woke up."

"What's your location, ma'am?"

"I'm . . . in the laundry room."

"Okay . . . I'm showing an address of 22 Island Circle, is that correct?"

Close enough, I thought. "Yes, that's it."

"Are you able to get out of the house safely?"

I looked around for Barney but he had disappeared. "Um, I don't know."

"I'm sending help now. Stay where you are."

I slid my hand down my hip and felt for my holster. "Okay. I'll search the house."

His voice rose. "Excuse me? No, you need to stay right where you are. You need to —"

I interrupted as I felt my fingers close around the handle of my pistol. "It's okay, I'm a sheriff's dep—"

But before I could finish I looked down at my hand. I was holding my little flashlight out in front of me, absentmindedly fluttering my thumb around its base looking for the safety release.

The operator's voice cut through. "Ma'am? You need to stay put, do you hear me?"

Just then the room started spinning.

"Yeah," I whispered as I let my head touch the floor with a gentle thud. "I hear you."

■ ■ ■ ■

I'm not completely sure how long I lay there before they arrived, but it felt like an eternity. I spent the entire time straining to hear any sounds from inside the house, which wasn't easy since the ringing in my ears wouldn't stop and I felt like I'd been injected with a dose of morphine big enough to take down the Jolly Green Giant. There were literally waves of sleepiness washing over me.

I tried not to think about the fact that I'd just mistaken my flashlight for a pistol, or that I even thought I was carrying a pistol in the first place. Instead, I concentrated on what I'd learned in law enforcement training about concussions and ran down the symptoms: Trauma to the head? Yep. Extreme Lethargy? Yep. Mental confusion? Well, I'd come back to that one, but it wasn't looking good.

I closed my eyes and sighed.

It was bad enough some low-life punk had snuck up on me, and worse still that he'd hammered me to the ground with a big-bosomed Buddha, or that he'd taken the time to light a couple of candles, which was super creepy, but the worst part was the possibility that he might still be lurking around inside the house somewhere. You'd think the thought of that would have sent me into a total panic, but it didn't. I just kept telling myself everything would be fine as long as I stayed calm and alert.

Barney Feldman had taken up his post again, purring loudly and watching over me with a serene expression on his face. That made me feel better, too. I figured if there actually was somebody in the house Barney wouldn't have been so relaxed. Just as I was congratulating myself for staying awake in spite of the overwhelming urge to sleep, I felt something press my hand gently. I opened my eyes to find, not Barney Feldman looking down at me, but Deputy Jesse Morgan. He was kneeling at my side.

"Dixie? You okay?"

I thought for a moment. I've known Morgan for years. He's one of the Key's few sworn deputies, which basically means he's licensed to carry a gun. He's about as fun as a barrel of monkeys, minus the monkeys, but he's tall and lean, with sharp cheekbones, broad shoulders, and a buzzed, military-style haircut — exactly the type of guy you want around if there's any trouble.

I said, "I'm fine . . . sort of."

"You've got a pretty good bump there."

41

I reached up and ran my fingers through my hair. There was a tender bulge the size of a small plum on the very top of my head.

I said, "Yeah, I was here taking care of the Kellers' cat, and somebody snuck up and hit me."

He frowned. "Somebody hit you?"

"Yeah, with a statue. It was a fat bald woman, and her toes were painted red."

He raised an eyebrow. "A fat, bald woman with red toes hit you?"

Morgan's not the brightest bulb in the box. I shook my head. "No, the statue. Dick Cheney hit me."

He squinted his eyes and nodded. "Uh-huh."

"He was about my height, more or less, and dressed head to toe in black."

"Dick Cheney."

"Yeah, one of the masks . . . he had one of the masks on. And I left the front door unlocked, so I don't know if he was already here or if he snuck in after me."

He nodded. "Okay, I think we better get you to a hospital."

"No!"

I pushed over to my side and tried to stand up, but Morgan held me there. "Whoa, slow down now, little lady, let's call an ambulance first."

I decided to ignore the "little lady" comment and suppressed the desire to sock him in his little man parts. I said, "No. No way. I am *not* going to the hospital. And we need to make sure he's not still hiding in the house somewhere!"

Morgan put his hands on both my shoulders and looked me squarely in the eye. "Dixie. You've got a concussion. Believe it or not, the first thing we did was search the house. There's nobody here."

I squeezed my eyes shut a couple of times and then nodded. "Okay, good. But I don't have a concussion, so no hospital."

"I'm pretty sure you do, and anyway that's my call, not yours."

"Believe me, I'd know if I had a concussion, and I don't."

He raised an eyebrow. "You told the 911 operator you're a sheriff's deputy."

"No, I didn't."

"Yeah. You did."

I didn't remember doing that, but then again, I didn't remember *not* doing it, either. I shook my head slowly. "No. She must have heard me wrong."

"You mean *he*?"

"Yeah. He. Whatever."

Morgan's sharp features seemed to soften and he tilted his head to one side, the way you might do if you were trying to soothe a small child. "Dixie . . . you reported an 11-99."

That stopped me. 11-99 is scanner code for "Officer Needs Assistance." I didn't remember saying that, either, but I tried to shrug it off. I said, "Well, what was I supposed to say? There's no scanner code for 'Cat Sitter Needs Assistance.' "

Just then, Deputy Beane appeared in the doorway to the laundry room. I probably wouldn't have recognized her but I remembered her hair — straight and jet-black, cut in a short bob that framed her face like a helmet. We had met before.

Morgan looked up at her and said, "Anything?"

She shook her head. "No. And I talked to a couple of neighbors. Nothing."

"Okay," Morgan said. "Dixie, I believe you know Deputy Beane."

She nodded at me. "Hi. You all right?"

"Yeah, I'm fine."

Morgan said, "Dixie was just filling me in on all the details. Seems she reported an 11-99 because a fat, bald, naked woman with red toes broke in and hit her over the head with a statue."

I started to interject but he held up one finger. "Oh sorry, no, I got that wrong. It

44

was Dick Cheney. Dick Cheney broke in and hit her on the head with a statue. He was wearing a mask, and he had red toes. I forget, was he naked, too?"

Beane's eyes widened as she looked at me expectantly. I couldn't tell if she was thinking I needed immediate medical attention, or if she was waiting to find out if Dick Cheney had been naked, too.

I sighed. "No, he was not naked. And it wasn't *actually* Dick Cheney. He was wearing one of Mrs. Keller's masks that reminds me of Dick Cheney, so that's what I call it. And he hit me with this little statue that had red toes."

They both just stared at me with blank expressions.

"I know it sounds crazy, but I'm telling you the truth. I admit I must have been a little loopy when I called 911, but if I had a concussion, would I be sitting here talking to you like a normal person?"

Morgan's eyes narrowed a bit. "I'm not so sure you are, but let's try this. What's your name?"

"Huh?"

"You heard me, what's your name?"

"Oh, give me a break. You know exactly who I am."

His expression didn't change. "What is

your name?"

I knew what he was up to. A person with a concussion can seem perfectly normal on the outside, while on the inside circuits can be overloading and burning out and blood can be pooling up in all corners of the brain and then before you know it you're a vegetable. One way to determine if someone's had a concussion is if they have trouble answering basic questions.

"I'm waiting."

I sighed. "All right. My name is Dixie Hemingway."

"And where are you?"

"I already went over this with 911. I'm in the laundry room."

"Funny. I mean what town are you in?"

I blinked. "Oh. I'm in Siesta Key."

"What state?"

"Florida."

"Who's house is this?"

"Buster and Linda Keller's."

He nodded. "Okay. So far, so good. What's one hundred minus thirty-seven?"

My eyes glazed over. Math is not exactly my best subject. I can barely balance a checkbook.

I said, "Uh . . ."

Morgan stood up. "Yeah, we're calling an ambulance."

"Wait a minute, I got this . . . seventy-three?"

He nodded at Beane, "Go ahead and call Dispatch while I start a report."

She pulled her radio out of its holster while I swiped at Morgan's ankles, feeling like Barney Feldman under the hall credenza. "Sixty-three! Sixty-three!"

Morgan looked down and sighed. "Dixie, are you sure you're okay?"

I looked around and thought for a second. I had mistaken my flashlight for a pistol, I'd told the 911 operator I was a sheriff's deputy, my head was throbbing, the room was rotating slightly, and there was a distant ringing in my ears that sounded a little bit like the coronation bells at a royal wedding.

"Yes," I said. "I'm totally fine, and I promise if I notice anything weird I'll go straight to the doctor."

He shook his head slightly. "Okay. I don't like it, but I guess I'll just have to trust you on this one."

I held out my arms. "I could use a little help getting up, though."

Beane stepped in and they both pulled me to my feet and stood on either side while the blood rushed back into my legs.

He said, "You good?"

I gave him a nod and a smile. "I'm good."

"Okay, let's have a look around and see if you notice anything out of place."

I steadied myself with one hand on his shoulder. "Well, I can tell you right off the bat, those candles in the living room . . . they weren't there before."

Morgan glanced at Beane and then frowned. "What candles?"

4

I was standing at the entry to the living room just beyond the Kellers' kitchen, with Deputy Morgan on one side of me and Deputy Beane on the other. Luckily the ringing in my ears had subsided a bit and the room was only barely rotating now, but my eyes were wide as saucers. I was holding one arm out in front of me with an open palm, like I was about to shake hands with a ghost.

"They . . . they were right there."

Morgan said, "A candle."

"*Two* candles. And they were both lit."

The coffee table was one of those big square modern things you see in fancy catalogs, with iron legs and a massive slab of white stone polished to a glassy finish, and just like everything else in the Kellers' house it was completely clutter-free — no old magazines piled up, no TV remotes, no half-finished crossword puzzles, and most importantly, no tapered candles in the middle.

Morgan walked around to the other side and squatted down to peer underneath it. "And when did you see these candles?"

"Right when I woke up. The first thing I noticed were those curtains moving in the wind, but then . . ."

I glanced over at the curtains. They were not moving in the wind. Not even slightly. They were not moving in the wind because there was no wind. The doors to the garden outside were completely closed.

Morgan folded his arms over his chest and looked down at his shoes. "You saw the curtains moving?"

"Yeah, because those doors were open . . ."

"And where was the cat?"

"I don't know."

"And you saw all this before or after you got the concussion?"

I cast him a sidelong glance. "I do *not* have a concussion. And I told you, it was after."

He studied my face for a moment and then said, "Bright red toes, huh?"

I sighed. "Look, I know it sounds crazy, but I'm not making this up. As sure as I'm standing here, those doors were open and there were two lit candles on that table."

He looked around the room. "Well, I hate to tell you, Dixie, but I'm standing here, too, and I don't see any candles anywhere."

I tried to think of a smart-ass reply — something I'm normally pretty good at — but my brain just wasn't cooperating. "Well, they must have . . . taken them when they left . . . ?"

Even as I said it I knew how ridiculous I sounded, but there had to be a logical explanation and that was the only thing I could come up with. Deputy Beane went over and parted the curtains with the back of her hand.

She said, "These doors are all locked. And they're latched from the inside."

Morgan nodded. "Okay, it's all starting to make sense now."

I turned to him. "It is?"

"Yep. Somebody snuck in here and clobbered you over the head with a statue. Then they opened these folding doors. Maybe they needed some fresh air or something." He pointed toward the laundry room. "Then, while you were taking your beauty nap in there, they came in here and lit a couple candles." He looked around and nodded with a smug grin. "Now, as to why they lit those candles, I have no idea. Who can say what motivates the mind of a criminal? All I know is, when they got done doing whatever they were doing, maybe they took a nap or watched a movie, they locked everything up and took the candles with them. Happens all the time."

I rolled my eyes. "What are you trying to say, that I was hallucinating?"

"Dixie, you have to admit, none of this makes sense. And there's nothing missing."

I said, "What do you mean, there's nothing missing?"

"Look around. There's expensive artwork all over this place and none of it's been touched. There's even a jewelry box in the master bedroom full of stuff that no criminal in his right mind would leave behind. I'm sorry, but this just doesn't look like a burglary."

"Then how do you explain what happened to me?"

He paused for a moment. "Dixie, how were you feeling before you got here?"

"Huh?"

"You know, how were you feeling? Like, light-headed or dizzy or anything?"

I folded my arms over my chest. "Seriously. You think I fainted?"

"Well, don't take this personally, but you don't look too good."

I raised my finger and wagged it in his

face. "Really? You wouldn't look too good, either, if you'd been knocked out cold and left for dead!"

"Listen, I'm just saying it's a possibility, that's all. If you blacked out, that might explain all the, uh . . . visions."

"Visions . . ."

"The fat lady and the red toes and the candles and everything. Maybe you hit your head when you went down."

I nodded. "So you're saying the whole thing was a dream."

"Yeah. Basically."

I sighed. There was no point arguing with him, and also I had to admit he was right: none of it made any sense.

He came over and gave me a little pat on the shoulder. "Look, if it'll make you feel better, we can go through the house one more time and look for anything missing, and I can always check for fingerprints."

"Wait!" I put both hands up like I was stopping traffic. "Barney Feldman!"

Morgan shot Beane a worried look. "Barney Feldman?"

I rushed over to the folding doors and looked outside. "Yeah. The Kellers' cat. He's spoiled rotten but if there's an open door he'll go busting out like an escapee from a torture chamber. I guarantee you, if these doors were open at any point, he'll be outside hunting around in the garden and then we'll know I didn't make this whole thing up."

As I ran into the kitchen I heard Morgan say, "What ever happened to names like Whiskers and Tommy?"

I got down on my hands and knees and peered under the cupboard. "Barney?"

All I could see were a few cat hairs and the stubby eraser end of a pencil, so I rushed back into the living room and checked under the couch and both armchairs, but he wasn't there, either. Morgan and Beane were still standing right where I'd left them, watching me like I was some kind of lunatic.

I said, "Hello? A little help?"

They followed me through the living room, and as soon as I turned the corner down the hallway I saw a flash of something under the antique credenza. I stopped about a foot from its edge, and sure enough a single black paw took a couple of swipes at the tips of my toes. I knelt down and held out one hand like a peace offering, and Barney came squeezing out from under the credenza, as sweet as can be and purring like an electric razor.

Deputy Beane adjusted her belt and said,

"Well, mystery solved."

I stood up and leaned over the credenza while Barney rubbed up against my shins. Maybe Morgan was right, maybe the whole thing was a dream. I must have looked like I was about to burst into tears, because Beane started rocking on her heels while she tried to think of the right thing to say.

Morgan said, "Listen, Dixie, people faint all the time. It happens to the best of us, right?" He looked over at Beane for support, but she just widened her eyes and shook her head slightly. He frowned. "Okay, maybe not Beane here, but it's definitely happened to me."

I rolled my eyes. "Oh, please. You've never fainted in your life."

He glanced down and mumbled, "When my wife was giving birth, she was in labor for sixteen hours. I went down about hour nine."

"Okay, but that's not exactly the same thing."

He shook his head. "Look, the point is it's no big deal. You came in, you saw all these creepy masks everywhere, you got a little woozy, and then, bam, you hit your —"

"Ha!"

I cut him off. Something about the way he said "creepy masks" had loosened something

55

in the back of my mind. I clapped my hands together triumphantly. "Dick Cheney!"

He frowned. "Now we're back on Dick Cheney?"

"Yes! I just realized, Mrs. Keller told me that mask cost her a small fortune. It's rare, and it's probably worth a hell of a lot more than anything she's got in that jewelry box. I can't explain the candles or the curtains or how the guy got in here yet, but I can tell you one thing for certain: I know exactly why he was wearing that mask — he *stole* it!"

I swooped Barney up in my arms and marched down the hall toward the front door with Morgan and Beane following close behind.

I said, "I guarantee you, with that mask and the right connections somebody could make a killing on the black market. Whoever it was knew exactly what they were doing."

As I came to a stop in the foyer, my throat made a little squeak, kind of like the sound sneakers make on a hardwood floor. Morgan and Beane said in unison, "What?"

I pointed up at the wall just opposite the front door, directly at the spot where Dick Cheney had been hanging when I first came in.

He was still there.

5

I've always loved animals, but pet sitting just sort of fell in my lap. A friend had the cutest tomcat, Rudy, a tiger-striped fellow she'd found under an RV parked behind her apartment building, and she asked if I might be able to stay with him while she went on a business trip to San Francisco. It took my brother Michael about two days to talk me into it. The thought of leaving the house made me sick to my stomach, but I knew he wouldn't give up, so I packed an overnight bag with the bare essentials — toothbrush, sunglasses, Prozac — and stayed with Rudy in a condo on the bay for five days.

I spent most of my time lying in a chaise lounge on the balcony, gazing out at the water and wondering what in the world I was going to do with the rest of my life, while Rudy stood squarely on my chest and gazed into my eyes, purring like a squeezebox stuck on the same low, growly note. To this day, I'm completely convinced it was Rudy who planted the idea in my head of starting a pet-sitting business. The thought of returning to law enforcement was about as attractive as a root canal, and I remember thinking at the time how much quieter and simpler life would be as a cat sitter.

It hasn't really turned out that way.

As I rolled my bike down the Kellers' driveway, I couldn't stop shaking my head. I like to think I'm not a dainty, delicate flower susceptible to the occasional bout of swooning or case of vapors because of my dainty, delicate composition. I may not exactly look like an Amazonian warrior, but I'm no lightweight. I mean, I'm an ex–sheriff's deputy, for God's sake.

I don't faint.

In fact, I couldn't think of a single solitary time I'd even come close to fainting . . . well, except maybe once at church when I was about thirteen years old, but that doesn't really count. I was in the throes of puberty, plus I'd eaten so many gingerbread cookies I think my body had gone into sugar shock. Still, when I turned south on Island Circle Road and made my way along the sandy edge of the neighbors' yards, I wondered if maybe something like that hadn't happened again.

Morgan and Beane had followed me through the whole house looking for any indication that there might have been a robbery, and they'd been right. There was nothing missing. And just like Morgan had said, Mrs. Keller's jewelry box was sitting on top of her dresser, practically spilling over with what looked to me like some very expensive jewelry, including one ring with a ruby the size of a dimestore gumball. I'm no expert, but I'm pretty sure it was probably worth more than my entire earthly possessions put together.

The final straw, however, had been good ol' Dick Cheney, hanging there on the wall and looking down at me with that smug, teasing scowl, as if to say, *What are you lookin' at? I've been here all morning.* The problem wasn't so much that Mrs. Keller's prize Tibetan mask hadn't been stolen — in fact I was relieved it was still there; I'm sure Mrs. Keller would have been absolutely heartbroken if it was gone — but the fact that it was hanging exactly where it was supposed to be was just downright . . . well, I don't know . . . *bizarre.*

Even if my attacker had had no intention of stealing it, why would he have carefully hung it back on the wall before he made his getaway? And what exactly was he getting away *from*?

At the end of the Kellers' block, there was an empty lot with a few scrub oaks and a couple of squat palm trees. I parked my bike in the patchy grass by the road, dropped my backpack, and sat down Indian-style next to the stop sign. There were a few cars going by on Canal Road, so I knew there'd be some raised eyebrows — I must have looked like a half-drunk party girl who didn't quite make it home the night before — but I didn't care.

I leaned my head against the post and sighed. I tried to remember what it had felt like, that time I'd fainted at church. My grandparents had taken us all to the annual Christmas party, and I was hovering around the buffet table, happy as a conch in my new pink taffeta dress, munching down on what for all I knew was my hundredth gingerbread cookie.

I had just taken a giant swig of Coca-Cola when all of a sudden there was a strange, tingling sensation in the tips of my fingers. It started slowly, traveling over my hands, but then it picked up speed as it moved up my arms and shoulders and across my chest. Meanwhile, the room had started to spin, and I could feel a bead of sweat rolling down the side of my neck.

I remember thinking if I could just find a chair, everything would be okay, but there was nothing nearby. My only choice was to plop down right there on the floor, but I was at the ridiculous age when the idea of making a scene seemed like the most appalling thing in the world, so instead I managed to make it over to the far end of the buffet table where there were a couple of bushy plastic trees in chocolate-brown pots shaped like giant elephant's feet. As discreetly as possible, I lowered myself down to the floor behind them, and the last thing I remember was watching the party through the dusty plastic leaves as I tried to keep my breathing as steady as possible.

When I finally woke up, I was all alone and curled up in a ball. Apparently I'd crawled behind the red paper cloth that was spread across the buffet table and slept through the entire party, not to mention the Christmas concert after, and the whole congregation was out scouring the neighborhood for me, including the preacher.

My poor grandmother had been so upset she'd worried dime-sized holes in both pockets of her sweater, and after that she monitored my sugar intake as if it were her life's mission and I was her own personal science project. Whenever she made one of her famous key lime pies, I was only allowed the tiniest little hint of a sliver, much to my brother's delight, I might add, since of course that just meant more for him. As a result, to this day I can easily eat a whole pie in one sitting if left to my own devices.

I didn't remember feeling any tingling in my fingers at the Kellers', and I certainly hadn't noticed anything spinning or getting blurry. I was totally fine. But I could still feel the adrenaline that shot through my body when I turned and saw that wild-eyed mask looming in front of me, its jagged teeth and flaring nostrils, its arm raised in the air, that little stone statuette poised and ready to come barreling straight down on top of my skull.

And that was another thing. If it was a dream, wouldn't the details have been a little more . . . *normal*? I could understand if I'd imagined my mystery attacker coming at me with a baseball bat or a tire iron, or maybe even one of those wooden sticks you see in kung-fu movies, but a naked, bald she-Buddha with huge, bowling-ball breasts and painted toes?

Really?

The only thing that kept me from deciding I wasn't one hundred percent cuckoo for Cocoa Puffs was the bump that was still throbbing away on top of my head. I reached up and gently touched it with the tips of my fingers. Of course, all it meant was that I'd actually been hit, it didn't exactly say *how*. Either I'd been attacked and the whole thing was real, or I had fainted and the whole thing was a dream.

Wait a minute, I thought. *For all I know, I'm dreaming RIGHT NOW.*

I took a deep breath. It probably goes without saying, but my imagination can get a little out of control sometimes. I decided there was no point torturing myself, and the sooner I got on with my day, the better.

I stood up and glanced back at the scene of the crime, or — I thought with a sigh — the *alleged* crime. Morgan's cruiser was still idling in the Kellers' driveway, its emergency lights silently flashing red and blue, and Morgan and Beane were sitting inside with their heads bowed, busily filling out their reports. Practically every single move a deputy makes has to be written down and submitted to the department, and then it all gets printed out and duplicated and triplicated. The standard joke is that if you're not going through at least a tree a day you're not doing your job right, so I figured they'd be a while. I wondered if they were writing things down like, *Hysterical woman fainted,* or *Hallucinating cat sitter.*

Before he'd let me go, Morgan had issued a couple of orders while I was locking up the Kellers' house. One, I was to walk, not ride, my bike for the rest of the day, and two, I was to go to the doctor and get my head inspected as soon as possible. In return, he had agreed not to throw me in the back of his squad car and escort me to the hospital himself — in handcuffs if necessary.

I didn't like the thought of that one bit, so I flipped the kickstand up on my bike and walked it all the way to Canal Road until I was completely out of sight. Then, with one more quick look back, I hopped up on the seat, leaned on the pedals, and sped off as fast as I could.

If there's one thing I've learned from cats, it's that taking orders is for the birds.

6

I managed to make it through the rest of my morning without fainting or hallucinating or getting attacked by any more mask-wearing mystery bandits. The Hendersons' Siamese, Constance, had tipped over a cup of pencils that Mr. Henderson keeps on his desk — at least I was pretty sure it was her, though she adamantly denied it — and Rocky, a short-haired tomcat who shares an apartment with a couple of other bruisers from our local football team, the Millionaires, managed to slip out the door when I was coming in, but I snatched him up before he got too far.

Looking back, considering the morning I'd had, it's amazing I was just continuing on with my day as if nothing had happened. But I have experience forging ahead when things get rocky. It's one of my many talents, and by the time I rolled up to Hector and Elva Castillo's house I was actually feeling relatively normal. Luckily my hair was doing a commendable job of concealing the bump on my head.

Hector and Elva are both science teachers at the local high school. They live with their dog, Sophie, at the top of the Key in a modest Florida-style cottage with pink siding and tall snow-white shutters. In the front, wide wooden steps lead up to a wraparound porch filled with potted bananas, sweet agave, and blooming angel's trumpets, and if that's not enough to make you feel like you've made the cover of *Heaven on Earth* magazine, there are four wicker rocking chairs just begging you to come and have a look at the sparkling, emerald-green waters of Roberts Bay.

As soon as she heard me on the steps, Sophie started yapping up a storm, not in a particularly menacing way, but with just enough of an edge to make it clear that I was entering protected territory. She's a Baja terrier, which I'm not sure is an actual breed, but that's what the Castillos call her because she's typical of a lot of the dogs where they found her: Baja California. She's shaped like a Jack Russell, no bigger than a toaster oven, but with a brindled coat and an attitude the size of a two-hundred-pound opera diva.

I let myself in the front door and Sophie immediately launched into her traditional dance of welcome. She stood up on her hind legs and hopped around in circles, waving her paws up and down like she was conducting a marching band, and then she crouched down low with her rear in the air and growled a rumbling, contralto *rrrroooooooo!*

I slipped my backpack off and answered her with a *rrroooooo!* of my own, but as I hung my keys on the coatrack by the door, I kept one eye on her. Sophie's an interesting character; in fact, sometimes I wonder if she didn't apprentice at the paws of Barney Feldman, because you have to mind your p's and q's when she's afoot. Don't get me wrong, she's one of the sweetest dogs I've ever known, but occasionally she gets a mischievous gleam in her eye, and then *look out.*

She attacks shoes — not in the funny, playful way that Barney Feldman attacks ankles — but in a crazy, possessed, search-and-destroy, shock-and-awe kind of way. It usually only lasts about ten seconds or so, and then she's back to her sweet, lovable self, as if nothing ever happened.

Hector found her when she was just a puppy, trotting along the road, thoroughly exhausted and filthy, wearing a ratty old collar and a tag with her name on it but nothing else. Eventually they came to the conclusion that at some point in her young life Sophie must have been kicked, and probably more than once.

Now, even after years have passed and the Castillos have showered her with all the love a soul could ever hope to have, there's still something hidden deep inside her, some lingering sense of injustice that makes her want to lash out at the world every once in a while, maybe as payback for the lousy cards she was dealt when she was a pup.

I don't blame her. I feel the same way sometimes.

Once I was relatively certain she wasn't in attack mode, I headed through the living room while Sophie skipped along, giving me a breakdown of her morning so far with a series of half woofs and high-pitched yips, but when we got to the kitchen she ran ahead to her water bowl and stood over it, waiting silently.

I said, "Sophie. Really?"

Another of Sophie's little quirks is that she's very particular about her water bowl. It has to be absolutely spotless. No tiny specks of dirt. No dust. Not even one of her very own hairs lying innocently at the bottom. If it's not perfectly pristine, she won't touch it. And it doesn't help to just fish out whatever offending object there is and call it a day. No, the bowl must be taken to the sink, emptied, thoroughly rinsed, and refilled with fresh water.

Sophie took a couple of desultory sniffs at the air above her bowl and then looked up at me with a vaguely accusing look in her eye. I knelt down to get a better look, and sure enough there was a tiny dust bunny floating on the surface of the water.

I laid the back of my hand over my forehead and cried, "Oh, the humanity!"

She trotted behind me to the sink and waited patiently while I threw out the ruined water and refilled the bowl, then as soon as it was back down on the floor she lapped at it like a dehydrated camel, pausing only to wag her tail and give me a look of grave gratitude, as if she'd just crossed the Mojave Desert and I had saved her from a slow, unthinkable death.

Hector and Elva are up and out of the house early, so Sophie gets breakfast before they leave for work, and then she goes back upstairs for a snooze until I arrive. All that's required of me is a thorough water bowl inspection and a good brisk jaunt around the neighborhood.

We walked all the way to the end of Gulfmead Drive, which this far north isn't really a drive at all, more like a flattened trail of sandy soil and crushed shell just wide enough for a car to fit through, dotted here and there with tufts of clover and sedge weed. Since it dead-ends at the bay, there's hardly any traffic — just the locals and the occasional adventurous tourist — so I unsnapped Sophie's leash and she went zigzagging ahead of me, peeing on everything in sight to let the neighbor dogs know she'd been by.

With Sophie playing on her own and nothing but the crunching sound of my sneakers on the road to distract me, I had to allow for the fact that there'd been a nagging voice in the back of my head all morning. So far I'd done a pretty good job ignoring it, but now it was getting louder and louder. It was a jumble of questions and rambling thoughts and theories, but the overriding theme was: *Huh?*

There was no point trying to re-create the whole scene of what had happened that morning, but I couldn't stop myself. And even though low blood sugar was probably the most logical explanation, I just couldn't accept the idea that I'd just fainted and dreamt the whole thing.

For a moment I even toyed with the idea

of going back and seeing if I could get some answers out of Barney Feldman. He was my only bona fide witness, and I'm a firm believer in the notion that our animal friends are perfectly capable of communicating with us, even on a very sophisticated level. The only problem is that we haven't quite figured out how to listen yet. In my opinion, if we ever do, the world will be a vastly better place.

Sophie was chasing after a swallowtail butterfly she'd roused from a spindly spice bush growing on the side of the road, and as she raced by in hot pursuit I swooped her up in my arms and cradled her like a baby.

I said, "Hey, any chance you speak Maine Coon?"

She looked up with soulful brown eyes and blinked a couple of times, which I wasn't sure meant yes or no or *Can you please put me down I'm in the middle of something?*

I said, "Listen, there's somebody I'd like you to talk to. Would you be up for that? He's the only one that can tell me what really happened."

She perked her ears up and tilted her head to one side, trying her best to figure out what the hell I was talking about, but I knew

I wasn't getting through to her. Without an interpreter, I didn't think I'd get much information out of Barney Feldman. But then again, there was one other option . . .

Contrary to what some people might tell you, I'm no dummy, at least most of the time. The moment I hopped on my bike and pedaled away from the Kellers' house, I knew my brain had gone into autopilot, and I could still feel it working quietly in the background, trying to connect the dots.

Maybe I'd been wrong this whole time. Maybe it hadn't been Levi parked outside my driveway at all. It certainly wouldn't take a genius to figure out that I have easy access to some of the island's swankiest homes, and the idea that I might have been followed to the Kellers' was starting to seem like a very real possibility, especially when I remembered hearing the sound of a car roll by in the street as I unlocked their front door.

I knew if Barney Feldman couldn't shed some light on what had happened, there was one person who could: Levi Radcliff. If there'd been another car in the neighborhood, like somebody lingering around waiting for me to leave so they could follow me, Levi would definitely have noticed it.

Sophie must have sensed I wasn't paying

attention to her anymore because she squirmed out of my arms and scampered off in search of her butterfly, and by the time we got back home she had pretty much tuckered herself out. I gave her a couple of kisses on the nose and then conducted one more water bowl inspection while she headed upstairs for her midmorning nap, which at the time seemed like a capital idea. The only thing that kept me from joining her was the angry growling coming from my stomach.

I needed food. It seemed like days since I'd eaten, and for all I knew the thoughts coming out of my head were just the fevered ramblings of a malnourished brain. I figured before I made any decisions about what had happened that morning or what I should do next — if anything — I'd better get something to eat first.

What I needed was a good, home-cooked breakfast with a healthy serving of TLC on the side, and I knew exactly where to find it.

7

I'm a creature of habit. Seven days a week, rain or shine, hell or high water, dogfight or fur ball, my alarm clock goes off at five a.m. and I roll right out of bed. I stagger blurry-eyed into the bathroom, splash cold water on my face, and pull my hair into a ponytail. If I think about it I dab on a little lip gloss and maybe some mascara, and then I walk like a zombie into the closet and get dressed in the dark. The order is always the same: Underwear, bra, cargo shorts, sleeveless white tee, and a fresh pair of white sneakers.

I might do a shot or two of OJ and then I'm out the door. All my pets get at least two visits a day, one in the morning and another in the afternoon — usually about half an hour each, or more if the client wants it. I'm usually done with my morning rounds by nine or ten. Then it's off to my home away from home.

The Village Diner is at the heart of the Key's "commercial" area, what we locals call the Village, thus the name. I've been eating breakfast there my whole life. Well, that's not exactly true. Before Todd and Christy left, I made breakfast at home. Pancakes were Todd's favorite. Christy was crazy for my avocado-and-mushroom omelets. You'd think it would have been the other way around, but Todd and Christy were full of surprises like that.

I almost feel like I work at the diner, I've spent so much time in one of its teal pleather booths. My reserved spot is at the very back on the right. As soon as I walk in the door, Tanisha gives me a wave and a wink from her little window in the kitchen to let me know she's already started on my order: Two eggs over easy with home fries and a biscuit.

I normally make a detour for the restroom to wash away the cat fur and the dog slobber I've accumulated, then I grab the newspaper and slide into my booth, where Judy's usually waiting for me with a pot of piping-hot coffee.

Judy is about my age and pretty much my best friend in the world, even though I never see her outside of the diner. She's smart-mouthed and long-limbed, with a sprinkling

75

of freckles across the bridge of her nose, and honey-brown eyes that look out at the world with a distant longing. She knows everything about me and all my tales of sorrow, and I know all hers, most of which have a man at the bottom of them. And even though she's not had the best of luck in the romance department, she's always cheerful because, as she puts it, "on the road of life, the grumpier you are, the more jackasses you meet."

She was leaning against the table with one hand on her hip, holding a coffeepot out from her waist and sloshing it around in slow circles. Her lips were pursed to one side and she had a particular look on her face — what I call the "Judge Judy." It usually means I'm in trouble.

I slid into the booth and pushed an empty coffee cup toward her. "What are you looking at?"

"Well, first of all I'm looking at that Fu Manchu mustache you've got going on."

I brought one finger to my lip and pulled away a small white tuft of fur that was clinging to my upper lip. "Oh, dammit! That's probably been there all morning."

Judy nodded as she poured my coffee. "Probably. And then I'm also looking at that pretty little bump on top of your head."

I sighed. "Great. Is it that obvious?"

She grinned triumphantly. "No, but your friend Captain Morgan was in here a little while ago and told me all about it."

"Are you kidding me? Isn't that like a breach of confidence or something? And he's a deputy, by the way, not a captain."

She shrugged. "Deputy, captain, colonel. All I know is, I'm a sassy waitress in a small-town diner. If anybody's got local gossip, they're pretty much required to hand it over."

I heard Tanisha ring her order bell as I took a sip of coffee. "So how much do you know?"

"Not much, I made the mistake of telling him he should be a little more professional, that people could be listening, but that was before I realized he was talking about you. If I'd known I would have kept my big mouth shut."

"Well, what did he say?"

The order bell rang again, this time with a little more *oomph* to it, and Judy held up one finger. "Hold on, that's probably for you."

She zigzagged down the aisle, picking up plates and topping off cups of coffee here and there, and then in the blink of an eye returned with my breakfast. Tanisha must have known I'd had a rough morning, too, because sitting next to my eggs were two biscuits instead of one. They were topped with twin pads of melting butter and dollops of Tanisha's homemade peach marmalade. One bite and my eyes rolled right up into the back of my head. I could barely hear Judy over the moans of sheer ecstasy coming out of me.

"He said he found you passed out on the floor in the Kellers' laundry room and that you had a nasty bump on your head, but other than that he wouldn't give me the details. Dixie, what the hell happened?"

I dabbed at the crumbs on my lips and took a sip of coffee for dramatic effect. "I don't know."

She shifted her weight to one side and crossed her arms over her chest. "What do you mean, you don't know?"

"I mean, I don't know."

"Dixie, I'm in no mood for games. I've been worried sick about you."

"Seriously, I have no idea what happened. Believe me, I wish to hell I did."

I told her the whole story, how everything seemed fine when I arrived at the Kellers, how I'd given Barney his breakfast and taken out the trash, and how Dick Cheney had been waiting for me with his red-toed, baldy she-Buddha. The whole time I was talking, her eyes got wider and wider until finally she interrupted me.

"Wait a minute, somebody broke in to the Kellers' house, put a mask on, and *attacked* you?"

I shrugged. "Maybe. Maybe not."

Her eyes narrowed. "I'm gonna add another bump to that head of yours if you don't stop foolin' around and tell me what happened."

"I'm telling you! Here's everything I know: I passed out, and at some point or other I woke up, the doors in the living room that lead out to the back garden were standing wide open, and there were two candles on the coffee table that weren't there before. And they were lit."

She frowned. "You sure you weren't the one that was lit?"

"Hold on, it gets weirder. When the cops showed up, those doors were shut and locked, the candles were gone, and the mask was hanging right where it's supposed to be. So in other words, I may have fainted and dreamt the whole thing."

She eyed me for a second and then sighed as she slid into the booth opposite me. "Hmm."

"Yeah. Hmm is right. So I have no idea,

and there was no sign of a break-in, either. Nothing missing."

She put her elbows on the table and brought her hands together like she was about to say a prayer. "Now I know why Captain Morgan wouldn't give me the details."

"And this is gonna sound crazy, but Judy, I halfway think somebody followed me there. Do you know Levi, the paper guy?"

She nodded and started to speak but I interrupted her. "Well, he was parked outside my driveway about five this morning, at least I thought it was him because that's what time the paper usually comes . . . only now I'm not so sure. Either way, I'm wondering if maybe he saw something suspicious. Or maybe he saw somebody lurking around outside the Kellers' house . . ."

Her eyes narrowed slightly and she looked down at the table for a brief moment. I could tell she wasn't convinced. "Honey, I think you better go see a doctor."

"Now you sound like Morgan."

"Well, Dixie, did you faint or not?"

I didn't know whether to nod, shake my head no, or shrug, so I did a combination of all three.

She put one hand on top of mine and

sighed. "Maybe you just need some food in you and a little rest. Just stop thinking about it and maybe it'll all make sense tomorrow. You've just been working too hard, that's all."

I felt my eyes start to well with tears, much to my surprise, but I rubbed my eyelids with my thumb and forefinger so Judy wouldn't notice. If she did, she pretended not to.

"And I know you don't want to, but you need to stop by Dr. Dunlop's office and let him take a look at that bump on your head. It looks like you're growing a little horn, and it's high time you got your head examined anyway." She slid out of the booth and straightened her apron. "Now eat your breakfast and don't worry. I'm gonna fetch you a couple of slices of bacon. That'll get you feeling back to normal in no time."

I nodded. "Okay. And bring me the newspaper, will you? Maybe that'll help distract me."

She reached over and picked up my coffee cup. "Well, I would if I could. That's what I was gonna say before. The damn paper never came this morning."

She turned and took two steps toward the kitchen, and froze.

As our eyes met she whispered, "Oh,

Dixie, you don't think . . ."

I remember reading once about Carl Jung, the Swiss psychologist who blew everybody's minds in the 1920s when he came up with the whole idea of synchronicity. The way Jung saw it, anybody with a central nervous system was part of a collective unconscious, maybe even some kind of world soul, where the thoughts and actions of one being could touch, on some basic level, the thoughts and actions of every other being on earth. Of course, that just freaked everybody out because it meant that two seemingly unrelated events could actually have some kind of relationship with one another, even if you couldn't exactly draw a straight line between them.

I think on any other day, the fact that the diner hadn't received its morning newspaper wouldn't have registered as even the slightest blip on my radar, but the idea that I'd spent the whole morning with Levi hovering in the back of my mind made it stand out, and I knew Judy was thinking the exact same thing. She'd done a quick poll of her other tables, and the results made the hair on the back of my neck stand up: more than half of her customers hadn't received their morning papers, either.

After I wolfed down my breakfast, including two scrumptious pieces of Tanisha's world-famous, lip-smacking bacon, I took a cup of coffee out to the bench on the sidewalk just outside the front door and slipped my phone out of my pocket. I had no idea what I was doing or what I hoped to accomplish, but that's never stopped me before.

"Hello, and thank you for calling the *Sarasota Herald-Tribune.* If you're a new customer, press one. If you're calling to cancel your subscription, press two. If you plan on being out of town and would like to stop delivery, press three. If you didn't receive your paper today, press four."

The woman on the recording had a smooth, silky voice. I pulled the phone away from my ear and pressed four.

"Thank you. You have chosen to report a problem with your delivery. Please enter the telephone number associated with your account, beginning with the area code."

"Oh, shoot."

I tried my best to remember the diner's telephone number, but after I punched it in, the voice said, "I'm sorry. I don't recognize that number. Please enter the number associated with . . ."

I hung up and sighed. There was no point

going on. First of all, the chances of getting an actual human being on the phone were pretty slim, plus I didn't think my silky-toned friend would ever say, *Press five if you think your paperboy may be in danger.*

Just then Judy popped her head out the front door. "Any luck?"

"No, I couldn't get a connection with a real person."

"Ha. Story of my life." She stepped out and leaned her hip against the bench, squinting into the sun. "Tanisha says he lives in her neighborhood."

"Who, Levi?"

"Yep."

"Where does she live again?"

"Grand Pelican Commons. She walks her dog past his place every night, so she said she could stop by and check on him when she gets off here."

"Grand Pelican Commons. Isn't that the trailer park across the bay?"

She tipped her chin up. "I think the preferred term is 'mobile home community.' "

That was all I needed. I stood up and gave her a quick thumbs-up. "Perfect! Then I'm off the hook. I was starting to think I was overreacting anyway."

She nodded. "Well, it certainly wouldn't

be the first time."

"And just because a few people are missing their newspapers doesn't mean diddly."

"Nope. Doesn't mean a thing, and Tanisha said he's kind of wild anyway. Probably up late partying and just called in sick or something."

I passed her my coffee cup and pulled my bike out of the rack next to the bench. "Well, if your paper ever shows up let me know."

"Yes, ma'am. And if you faint while you're on that bike and veer into traffic and get your head busted open like an overripe watermelon, be sure to give me a call."

"Yeah, yeah, yeah. I'm on my way to Dr. Dunlop's now."

"Seriously?"

"Yes, seriously. I'll stop by on my way home."

"Good girl. Let me know what he says."

"Okay. And tell Tanisha I said thanks."

She swung open the door to the diner but stopped it with her foot. "For what?"

"For checking in on Levi. What do you think?"

Her eyes narrowed as I pedaled off, and I could feel her watching me all the way down to the end of the block.

■ ■ ■ ■

This time of year, when the sun hangs just a few feet over your shoulders and the heat feels like it has weight to it, anybody with a lick of sense stays indoors in the middle of the day. If they absolutely have to go outside, it's only for as long as it takes to walk from their air-conditioned house to their air-conditioned car, and then they park as close as possible to the front door of their air-conditioned destination. It's only the tourists who don't know any better.

I reminded myself of that as I pedaled through the throngs of heat-soaked vacationers wandering around the center of town: gaggles of teenagers in flip-flops and Ray-Ban sunglasses with candy-striped towels like sarongs around their waists, hand-holding gray-haired couples with blissful smiles and dabs of chalk-white sunblock on their noses and ears, parents with kids in tow all happily negotiating their melting ice-cream cones, and young lovers without kids in tow happily negotiating their four-wheeled beer coolers down to the beach to work on their tans.

It was like riding through an obstacle course, but as soon as I got down to the end of the Village, the crowds thinned out and I was able to pick up speed. By the time I got home I was drenched in sweat. Normally I would have gone right upstairs to my apartment, taken a nice long shower, and collapsed in bed for a quick nap before I was out again for my afternoon rounds, but not this time. I rolled into the carport, leaned my bike under the steps, and hopped right into my Bronco.

With the air conditioner on blast, I took Midnight Pass all the way up to Stickney Point, where I hung a right and crossed over the bridge to the mainland. Then I headed down Tamiami Trail, past the clusters of thrift shops and burger stands and street-side fruit vendors, all the way down to Old Wharf Way, which isn't easy to find because it's often confused with New Wharf Way a mile or two farther south, but also because the road sign got knocked down in a storm almost a decade ago and no one's ever bothered to put it back up.

You have to know where you're going to find Grand Pelican Commons.

8

I'm not one of those psycho lunatics who wanders around in a deranged fog of insanity, following every random impulse that pops into her head or listening to imaginary voices from God knows where. I am fully cognizant of my occasional lapses in judgment, and furthermore I know there were any number of things I should have been doing instead of driving around looking for Levi, but as I made my way down Old Wharf, I couldn't stop thinking about something that had happened almost twenty years earlier.

Back then, the school day started at 8:15, so my alarm was set to wake me up every morning at exactly 7:00 a.m. I'd roll out of bed and stumble downstairs to find my grandfather sitting at the breakfast table in his blue-jean overalls and plaid work shirt, his reading glasses perched on his nose, Lucky Strike dangling from his lips, and a piping-hot mug of coffee at his side. My grandmother would still be rustling around upstairs, but he would already have read through more than half of the morning newspaper, including the funnies.

It always made me think of Levi, who was probably about fourteen and had been delivering the paper for a couple of years by then, and how early he must have had to get up to deliver those newspapers on time. Just the idea of it made me want to crawl back in bed and hide under the covers. At that age I couldn't imagine anything more inhumane than making a teenager rise before the sun, but here Levi was doing it every day, every week, fifty-two weeks a year.

His mother always chauffeured him around town in her old Dodge minivan, with Levi sitting in the back and pitching the papers out the open hatch like the professional baseball player we all thought he'd be one day. I remembered one morning her van wouldn't start. She had accidentally left the headlights on the night before and the battery had drained out dead as a doornail.

Levi didn't give up. Instead of calling up his boss at the *Herald-Tribune* and saying he wouldn't be able to deliver the papers that day, he got on the phone and rounded up a group of his friends from the baseball team. They all got dressed and came over with their wagons in tow, loaded them up with newspapers, and zigzagged all over the island on foot, each with his own portion of Levi's delivery route. If your address was on Levi's list, you got your paper.

Well, it was all anybody talked about for days. They might not have gotten their papers as early as usual, but not a single person with a subscription to the *Herald-Tribune* went without that day, and the following Sunday they published a whole spread of letters to the editor from the community, including one from the mayor of Sarasota, thanking "the Radcliff boy" for his can-do spirit, his hard work, and most of all, his dependability.

It was that famous dependability I was thinking about as I turned onto the main drag of Grand Pelican Commons. The Radcliff boy was older now, and yes, he'd been through some hard times if the rumors of drinking and partying were to be believed, but I couldn't think of a single day in the past twenty years that the morning paper hadn't shown up on time.

Of course, as soon as I started checking all the driveways for Levi's car, I started wondering what I was getting myself into. It wasn't that I didn't think I could figure out which trailer was his — Grand Pelican Commons isn't exactly a sprawling metropolis — but once I figured out where he lived, what in the world was I planning on saying if I found him?

Oh, hi. Remember me? Your first sort-of-girlfriend? I just wanted to make sure you were okay because some people didn't get their papers this morning and there was a lunatic attacking people with a she-Buddha . . . either that or I fainted and had a really weird dream. By the way, were you outside my driveway this morning? Did you happen to notice any burglars or art thieves hanging around?

I hadn't been in this part of the city for years. In high school, Michael had taken trombone lessons from a matronly ex-Navy machinist who lived in an Airstream trailer with about twenty pet canaries. While she and Michael practiced what sounded to me like a whale's funeral, I would keep the canaries company and my grandmother would work on her crossword puzzles in the car. Back then, everything was brand-new and meticulously maintained, but now I barely recognized the ramshackle collection of trailer homes and lean-to sheds that dotted the street.

There were a few trailers hanging on to better days, though. One was freshly painted, with rows of begonias on either side of a winding stone path that stretched from the curb to the front steps, and I wondered if maybe that one wasn't Tanisha's. There was an impressive vegetable garden on the trailer hitch side, with vines of climbing tomatoes scrambling up a trellis and cascading over into the yard, and the front door had an oval sign hanging next to it with bright orange lettering, but from this distance I couldn't quite make out what it said.

Just then the door of the trailer swung open and a little towheaded boy appeared. He hopped up on a pogo stick and maneuvered down the two short steps into the yard with confident ease, even though he couldn't have been much older than seven or eight. I remembered Tanisha's sister, Diva, had moved in with her recently and was babysitting during the day to make extra money.

When the little boy noticed me, he raised one hand and gave me a quick wave, looking much like a cowboy on a bronco bull. Luckily the yard was carpeted with a thick bed of lush green grass, so I figured if he fell it would be a nice soft landing.

Just past that trailer the asphalt ended abruptly and turned into a dusty narrow road with wheel ruts down the middle. It led about a hundred feet through a stand of pines, eventually widening into a weedy clearing where there was a sky-blue trailer shaped like a boxcar. It was faded, with what looked like coffee stains spilling down its corrugated metal siding.

I inched the Bronco forward a bit, just parallel to a sign that read PRIVATE PROPERTY, and whispered to myself, "What in the world am I doing here?"

A voice in my head said, *Nothing good. Turn around.*

I ignored it. Putting aside for the moment that my mask-wearing assailant was probably a figment of my imagination, if it turned out there was even the slightest connection between that and the fact that Levi hadn't finished his paper deliveries that morning, I'd never have been able to forgive myself if I didn't at least make sure he was okay.

The closer I got to the trailer, the more certain I was that this was the right place. There was a sad stack of old tires about five feet high in the middle of the weedy yard, and parked at a forty-five-degree angle between that and the trailer, its front bumper practically touching the front door, was Levi's dark brown Buick LeSabre convertible.

I breathed a sigh of relief as I pulled over to the side of the yard and shut the engine. At least he'd made it home, which meant I could rule out some of the other possible scenarios I'd come up with since I'd left the diner: that shortly after he'd pulled away from my driveway that morning, Levi had been run off the road, tied up, and thrown off the bridge into the bay, or he'd been locked in a basement chamber somewhere, all to keep him from coming forward as a witness after the Kellers returned from their vacation in Italy to find my lifeless body in their laundry room.

Like I said, my imagination can get a little unruly sometimes.

I dropped my keys down into the Bronco's center console and stepped out into the weedy yard. The sun was in her full midday glory now, and the heat bouncing off the front of the trailer made me feel like I'd walked into a giant rotisserie oven. To the right of the front door was a single window about four feet square, covered with a flimsy sheet of plastic held to the casing with a double-wide framing of gray duct tape. A lime-green fitted bedsheet was tacked up behind the glass, blocking the view inside except for one spot in the lower left corner where the sheet was balled up in a knot. As I squeezed myself around the front of the LeSabre and climbed up the few steps to knock on the front door, I had the distinct feeling I was being watched.

"Excuse me, can I help you?"

I spun around to find a squat, pasty-faced woman in her early twenties, with crispy, dyed-red hair and puffy eyes, looking up at me with her head cocked snottily to one side.

"Oh, hi," I blustered. "I didn't hear you come up."

"No kidding. This is private property, you know."

"Yeah, sorry. I was just looking for Levi."

She gave me a once-over. "Oh, yeah? What do you want with him?"

"Well, it's a little weird. He was parked outside my house when I was leaving for work."

"Oh, he was, was he?"

She was wearing flip-flops and a grubby white button-down with a black silhouette of Mickey Mouse across the front, buttoned all the way up to her neck. It was either a nightgown or an extremely large man's dress shirt, because it fell halfway down her bare legs.

I said, "Yeah, so I just wanted to know if maybe he'd seen anything unusual."

"What's the matter. Can't you read?"

"Excuse me?"

Folding her arms across her chest, she said, "The sign clearly says NO TRESPASS-ING."

I thought about saying that, actually, the sign clearly said PRIVATE PROPERTY, but I doubted it would win me any points. Instead I nodded. "Oh, I know. I just need to talk to Levi. This is his place, right?"

"So, you're a *friend* of Levi's?"

As she said "friend," she held her hands up and made little fat quotation marks in the air with her pudgy fingers.

"Well, not exactly. But —"

"Uh-huh. You're the girl that was here last night. What's the matter, forget your pant-ies?"

I sighed. This wasn't going well at all. I stepped forward with my hand out and said, "Hey, I think maybe we're getting off to a bad start. I'm Dixie Hemingway."

Her upper lip curled into what at first I thought was a smile but turned out to be a sarcastic snarl. She stepped back and put her hands on her hips. "Bitch, I don't know you. You're trespassing on my neighborhood and my man, so you better get the hell out of here before I call the cops."

For a split second I thought about leaping off the steps and pummeling this fire-hydrant-shaped Sasquatch of a woman into the ground, but luckily I managed to control myself. I took a deep breath and gave her as pleasant a smile as I could muster.

I said, "Okay, there's no need to call the cops."

"I'll call the cops if I want to. This is America. I got free speech."

I raised an eyebrow. "Yes, I understand that, but the cops probably have more important things to deal with. I just need to talk to Levi for one second and then I'll be out of your hair."

Given the state of the chemically altered mess on top of her head, it was all I could do to keep myself from holding my fingers up and putting air quotes around the word *hair,* but the woman's cheeks were turning beet-red as it was, plus every once in a while I do actually manage to conduct myself with a modicum of composure.

She squinted and tipped her chin at the trailer. "I'm sure he's still too drunk to talk anyway, but that don't matter because I'm gonna count to five and if you ain't out of here by then, you're gonna be sorry you ever met me."

Before I could stop myself I said, "Believe me, I already am. But more than that, I'm sorry you're so tortured."

Her eyes widened as I turned on my toes and rapped on the front door of the trailer with four confident knocks. Actually I had planned on four, but I only made it to three because as I knocked it swung open. At the same time, I caught a glimpse of the woman's shadow approaching from behind. For a split second, I considered the idea that I was about to receive my second beating of the day.

But something stopped her.

It was a man, flat on his stomach on the trailer's pale blue linoleum floor. I couldn't see all of him, just his naked legs. The rest was hidden behind the door and blocking it from opening completely. Something clenched shut at the top of my throat, and as I reached for the doorframe, I noticed the man's toes were splayed out spastically and the pale white soles of his bare feet were facing up, perfectly still. He was lying in the center of a pool of blood that stretched almost the entire length and depth of the trailer.

Just before the woman screamed, I muttered under my breath, "Okay, you win. Call the cops."

9

I never found out if my little fiery-headed friend had planned on giving me another beating or not, because after she screamed, the full weight of her body slammed into my back and pushed me forward into the trailer. Luckily my instincts kicked in and I grabbed on to both sides of the doorway and held on with all my might. That turned out to be just enough to keep us both from falling facedown in all that blood.

Sasquatch had taken one look at what was inside the trailer and conked out like a light, and now she was draped piggyback over my shoulders. I managed to get over to the left against the doorjamb, then, holding myself upright with one shoulder and squeezing my other arm between us, I maneuvered around until I had her in a tight bear hug. As gently as possible, I slid down to the shallow steps in front of the door and leaned her heavy body up against the front bumper of Levi's LeSabre.

The first thought that flashed across my mind was something like, *Well, this is the story of my life,* but I didn't have much time to indulge in that.

The woman's hot breath had left a moist spot on the side of my neck, and as I wiped it away with the back of my hand, her head plopped over and came to rest on the hood of Levi's car. I reached out and pulled her shirt across her shoulder, scrunching it up under her cheek so her face wouldn't get char-grilled on the hot metal. A few of the top buttons of her shirt popped open, and I saw a crudely drawn bluish black tattoo across the top of her chest, although I couldn't tell what it was. Her eyes were closed and her jaw was slack, but there was a look of pained terror stuck on her face. For a moment, even though I had no idea what her story was, I felt sorry for her.

It's funny how the mind works in a situation like this. Here I was, just inches from a lifeless body lying in a pool of blood, and yet my main concern was the safety of this unpleasant beast of a woman. While I fished my cell phone out of my pocket, I braced one arm against her shoulder and locked my elbow so she wouldn't tip over and break her neck.

I flipped the phone open and gingerly dialed the numbers with my thumb.

"911. What's your emergency?"

I leaned back and peered around the edge of the open door. The blood had seeped up against the toe kick of the doorframe and had already dried to a dark burgundy around the edges. The man's face was turned toward me, as white as marble, his mouth slightly askew, his eyes wide open in frozen astonishment.

I said, "My name is Dixie Hemingway. I'm at Grand Pelican Commons. There's been a murder."

It was Levi Radcliff.

The quiet that develops in the presence of a dead body is like no other in the world. I could see straight down the dirt road to the main drag of Grand Pelican, where a group of kids had appeared with a couple of hula hoops and a basketball. They were mostly boys, probably around ten years old or so, but there were a few girls as well, all in bathing suits, shiny wet with their hair slicked flat, screaming and giggling the way kids do. I imagined they'd probably been playing with a garden hose to cool off.

At the edge of Levi's dusty yard, there were three squirrels racing around in the brush at the foot of the pines and chattering at one another, and there was a loud whispering like the white noise of a broken radio coming from above as the pine needles shimmied in the steady breeze off the coast. None of that, however, could drown out the silence of the body lying not three feet away from me.

When Michael and I were little, Siesta Key was practically deserted compared to what it's become in the past thirty years or so. Back then we could wander around for hours by ourselves. The entire island was as safe as our own front porch, and if you wanted a little excitement or drama, you were plumb out of luck.

But that didn't stop me. I managed to get myself into trouble on a daily basis without even trying. If there was a hornet's nest hidden in a tree, that was the tree I'd climb. If a fight broke out at school, I was the primary witness. If a newborn bird was pushed out of its nest, you could bet the farm I'd be standing nearby, and then I'd be saddled with the inevitable heartbreak of trying to keep it alive. My grandmother called it the Hemingway Curse, and I think it haunts me to this very day. Basically, if there's a wrong place to be, I'll be there, and if there's a bad time for it, I'll arrive promptly.

At almost the exact moment I hung up with 911, I heard the sirens start up from the north, thin and distant at first, so I knew the crew was probably coming from Sarasota Memorial. The operator had asked me all the standard questions: Was the victim stable? Was he conscious? Was he breathing? Was I able to perform CPR?

All I could do was hang my head between my knees, shaking slightly and muttering, "No," over and over again while she went down the list. It's standard procedure to dispatch an ambulance crew no matter what, even if the person reporting the victim is one hundred percent certain there's no hope. As fragile as the human body is, it's also amazingly resilient, and even in cases where every organ in a person's body has ground to a stop — the lungs, the heart, even the brain — with the right equipment and a little luck, a skilled emergency crew can work miracles.

But I knew, in Levi's case, it was hopeless. The massive pool of blood was bad enough, but the way its edges had dried meant he'd been lying there for at least a few hours. The back of his legs had taken on a milky translucence, while gravity had drawn what little blood was left down toward the floor, turning the front of his legs a pale eggplant-purple, something that only happens after a body has long stopped. His knees were pressed into the hard tile floor, and there were rings of white skin where the blood couldn't reach without the will of his heart to force it there.

Before the 911 operator had hung up, telling me to stay where I was and not to touch anything, she had asked if I was alone. I said yes, which of course wasn't true, but it might as well have been. Sasquatch was still propped up against Levi's car. She'd been snoring quietly the whole time, but as the sirens grew closer they must have roused her, because she raised her head abruptly and looked around with glazed, frightened eyes.

I tried to give her a comforting smile. "It's okay. The police are almost here."

She blinked a couple of times and frowned, and then, before I could say anything else, she looked down at the pool of blood in the open doorway behind me and her gaze traveled to Levi's legs.

"No . . ."

Her eyes widened as she pushed herself up onto the car and shook her head from side to side. "No. No. No . . ."

I said, "It's okay, try not to panic."

She climbed over the side of the hood and

slid down to the ground, her eyes glued to Levi's body the whole time, but now she looked directly at me.

Her voice was trembling. "What happened?"

"I called 911 right away. They're almost here."

Just then, an ambulance came around the corner of Old Wharf Way and headed through the trailer park toward us. The woman looked over her shoulder and then back at me, and for a moment I thought I saw something flash in her eyes, something subtle . . . It was *triumph.*

She shook her head as she pushed herself off the ground and backed away.

I said, "Hold on. You should wait —"

But she wouldn't let me finish. The next thing I knew she was running across the yard, shrieking at the top of her lungs and windmilling her arms at the emergency crew like she was some kind of innocent damsel in distress and they were her only hope of survival. As the ambulance slowed to a stop in front of her, she fell to the ground in the middle of the road and crawled forward a few more feet on her hands and knees, sobbing, her head flailing violently up and down, her screams piercing the air.

10

I was sitting in the passenger seat of the Bronco with my sunglasses on and my legs tucked up under me. The sun was still glaring down like a blowtorch, but that wasn't why I was wearing glasses. I needed something to hide behind.

The group of kids playing in the street had moved closer and were standing in a huddle at the head of the dirt road, watching with quiet faces, and I noticed the little blond-headed boy with the pogo stick beyond them. He was by himself, standing on his toes in the grass at the edge of his yard like he was afraid to step into the street. The squirrels had retreated into the treetops to view the proceedings from a safer distance.

It hadn't taken long before practically the entire dirt road leading up to Levi's trailer was filled with a line of emergency response vehicles with all their lights flashing. The ambulance had pulled in just behind Levi's car, but the two sheriff's cruisers had parked just shy of the yard, probably to minimize the possibility of disturbing potential evidence. A couple of unmarked sedans had appeared moments later and were idling behind the cruisers.

Two of the deputies led Sasquatch over to the side, and another officer — he must have been new to the force, because I didn't recognize him — was standing a few feet to the left of the Bronco, pretending not to watch me. I couldn't help but notice he'd situated himself where he could see my hands. I was probably just being paranoid, but I got the distinct feeling he'd been told to watch out for any sudden movements.

Standing on the bottom step of Levi's trailer, surveying the scene, was a tall, lanky man with dark skin and sad, drooping eyes — Sergeant Woodrow Owens. He stood there quietly for a few moments, and then turned and motioned to one of the officers to join him. After they spoke, the deputy nodded and pointed in my direction, but Owens didn't look over.

I sank down in my seat and sighed. Sergeant Owens had been my commanding officer when I was on the force. After Todd and Christy were killed, while everyone else

108

at the station was waiting for me to pull out of the depths and return to my old self again, it was Owens who had called me into his office and dismissed me from service. It hadn't surprised me one bit. We both knew I was too fragile, too unstable, too "fucked up" (his words, not mine) to continue in any capacity as a sheriff's deputy.

There was a fly skating along the inside of the windshield, buzzing back and forth in a vain attempt to escape to the outside. The Bronco was broiling hot, but I couldn't bring myself to turn on the AC. The idea of starting the engine and letting it idle while less than a hundred feet away the officers were inspecting the scene of a murder felt wrong, so I had the windows on both sides of the car rolled down all the way. That didn't seem to help the fly one bit, though. He just kept skittering from side to side, convinced he was trapped and that the only way out was forward.

I looked over at Levi's trailer and felt a tremor of panic begin to rumble somewhere deep inside me, threatening to turn into a scream. I knew right then and there if I wasn't careful I'd fall apart, and for a couple of seconds I had an overwhelming urge to kick the car door open and just run . . . run right into the woods and keep on running until the whole thing was far behind me.

Luckily, I managed to stay put. I was pretty sure racing through the trees screaming like a maniac might come off as a little weird, if not downright suspicious, so instead I closed my eyes and took a deep breath.

I imagined I was sitting on a stretch of white sand, gazing out at the still blue line where the ocean meets the sky, perfectly level and straight. I tried to see the waves rolling in, one after the other, and I timed my breathing to the sound they made as they crashed over the sand. It seemed to help. The tremor in the pit of my stomach quieted down, and the urge to scream slowly disappeared, except that every once in a while the image of Levi's astonished eyes would bubble up and my breath would catch.

I'm not sure how long I'd been sitting there when I heard someone say, "Miz Hemingway . . ."

Sergeant Owens was standing right next to my window, looking down with a pained expression on his face. His voice deep and slow as oozing honey he said, "Mind if I join you?"

I scooted over to the driver's seat as he went around the front and opened up the passenger door. Owens had never been much of a dresser, but as he slid in next to me I noticed he was wearing gray dress slacks with shiny black oxfords and a crisp white dress shirt. There was a hint of aftershave in the air, like mint and orange peel, and I wondered what he'd been doing when he received the call to come here.

He let the door close softly and then folded his hands in his lap. "Well . . ."

I said. "Okay, so this morning when I left my house, Levi was parked outside my driveway. At first I thought maybe he needed help, but then —"

He put his hand up. "Now, hold on. First of all, you okay?"

Just the sound of his soothing baritone calmed my nerves a bit. "Oh. I'm fine, sir, thanks."

He nodded. "All right. And you didn't kill that man in that trailer over there, did you?"

"Sergeant Owens, you know I didn't."

The corners of his mouth rose slightly. "Yes, ma'am. I figured as much, but it's my job to kick at every barking dog that runs by, if you'll pardon the expression. Did you know him?"

"Sort of. His name is Levi Radcliff. We went to school together."

Just then I heard a woman's voice and

looked up. Sasquatch was standing in the middle of several deputies, shaking her head and angrily wagging her finger in the air.

Owens said, "And you said he was parked outside your driveway this morning?"

"Yeah, he was there when I left for work. At least I think it was him."

"And what time was that?"

"About five a.m."

"That seems a tad unusual, doesn't it?"

"No, because he delivers the morning paper."

He nodded. "And did he seem all right to you at the time?"

"Well, that's just it. We didn't talk. I thought maybe he was having car trouble. I went over to see if he needed help, but then he pulled away, so I figured he was fine. I didn't think about it until later. I was at my first client this morning, Buster and Linda Keller —"

"Yes, Deputy Morgan submitted his report to me a little while ago."

"Oh. So you know about Dick Cheney?"

He frowned. "Dick Cheney?"

"That's what I call Mrs. Keller's mask."

"Ah. The one your imaginary assailant was wearing."

I nodded. "Yeah, except I'm beginning to think it wasn't so imaginary. When I was unlocking the front door, I heard a car go by in the street, then after I got attacked . . ."

He raised an eyebrow.

"I mean *allegedly* attacked, I remembered there'd been a car on the road behind me on my way there, too. It got me thinking maybe I'd been followed. I mean, you have to admit it makes sense. If a crook was on the lookout for wealthy people who are out of town, all they'd have to do is follow me around for a while. It wouldn't take long to compile a pretty good list of vulnerable houses to hit."

"Perhaps, but I don't see what any of that has to do with the situation here."

"Well, I had already decided to ask Levi if he'd seen anything. There aren't too many people out and about that time of morning, so I knew if there'd been anything suspicious, he might have noticed it. Then when I found out he never finished his paper route, it just seemed too weird to be a coincidence, and I got worried something was wrong —"

Just then Sasquatch's voice rose again, and I heard one of the deputies say, "Ma'am, I'm going to have to ask you to calm down."

I said, "She may need some medical attention. After I knocked on Levi's door, it swung open, and when she saw him she fainted right on top of me. I tried to calm her down when she woke up but she was too upset. She said someone came home with Levi last night, a woman, and she's convinced it was me."

"Yeah, I'd say she's not one bit happy with you."

"Is she his girlfriend?"

"Fiancée. She lives in one of the trailers up the road." He sighed as he reached up and massaged the bridge of his nose with his thumb and forefinger. "I still wish I understood what the hell you were doing here."

"I know it sounds crazy, but I just got worried. Judy — she's the waitress at the diner — she told me their morning paper never came, and then it turned out half the people in the diner didn't get their paper, either, and it's really unusual for Levi not to finish his route, and then . . ." I stopped and sighed. Apparently, explaining what the hell I was doing here wasn't so easy.

I said, "I guess you could say it was just a hunch."

He nodded. "Well, I've got a hunch there's somebody else who'll want to hear this, too. So you might as well save your energy."

He was looking across the yard. I turned and followed his gaze to the line of emergency vehicles. At the end was a black SUV with tinted windows. The driver's-side door swung open and out stepped a rangy, long-boned woman in her mid-forties, with pale skin and frizzy shoulder-length hair the color of a baked sweet potato.

I recognized her right away — Detective Samantha McKenzie, the sheriff's lead homicide detective. She was wearing a plain cotton skirt about the same ruddy color as her hair, and a plain, nondescript blouse with two vertical lines of small brown buttons down the front. Despite the mind-numbing heat, she had a thin gray scarf draped loosely around her neck, which I knew right away was probably to protect her freckled skin from the sun.

She had a cell phone in one hand, holding it out in front of her mouth like a walkie-talkie, and cradled in her other hand was another cell phone, which she was thumbing as she walked toward us alongside the line of cars.

One of the deputies trotted over to meet her as she snapped both phones shut and dropped them down in a canvas duffel bag slung over her shoulder, and then they walked across the yard together. The whole way, the deputy was talking under his breath, but when they got even with Levi's convertible, he waited quietly while McKenzie went up the two short steps and looked inside the trailer.

There was just a beat, like a millisecond, and then she turned and said something short to him. He immediately nodded and ran back across the yard to one of the squad cars and reached in for his radio.

I said, "So, his fiancée . . . does she have any idea who might have done this?"

He nodded. "Her name's Mona Duffy, and yeah, she seems to know exactly who did it."

I turned to him. "Who?"

He looked down at his hands and rubbed his fingers together as if they were aching. "Who do you think?"

Detective McKenzie had pulled a pair of sky-blue rubber gloves out of her bag. She pushed them down into one of the pockets on her skirt and then turned and looked in our direction, shielding her eyes from the sun with the back of her hand.

"Well," Sergeant Owens said, "shall we?"

11

There were several deputies working their way around the perimeter of the property, driving metal stakes into the ground with rubber mallets and hanging up a border of yellow and black police tape to mark off the crime scene. Two of the deputies had led Levi's fiancée down the road, and I imagined she was sitting in her trailer now, telling them how she'd found me over Levi's body, and more than likely how she'd narrowly escaped getting murdered herself.

McKenzie adjusted the scarf around her neck. "I understand you've had quite a day."

"Yeah, you could say that. I think I'm still in a state of shock."

We were standing next to the pile of old tires in the middle of the yard, and instead of looking me in the eye Detective McKenzie was gazing thoughtfully at a spot between my eyebrows and about an inch up my forehead, which I knew from previous experience is normal, at least for her. It always makes me feel slightly off-kilter, like I'm on a boat at sea and can't quite find my footing. I don't know if it's intentional on her part or not, but I have my suspicions.

She reached into her shoulder bag and pulled out a clipboard with a yellow-leafed notepad attached. "I won't keep you long. I got a full report from one of the deputies, but I'd like to clear up a couple of things. I imagine this is the last place on earth you'd like to be right now . . ."

Her voice ended with just the slightest hint of a question as she looked around the yard. The Sarasota ambulance was still parked directly behind Levi's car, but the two emergency medical technicians had walked down the line of responding vehicles behind us and were leaning against a couple of pine trees smoking cigarettes. Everyone else was keeping their distance, too.

On TV shows, they always act like the scene of a murder is a big party with lots of people, where the dead body is the center of everyone's attention and the investigators and crime photographers and law enforcement guys are all flitting around flashing their badges and cameras and guns at one another, busily pulling a wallet out of the victim's pocket, or lifting up the victim's shirt to reveal bullet holes or knife wounds.

In reality it's not so exciting, and in fact most of what goes on in those shows would be one hundred percent illegal in the real world. First of all, nobody looks like a part-time model — well, there might be a couple of exceptions — but I guarantee you nobody's running around touching a thing, especially if it's anywhere near the body, and only a few key people are allowed access to the actual scene of the crime. I don't care if you're the sheriff or the chief of police or the mayor of Munchkin City, if you don't have a really good reason to be there, you have to wait on the other side of the police tape with all the other gawkers, rubberneckers, and TV reporters.

There's only one goal on the mind of every crime specialist who first responds to the discovery of a dead body, and that is to treat the victim and every single thing he or she might have come in contact with as potential pieces of a massive and volatile puzzle — because that's exactly what it is. Everything is evidence. Every surface, every hair, every speck of dust, every fiber, every blade of grass. Even the slightest, seemingly trivial disturbance could result in a piece of the puzzle being lost, and that could mean the difference between finding an answer to what happened, and letting a murderer get away with . . . well, you know what I mean.

"Which reminds me," McKenzie said as she pulled a ballpoint pen out of one of the pockets on her skirt. "What are you doing here?"

I gulped. "Um, it's kind of a weird story."

She clicked the tip of the pen with the thumb of her left hand and looked me straight in the forehead. "Try me."

I told her the whole sordid thing, starting with Levi's car parked outside my driveway that morning and ending with Sasquatch fainting and nearly hurling us both headfirst into the trailer. To be on the safe side, I gave her the whole kit and caboodle in between, too, every detail along the way whether I thought it was relevant or not — every Dick Cheney, every imaginary candle and every big-eared, red-toenailed she-Buddha I could remember. I even threw in my brief history of fainting spells just in case.

After I finished she was quiet for a couple of moments. She looked up at the sky and mumbled in a kind of sing-song voice, "Where's Megan Granda?"

I think I was expecting her to say something like, *That's quite a story,* or even *Are you out of your cotton-picking mind?* But instead she just scanned the yard with a wry smile on her face and repeated under her breath, "Where's Megan Granda?"

I had no idea who or where Megan Granda was, but I figured I should probably just play along, so I shook my head slightly and shrugged. "Uh, I don't know."

At that, McKenzie frowned slightly, and then scribbled in her notepad as she muttered under her breath, "So when you first arrived, was there anyone else on the street that you recall?"

I shook my head. "No, at least not any cars. There was a little boy playing with a pogo stick in his yard, but other than that I didn't see anybody."

"And about what time did you arrive?"

"I'm not sure."

She looked down at her notes. "I'm told your call came in at exactly 10:27 a.m. Does that sound right?"

I nodded. "Yeah, and I think I was only here a few minutes before that. As soon as I saw Levi's car, I got out to knock on his door, and I probably only talked to his fiancée about twenty seconds before we saw his body . . ."

"And how did you know it was his?"

I frowned. It had been a while since I'd last had a full-fledged conversation with Detective McKenzie. I'd forgotten how her

121

mind careened from one thought to the other. I've never ridden blindfolded on a unicycle through a corn maze, but I would imagine it feels pretty much the same.

Before I could answer she said, with a note of impatience in her voice, "How did you know it was his car, how did you know it was his fiancée, and how did you know it was his body?"

I put my hands on my hips and thought, *Enough.*

The whole day was starting to feel like a parade of abusive lunkheads who refused for one reason or another to take me seriously, from Dick Cheney to Morgan to Sasquatch, and now this honey badger of a woman. I took a deep breath, composing an answer in my head like I was preparing for a school report.

I said, "I knew it was his car because he's been delivering the paper in it for twenty years. I knew Sasquatch . . . I mean, that woman, was Levi's fiancée because she told me, in her words, that I was trespassing on her man, and also because Sergeant Owens told me, and I knew it was Levi's body because I've known him since grade school and it had his face attached to it."

She didn't miss a beat. "It's good to see you again, Dixie."

I blinked. If my frustration was getting through, she wasn't letting on. "Uh, you, too."

"And how's your brother . . . it's Michael, right?"

"Yeah. Oh, he's great, thanks."

"And how well do you know him?"

Okay, I thought to myself. *You can do this.* I had a feeling she wasn't really interested in how well I know my brother. I tried to picture my brain working the way I pictured hers, like a tangled web of telephone wires and high-speed Internet cables wrapped around a nest of smoking cogs and spinning reel-to-reel tapes, with maybe a couple of fuses mixed in, throwing off sparks and little bolts of lightning. My mouth was fixed in a kind of dumb *O* as I mentally rewound our conversation a couple of beats.

"You mean Levi?"

She nodded. "You said you've known him since grade school?"

"Right. We had a few classes together, but we weren't really that close."

I realized I was still holding my indignant *Enough* pose, which consisted of my fists pressed firmly into my ribs and my head cocked to one side. Somehow, without my even realizing it, McKenzie had charmed me right back into submission, but appar-

123

ently my body hadn't caught up yet. I tried to relax my arms and slid my hands down into my pockets as nonchalantly as possible.

I said, "After graduation I didn't see him again except on his morning paper route. We're both up early, so our paths cross every once in a while, but that's about it."

"And how did you know where to look for him?"

"My friend Tanisha. She's the cook at the diner. She lives in this neighborhood, although I'm not sure which place is hers. She might be able to tell you more about him."

"Okay, that's helpful. So, you were about to knock on Levi's door . . ."

"Right, I was just about to knock and I was trying to figure out what I would say to him, and then all of a sudden his fiancée was there. She said this was private property, and I told her I was just checking on Levi."

"And where did she come from?"

"I don't know. I turned around and there she was, just to the left of his car." I pointed at the driver's-side door of Levi's LeSabre.

"And what were her words, exactly?"

"She was pretty upset right from the start. I think she said, 'Can I help you?' or something like that. I tried to tell her I was a friend of Levi's and I just wanted to make sure he was okay, but she was hell-bent on getting rid of me. Apparently, Levi came home last night with another woman, and she thinks it was me."

McKenzie flipped a page over in her pad, and without looking up said, "She says you and Levi came home last night around 11:30. Does that sound right?"

I shook my head slowly. "No. That does *not* sound right. Detective McKenzie, I don't know who that woman was, but it definitely wasn't me. I was not here last night."

"Well, then, you'll forgive me, but I do need to ask . . . where were you?"

"I was home."

"And were you alone or was there someone with you?"

I felt my ears turning red. "Yes."

Her eyes narrowed slightly. "Yes, you —"

I cut her off. "Yes, there was someone with me, and no, I was not alone."

"And you don't by any chance happen to know where we might find someone in Levi's family . . . his parents, or a sibling perhaps?"

"No. I'd think that would be a good question for his fiancée."

She nodded and then leaned in slightly. "Just between you and me . . ." She looked over her shoulder and lowered her voice. "Sasquatch — I believe that's what you called her — is a bit unstable."

One of the deputies stepped up and whispered something in McKenzie's ear. She nodded curtly and put her hand out. "Thanks for your time, Dixie. I think I'd better go have a talk with her now."

I nodded mutely.

"In the meantime, I need to ask that you not talk about this to anyone, at least not until we've had a chance to locate the next of kin."

Just then, a black and white van pulled in behind the row of cars. I figured it was probably the department's new mobile forensics unit, which they'd been able to purchase recently thanks to an anonymous donation. A woman in dark navy pants and a white lab coat stepped out with a bulky black briefcase. It looked very official and high-tech, like something you might keep the nation's nuclear codes in.

The woman was exquisitely beautiful, with jet-black hair pulled back in a tight ponytail, and almond-shaped eyes that were a deep obsidian-brown. She looked like a Chinese movie star, or — I'll admit it — like a part-time model from one of those TV crime shows. As I made my way back to the

Bronco, I heard her say, "Detective McKenzie? I'm Megan Granda."

In a daze, I got behind the wheel and backed up slowly until the nose of the Bronco was pointed out, then I headed toward the stretch of grass along the shoulder of the dirt road. I was wondering if I'd be able to make it through without making everyone move their cars when I looked up in the rearview mirror to find Detective McKenzie trotting along behind me and waving a finger in the air. I slowed to a stop as she came around to the window.

"Dixie, sorry." She put her hands on her hips and paused to catch her breath. "I just remembered one more thing. About this morning, are you absolutely certain it was Levi parked outside your driveway?"

I said, "I just assumed it was him because that's usually about the time the paper arrives, and it definitely looked like his car . . ."

"But you're not sure."

I shook my head. "It was so dark and foggy."

"It might help pinpoint the time of death . . ."

I don't think the reality of what had happened had actually sunk in yet, because the idea that there was a "time of death" sent a

127

tremor down my spine.

I said, "I wish I could say for sure, but he's the only person on the island I can think of that would've had a good reason for being there, right?"

She turned and looked in the direction of the trailer. For a second I imagined all those cogs and wheels in her head spinning in slow, deliberate circles, then she turned and for the first time looked me directly in the eye.

"Define *good.*"

12

The whole way home, I left the windows in the Bronco rolled down, and eventually — I'm not sure when — my little fly friend escaped back into the wild. The warm breeze felt good blowing through my hair, and the sound the wind made as it rushed through the car helped dampen the melee of thoughts that were spinning around inside my head. I could barely hold on to one before another would swoop in and knock it out of the way.

I kept seeing Levi's face, the way I remembered him from high school, the way he always smiled and gave me a wave whenever our paths crossed, but then the image of his body lying on the floor of the trailer would rush in, and then Sasquatch's angry maw would appear, telling me to get the hell off her property, and then Dick Cheney's scary eyes and gnashing teeth bearing down, and then Levi's car outside my driveway and candles and curtains and red-toed Buddhas, all bouncing around in my brain like Ping-Pong balls in a front-load washing machine.

I shook my head and tried to clear it all away. It had probably been a bit of an understatement when I told Detective McKenzie I was in shock, because as soon as I turned out of Grand Pelican Commons and headed up Tamiami Trail, my whole body started shivering slightly, despite the fact that the sun was straight overhead and it was easily ninety degrees in the shade.

The copper pod trees along Midnight Pass Road were all blanketed with their yellow orchidlike blossoms, filling the air with the scent of crushed grapes, and following along in the clouds over the treetops to the west was a lone osprey, its wings spread wide, coasting on the breeze. For a while I pretended he was my own personal escort, assigned to make sure I got home safe and sound. It felt good to think I wasn't alone.

Poor Levi.

I couldn't get the image of his lifeless body out of my mind. In spite of our brief encounter outside Mrs. White's ninth-grade history class (or maybe because of it) we hadn't really talked that much in the years following. Every once in a while we'd wind up in the same class or study period, and one of his buddies on the baseball team was the brother of one of my best girlfriends, so we often found ourselves at the same parties or sitting together at football games, but that was about the extent of it. He was tall, blond, good-looking, and he always seemed like a nice enough kid, even if, as Judy had said, he did have a bit of a wild streak in him . . . but in the era before cell phones and computer games, every teenager with half a pulse went through a wild stage. There wasn't much else to do in a sleepy beach town like Siesta Key.

Of course, there was drinking, and a lot of kids smoked pot, especially the older ones, but if there were harder drugs than that being passed around, I never saw them. Levi and his friends would stay out partying and carousing in the streets until all hours of the night, giving their parents heart palpitations and early-onset baldness, and sometimes they'd congregate in the parking lot at the old Ringling Shopping Center, but basically all they did was drink beer and make a lot of noise until the cops would roll through and order them all home. I remember hearing that Levi had been hauled in for public intoxication shortly after graduation, he'd even spent a night in jail, but other than that, there was no indication he'd ever wind up in more serious trouble.

But now, I wondered. As for Levi's money situation, he was clearly living hand-to-mouth. I don't know how much a paper delivery boy makes these days, but newspapers everywhere are struggling to make ends meet, so I doubt it's much more than minimum wage. Was it possible Levi had been forced to turn to more desperate means . . . drugs or petty burglary or something worse? It was a terrible thought, but why else would anyone want to kill him?

I suddenly realized I was sitting in the carport at my place with the engine idling, staring straight ahead like a zombie. I switched off the ignition and reached for my backpack, and just then I heard a car coming up the driveway. Right away I could tell by the sound of the wheels on the crushed shell who it was: Paco and my brother, Michael, in their four-wheel-drive pickup truck. Michael is a firefighter, just like our father before him. He's big and blond and broad, with pure blue eyes that can melt the hearts of either sex in a matter of seconds.

Paco, on the other hand, is slim and tall, with long muscles and deep olive skin, the kind of good looks that make your toes flutter and your eyelashes curl, plus he rides a motorcycle, which in my book only adds to his overall hotness factor. Women all over the island have fantasized about turning Michael and Paco straight, but there's little chance of that — they've been together almost fifteen years now. Paco is my brother-in-love.

Michael flashed me a toothy grin as they backed up to the edge of the deck. The fact that they weren't pulling in next to me meant only one thing: groceries.

"Hey, sexy," Paco said as he stepped out and shut the door with a hip bump. "You're just in time to help unload."

Normally, the vision of the two of them pulling in with a truckload of goodies is enough to make me forget all the troubles in the world, especially since they both happen to be really good cooks, but it wasn't working this time. I just stood there with my arms dangling helplessly at my sides.

I said, "Somebody killed Levi Radcliff."

Just like that. I hadn't meant to blurt it out so fast, but I couldn't help myself. Michael had hopped out of the truck on the other side and was halfway around the front fender when he stopped dead in his tracks.

"What?"

I felt my eyes start to sting with tears. I said, "Somebody killed him. This morning. I was afraid something was wrong so I went over to his place at Grand Pelican. The door was open and he was on the floor in a pool of blood . . ."

I had to stop and screw the heels of my palms into my eye sockets to stave off the waterworks, but then the next thing I knew Michael's big arms were folding around my shoulders. Instinctively, I tried to draw away, but he held on.

I said, "What are you doing?"

"I'm hugging you."

I snuffled, drawing the back of my hand across my nose. "Yeah, I know that. But *why*?"

His voice was steady as he hugged me a little tighter. "You know exactly why."

Long before any of us were twinkles in anyone's eye, my grandfather, Jesse Napoleon Hemingway, found himself on a business trip in Florida. He was twenty-two years old, newly engaged, and it was the first time he'd ever stepped foot out of his hometown of Manhattan, Kansas. He'd been sent here to convince a group of local businessmen to invest in the latest craze: portable steel sandwich shops, those shiny prefab diners shaped like railroad cars that started sprouting up all over the country in the thirties and forties. They could be shipped anywhere there was a mom and a pop with some cash and a dream of opening their very own restaurant.

The way my grandmother told it, that Florida air must have gone straight to my grandfather's head like a double shot of whiskey, because she never found out how many diners he sold on that trip — they never even discussed it. The day my grandfather returned home he presented her with the deed to a plot of land facing the ocean on the southern end of Siesta Key. My grandmother was none too pleased, especially since by her calculation they'd spent at least a hundred hours strolling hand in hand along the banks of nearby Walnut Creek, dreaming about their plans for the future, choosing names for their children, and discussing in which town (within a thirty-mile radius) they would build a home and spend the rest of their lives together.

In public, at least as a young woman, my grandmother was the model wife, quiet and demure — the way a young woman was expected to be in those days — but behind closed doors she let my grandfather know in no uncertain terms that there wasn't a snowball's chance in hell she was leaving Kansas, and if he wanted to go live in a spit of a sandbox on an island in the middle of nowhere like a hermit crab, he could plumb well do it by himself.

Luckily for me and my brother, my grandfather knew a thing or two about the art of persuasion, because if he hadn't worked things out between them, not only would we not have inherited this house, we would never have even existed. Using every sales trick in the book, he finally convinced her to make the trip to Florida to see it for herself. They stood shoulder to shoulder at the water's edge, holding their shoes in their hands as the waves lapped at their toes, and watched the sun set into the sea.

The sky turned colors my grandmother didn't even know existed, and she always said it must have been divine intervention, because the beauty of that moment took her breath away. She knew it was God's way of telling her she was finally home. Of course, it hadn't hurt one bit that my grandfather had phoned ahead for the local sunset schedule. He had timed their arrival perfectly.

Now, I live in the one-bedroom apartment over the carport that was built for visiting relatives from back home — it's small but it suits me just fine — and Michael and Paco live in the main house.

While Paco unloaded the groceries and Michael put on a pot of coffee, I slumped down on one of the barstools in the kitchen and laid my head down on the big butcher-block island. I told them everything that had happened . . . well, almost everything. I left Dick Cheney out of the story. At that point, I still wasn't sure whether I'd fainted or not, and there was no point getting them all worked up about a home invasion or an assault with a deadly Buddha if in reality the whole thing had just been a little light-headedness on my part.

"Hold on a second." Michael slid a cup of coffee toward me with one hand while he dropped a single sugar cube down in it with the other. "What do you mean —"

I interrupted, "Michael, I don't want to talk about it."

"You don't even know what I'm going to say!"

"Yes, I do. You're going to say, 'What do you mean, light-headed?' "

He blinked. "Well?"

I laid my cheek back down on the table. "Ugh. I don't know. I just blacked out for a second, and then the next thing I knew I

137

was flat on my stomach."

I looked up at Paco just in time to see the faint smile on his lips fade. He was looking at the bump on top of my head.

"So you hit your head when you fell?"

I nodded. "Yeah, it hurt like hell but it's feeling better now."

He frowned slightly as he folded up a paper bag and pushed it down in the storage bin under the sink, mumbling, "You should probably get that looked at."

Michael sat down in the stool opposite me. "Dixie, I still don't get it. You find out somebody didn't get their morning paper, so you race over to Levi's house?"

I said, "Not *somebody*. A whole bunch of people. Nearly half the people in the diner said their paper never came, and you know Levi, he hasn't missed a day of work in twenty years."

"Okay, but still, I don't understand how you knew something was wrong. You said yourself you thought he was having car trouble. Wouldn't that explain it right there? I mean, it just doesn't add up."

I turned to Paco for help. I can usually count on him to take my side in these kinds of things. He knows as well as I do that Michael tends to worry too much, but he just shrugged. "Do you want to tell him, or should I?"

I said, "Tell him what?"

He cocked his head to the side and grimaced slightly. "Sorry, kid."

"Okay, first of all, don't call me 'kid,' and second of all, I have no idea what you're talking about."

I could feel my cheeks getting hot. Paco is an undercover agent with the Sarasota Investigations Bureau, which means he helps catch drug dealers and smugglers and all kinds of assorted bad guys. Technically I'm not supposed to know, but I figured it out a long time ago and now it's just a house rule that we don't talk about it. Sometimes he disappears for days or even weeks, during which time Michael and I walk around on eggshells chewing our fingernails. It's a dangerous job. He's fluent in at least five languages (including Korean), and his IQ is probably higher than my checking account balance.

In other words, he's smart.

As Paco and I stared each other down, Michael was looking back and forth between us like a spectator at a tennis game. "Okay, what's going on?"

I rolled my eyes. "I give up. You tell him, if you think you know so much."

He sat down next to Michael and put one

hand on his shoulder, as if to steady him. "Somebody broke into the Kellers' house and hit her over the head. That's why she blacked out."

I bolted upright as Michael's jaw fell open and we both said, "What?"

Michael said, "Dixie, what the hell?"

I said, "Paco, you really think so?"

He nodded. "And I was just reading in the paper, there's been a string of break-ins on the island the past few weeks. They've been targeting vacant houses."

Michael sawed both his hands in the air like a referee on a football field. "Whoa, whoa, whoa! What the hell are you guys talking about?"

Paco shrugged. "I can tell by that bump. When people faint, they usually just keel straight over, so lots of times they'll have a bloody nose, or an injury to the back or the side of the head." He turned to me. "I don't know how you could've hit the very top of your head unless you were doing somersaults or backflips when you fainted."

Michael's eyes narrowed. He pursed his lips to one side and with a slow, sarcastic edge to his voice said, "Dixie, were you doing somersaults or backflips when you fainted?"

I looked at Paco and then back at Michael, and then reached up and gingerly touched my walnut-sized bump.

I said, "Huh."

13

It's probably only a couple hundred feet, but the walk from Michael and Paco's kitchen to my front door felt like a hundred miles, mainly because my head was spinning all over again — not because I was dizzy, but because I was completely lost in thought as I ambled across the courtyard.

Paco had admitted he was really only making an educated guess about how I got my bump, but he'd also said he was beginning to recognize all the little telltale signs I exhibit when I'm not telling the entire truth . . . something I sometimes do to protect Michael. Being my older brother hasn't always been a bed of roses, and he's got a light sprinkling of gray hair on his head to prove it.

I made a mental note to figure out exactly *which* telltale signs Paco was referring to, but for now I knew he was on to something: When I woke up and found myself on the floor of the Kellers' laundry room, I was flat out on my stomach with my cheek smashed into the floor, which Paco said would indicate that I'd fallen straight forward. But if that was the case, why was there a bump on the very top of my head and not a gash on my cheek? Or a black eye? Or, at the very least, a bloody nose?

I didn't want to jump to conclusions, but if Paco was right, it could mean only one thing: I wasn't hallucinating when I saw Dick Cheney. And it wasn't just a dream that he bonked me on the head with a small stone figurine. As for the lit candles on the coffee table and the open doors in the living room — well, it was anybody's guess. After a blow like that it was a wonder I hadn't seen a halo of stars and yellow tweety-birds flying around my head.

During my deputy training, we were subjected to a lecture by a retired medical examiner visiting from Orlando who had made a name for herself in the field of forensic osteology. With me wincing the entire time, she had gone down a list of practically every bone in the human body, along with a corresponding list of all the various ways in which each of those bones is most typically broken. When it came to injuries to the top of the skull, she said in nearly every case it was the result of either a physical attack or, strangely enough, falling debris.

It had stuck with me all these years mainly because one of her cases had involved a man who'd been mysteriously killed while taking a stroll all alone in an open field. He had died of a cerebral hemorrhage, and the only sign of injury was a curious dent in the top of his skull. To everyone's utter horror (including my own) it was later proven that a tiny frozen chunk of wastewater, dropped from an overpassing plane, had landed right on top of him. Ever since then, whenever I hear a plane overhead, I don't exactly run for cover, but I keep my eyes open.

"Mreeep?"

Just as I was about to unlock the front door, I felt something furry brush up against my ankle and looked down to find Ella Fitzgerald gazing up at me. Ella is technically my cat, but it didn't take her long to figure out all the good stuff comes out of the main house, so she spends most of her time hanging out with Michael and Paco. She's a true Persian mix calico — meaning she's got some Persian in her bloodline and her coat has distinct patches of black, white, and red. She earned her name by the funny scatting sounds she makes.

I said, "Oh, my goodness, Ella! Fancy meeting you here!"

She said, *"Thrrrip mrack!"* and then walked her paws up my legs, being careful to keep her claws in, and arched her long body as she flicked her snow-white whiskers at me. I handed her the little piece of smoked salmon that I'd snatched out of Michael and Paco's fridge and winked at her.

"Thanks for coming up with me. I could use a little company right now."

She downed the salmon in one quick gulp and then squinted her eyes, which in cat language means, *I love you.* Or it means, *I love salmon.* Either way, I knew it was a dirty trick on my part, but I didn't feel like being alone and I knew Ella would follow me upstairs if she sensed I was hiding something yummy. When I handed it over I expected her to go right back down, but instead she waited while I opened the door.

"Oh, you wanna hang out for a bit?"

She tilted her head and eyed me curiously, as if to say, *Of course. Our love is deeper than salmon,* and then trotted in.

As soon as I shut the door I started peeling off my clothes. I left one shoe on the jute rug by the front door and another in the middle of my ragtag collection of furniture — a puffy couch, an old leather lounge chair, and a walnut coffee table that once belonged to my mother — and then I left both my socks on the floor just beyond the breakfast bar that separates the living room from the galley kitchen. As I stumbled down the short hall, I threw my shorts into the wicker basket in the laundry alcove and flung my T-shirt and bra into the bedroom before making a quick right turn into the bathroom.

I grabbed a towel and draped it over the handle to the shower door while I turned the water all the way up to Niagara Falls level. Ella slinked in behind me and curled up on the bath mat, and while I waited for the water to get hot I opened the mirrored doors of my medicine cabinet and stared at my meager collection of soaps and lotions. As soon as the shower filled with steam, I stepped in with a deep sigh, sliding the door behind me like I was closing the curtain on a very bad play.

I stood there and let the warm water stream over me, imagining it washing the whole morning right down the drain. That seemed to work for a couple of minutes, but as soon as I felt my body start to relax, a lump formed in the base of my throat and my eyes started to sting with tears.

"Oh, my God, don't be ridiculous," I said

out loud as I grabbed a bottle and squirted some shampoo on my palm. "You barely knew him."

But it was no use. As I worked my hair into a lather, I cried.

I cried like a baby.

I cried not just for Levi, but also — I'm ashamed to admit — for myself. I like to think I'm tough, but seeing Levi's lifeless body had thrown me for a loop, and now it dawned on me that even though we hadn't been close, even if he hadn't known it, Levi was something special to me. He would always be the boy who gave me my very first kiss, that first rush of breathlessness, that first taste of sex and love and deep, unquenchable need . . . at a time in my life when the world was simple, when life was good and innocent and never-ending.

Well, at some point, standing there thinking all those soapy thoughts with a frothy mix of shampoo and tears streaming down my cheeks, I caught a glimpse of Ella watching me quietly from her spot on the mat and realized I must have looked like a blubbering idiot, so I turned off the water and dried off as quickly as possible.

With the corner of my towel, I wiped the steam away from the mirror and parted my hair to check out my injury. It had gone down a bit, which was good, except now it looked like an angry nipple on the top of my head, or maybe a bite from one of those giant mosquitoes they're always talking about on the Nature Channel.

Ella rolled over on her side next to my feet and stretched herself out full-length as she lapped gently at the water droplets on my toes.

I said, "You know, you're lucky you don't have to be a human and deal with all the crap that comes with it. If I were you I'd be the happiest girl in the world. All you have to do is lie around and be cute."

She squinted her eyes and yawned, as if to suggest that it was, in fact, a pretty good life.

I padded naked into the bedroom and collapsed like a sack of grapefruit on the bed. There's a long high window along the back wall of my bedroom, and when the weather's warm, which is pretty much all year long, I keep it open so I can hear the ocean. Ella hopped up on the bed next to me and nuzzled her face against my cheek, and for the first time all day I felt safe and normal. I hugged her and gave her a kiss on the nose, a kind of thank-you for hanging out with me a while longer, and at that moment I made a decision.

I'd probably never know for certain what had happened to me at the Kellers' house, and furthermore, it probably didn't matter. I couldn't very well go back in time and change it, so the only thing I could do was forget about the whole thing.

But I couldn't forget about Levi.

Ella had scrunched herself up under my arm with her neck stretched across mine and her nose just under my chin. I lay there listening to the sound of her soft purrs mixed with the distant crash of the waves down below, and eventually I fell into a deep sleep.

I dreamed I was sitting on a beach chair in the middle of a tiny island, wearing a chocolate-brown full-length fur coat with my hair pulled back in a French braid. I knew I was dreaming right away because, one, I wouldn't wear a fur coat to save my life, and two, I was surrounded by about a hundred little hermit crabs, all sitting in their own tiny beach chairs and reading their own tiny newspapers.

I've been known to have some pretty wacky dreams, but I figured this was just my dream guide's way of making up for the lousy day I'd had so far. She probably thought I'd enjoy lounging around on a tropical island in a fur coat, and for now I didn't feel like arguing with her about the politics of fur, especially since the beach was pretty and the breeze felt so warm and relaxing. I leaned back in my chair and pressed my toes into the soft sand, waiting for whatever ridiculous gift she had in store for me next.

But then while I was waiting, the breeze picked up a bit and a couple of stray hairs dislodged themselves from my French braid. I reached up to smooth them back, and as my fingers played across the bump on my head, I felt a little jolt of pain.

Wait a minute, I thought to myself. *If this is a dream, why the hell does my head still hurt?* I looked around the island for my dream guide as I whispered, "This *is* a dream, right?"

14

The next thing I knew, my clock radio was blaring at me from my bedside table, and the song it was playing transported me right back to high school and Mrs. White's history class. At the start of every week, she'd serenade us with her own enthusiastic rendition of "Manic Monday" by the Bangles as she handed out our assignments for the day. We'd all groan and cover our ears, but we loved it.

I rolled over and smacked the snooze button with the palm of my hand and collapsed back down in bed. I don't take weekends off, so Mondays don't usually feel much different from any other day, but *manic* was as good a word as any for how my day had gone so far.

Apparently my nap had been pretty manic, too, because I'd thrashed around so much the blankets were wrapped around me like a straitjacket. I hadn't woken up enough yet to summon the energy to wriggle out of them, so instead I felt around for Ella, but she wasn't there.

"Kitty cat?"

I raised my head off the pillow and froze.

Out of the corner of my eye, I saw the outline of a man standing in the open doorway of my bedroom.

It's astonishing how fast the mind works. In less than a fraction of a second, all kinds of thoughts went zooming around inside my head, including a series of words that appeared like flash cards on a projection screen in front of me.

The first word was *STUPID.* Here I'd been wondering all morning if I'd been attacked or followed, and yet I hadn't bothered to lock the door when I got home.

The second word was *SCREAM,* which was funny because I'm not really a screamer. I'm more likely to deploy the rodent defense — completely still and quiet — but in this situation, alone in my apartment with a strange man not five feet from the foot of my bed, it didn't seem like such a bad idea.

The last word was *GUN.*

When I retired from the sheriff's department, I also retired my department-issue firearm, which I left on Sergeant Owens's desk along with my five-point deputy's badge. But like most officers, I kept a backup, and I still have mine: a Smith & Wesson .38 Special revolver. I store it in a velvet-lined case next to Todd's 9mm Glock, which hasn't been touched since he was killed. That case was right now directly underneath me in the hidden side drawer built into my bed.

Without even turning to look at the man standing in the doorway, I tried to calculate the odds of getting to my gun before he could get to me. Luckily, it would have been impossible.

The man whispered, "Dixie?"

My jaw dropped open.

He said, "Damn, babe. You must have been sound asleep."

As calmly as possible, I said, "Ethan, are you freakin' kidding me?"

He clapped his hands together like a prayer boy. "Sorry! I knocked first and called out, too . . . didn't you hear me?"

I sat up in bed, grabbing the sheet around me. "You nearly scared me to death!"

He leaned his shoulder against the doorway and raised one eyebrow. "Oh, really? Well, I guess that makes us even."

Ethan's ancestry is Seminole Indian. You can tell right away by his jet-black hair, which just barely brushes the top of his broad shoulders. He's in his early forties, tall, with eyes the color of dark brown coffee and eyelashes so thick you want to roll around in them. He was wearing dark pinstriped trousers, a crisp white button-down, amber cuff links, and a pale, rose-hued tie.

I don't know why, but the b-word is a little hard for me to wrap my mind around. *Partner* isn't good, either, it sounds like we're running a business together. *Beau* sounds too old-fashioned, and *life mate* just sounds ridiculous. Maybe it's because, in the grand scheme of things, Ethan and I haven't been "together" that long. And I say "together" in quotation marks because that somehow makes it easier.

You may have figured out by now that I have a few hang-ups about relationships, but anybody who knows me knows that the fact I'm even able to own up to it is a step in the right direction, especially considering my life with Todd . . . well, it was supposed to be forever.

Growing up, I completely bought into all the stuff we teach little girls about relationships and storybook love and romance. In fact, I swallowed the whole thing hook, line, and sinker — that every princess gets her prince, every beauty gets her beast, and every lady gets her tramp. And then, once you've got the date set, the dress picked, and the rings exchanged, it's all raindrops and roses and whiskers on kittens until the end of time. I guess I wasn't listening too good when the minister said "until death do you part."

I know. I sound like a reclusive old cynic.

I'm actually not, at least not most of the time, but after Todd was taken from me, I wondered if love was real, if there truly was such a thing as "happily ever after," and even if there was, I didn't think I'd ever find room enough in my heart for anyone else. It took me years to realize that love is eternal even if people aren't, and finding new love doesn't change that. There's always room for more love.

Whether he knows it or not, Ethan is one of the people who taught me that lesson, so I try to keep my reclusive tendencies under control when it comes to him. Although, judging by the look on his face now, I could tell I hadn't done a very good job today, so I did what any mature person in my situation would have done: I tried to change the subject.

"Ethan, ever hear of a thing called a telephone?"

He cocked his head to one side. "Oh,

really? So you're saying I should have called you?"

I nodded, but already there was a tone in his voice I didn't like one bit.

"So you're saying we should maybe call every once in a while to let each other know where we are?"

I nodded again, this time a little less emphatically. Ethan's an attorney. He runs his own firm, Crane and Sons, which he inherited from his grandfather. He's good at his job, and he handles a lot of big clients around here, not to mention a lot of the Key's most wealthy residents. He knows how to argue a case, so I could already tell I was done for. There was another problem, too: Ethan is drop-dead, holy smokes, seratonin-inducing gorgeous, so I tend to get a little dumb in his presence.

I muttered halfheartedly, "Yes. Yes, I am."

"Uh-huh. So, you think if something happens that isn't on the regular schedule, something out of the ordinary, we should give each other a heads-up? Something like that?"

I sighed. "Okay, who told you?"

He folded his arms over his chest. "Told me what?"

"You know damn well. Who was it?"

He smirked. "I'm not revealing my sources

— let's just say it's a good thing I stopped by the diner."

I stood up and wrapped the sheet around me. I was still thinking I might be able to get away with changing the subject. "That Judy! Can you believe what a blabbermouth she is? She can spread gossip faster than . . . faster than a . . ."

I looked at Ethan but the smile on his face had fallen away.

I knew he was right.

When a girl has a *b*-word and something unusual happens, it's normal behavior for that girl to call her *b*-word right away. Like, say for instance, that girl faints and hits her head so hard she sees things, or maybe she even gets bonked on top of the head by a masked intruder and has to call the police. Or maybe she discovers a dead body. Or maybe she's accused of murder. These are all things that might make a normal girl think, *Hey, you know what? I'll give my b-word a call. I'll bet he'd be interested in all this.*

I knew I should have called him the moment I woke up in the Kellers' laundry room, but I didn't . . . and I can't really explain why. I don't mean to shut him out. It's not something I do intentionally. It's just that having a partner in life still feels

relatively new, not to mention relatively surreal and bizarre and ridiculous and I don't
know what else.

But none of that mattered, because right
this very minute Ethan was boring a hole
into my soul with his dreamy, heart-
stopping, hurt-puppy eyes.

I melted.

"Ethan, I swear I meant to call you as
soon as it happened, but then the day got
away from me and I had to talk to the police
and then I was running late for the rest of
the day . . . and I just didn't want you to
worry about me."

As I was talking, I followed his gaze to the
top of my head, and when he saw the bump
there he shuddered. "Oh, no."

Before I could say a word he had wrapped
his arms around me and I fell into his body.
We just stood there for a full minute at least,
saying nothing. I could feel his chest rising
and falling against mine, and with every
breath it felt like my batteries were recharg-
ing. Finally, after I felt more or less like
myself again, I said, "How are you?"

He chuckled. "I'm good, thanks. You?"

I sighed and hugged him a little tighter.
"I'm good . . . now."

"Huh. You could have felt like this hours
ago if you'd called me sooner."

I pulled back and looked him in the eyes. "I'm sorry. I'm not a very good *g*-word, am I?"

"Not really, but I'll manage." He reached up and carefully parted my hair to the side. "How bad does it hurt?"

"Not much."

"It looks pretty gnarly."

"It's actually gone down a little. You should have seen it before."

"I'm glad I didn't."

Just then, Ella came curling around my ankles and squeezed herself between us, pausing with one paw on my foot and another on Ethan's, and then looked up at us with a high-pitched, *"Mrrrrap!"*

Ethan kissed me on the forehead. "I guess it's pointless to suggest you see a doctor."

"I already made the appointment."

"I don't believe you."

"Just pretend."

He whispered, "Come here."

Our lips touched, and I felt a flood of warmth spread through my entire body. In fact, I felt downright woozy. I was thinking I could stand there kissing him for the rest of the day if not for all eternity, and then it hit me.

My cell phone!

Ethan looked a little woozy himself.

"What?"

"I just remembered — Mrs. Keller called this morning."

He frowned. "So?"

I pulled away and glanced around for my cell phone. "So I should listen to her message. It's been such a crazy day I forgot all about it."

"Yeah, but what's the hurry?"

I tied the sheet around me and shuffled down the hall to the laundry room where I'd tossed my shorts. "I don't know. Maybe she knows something. I mean, with the day I've had, I wouldn't be surprised if she called to warn me about Dick Cheney. Maybe she got a call from the alarm company that there was a break-in."

As I grabbed my shorts off the washer and pulled my cell phone out of the back pocket, Ethan said, "Wait a minute. What break-in? And what the hell does Dick Cheney have to do with it?"

I cringed.

Of course. I should have known. Judy has a big mouth, but she's no dummy. She had probably only told Ethan that I'd hit my head and nothing more. She knew I'd kill her if she told him there was a possibility I'd been attacked before I could tell him myself.

As I flipped my phone open, I said, "Well, it's kind of a long story . . ."

He stopped midway down the hall, his arms dangling limply at his sides. "I've got time."

"Okay. Now, Ethan, don't freak out, but there's a slight possibility that maybe, just maybe, I sort-of kind-of didn't actually faint."

He blinked. "What do you mean, *sort-of kind-of?*"

I punched in the code for my voice mail. "I'm not sure, but it's possible somebody broke into the Kellers' house this morning and attacked me, and that's how I got hit on the head."

His jaw dropped open. "What? What the hell are you talking about?"

As I brought the phone to my ear, I flashed him a smile that was half disarming grin, half grimace, and held up one finger. "Hold that thought."

Just then, I heard the familiar beep announcing a new message, and in the few seconds between that and the sound of Mrs. Keller's voice, I could easily have hung up the phone. Or, I could easily have flushed it down the toilet. Or, I could easily have carried it over to the sink and run it through the garbage disposal. I could easily have

161

done any number of things, and then I would never have known what Mrs. Keller was about to say.

Instead, I kept my finger in the air to keep Ethan quiet, and listened.

15

"Good morning, Dixie. It's Linda. I hope you'll forgive me for calling so early in the morning . . . or is it late? I'm so turned around I have no idea what time it is. I wanted to let you know we arrived in Rome safe and sound. I'm afraid Mr. Feldman was none too happy to see us go, so I hope he's not being too naughty . . ."

I pulled the phone away from my ear and glanced at the message info as Mrs. Keller's voice rambled on. The screen said her message was only two minutes long, which for her is surprisingly brief. I love Mrs. Keller, but sometimes I wonder how Mr. Keller makes it through the day without flinging himself off a cliff.

". . . and we nearly left my purse in the taxi, can you believe it? Of course, it wouldn't have been the first time, but in Rome? That would have been an absolute disaster . . . but anyway, Dixie, the reason I called . . ."

There was a pause, and now her voice was quiet.

"Dixie, the reason I called . . . well, I hate to trouble you with this, but it's apparently urgent. A few weeks ago, I bought something at a gallery. Remember that little shop I told you about outside Tampa? Well, I know what you're thinking — I promised Buster I wouldn't buy any more masks — but, this was different, and I just couldn't stop myself. I even left my number with the gallery owner just in case he came across any more like it. Well, now I wish I'd never done that, because he called just before we left for the airport, full of apologies. It seems he made a mistake. His partner had already sold it to a collector there in town."

I was pacing up and down my short hallway while Mrs. Keller talked, and Ethan had moved over to the laundry alcove and was very slowly but deliberately bumping his forehead against the doorjamb.

"He said it was a communication error or some such nonsense, and of course I could have put up a fuss, but the man seemed so upset I didn't think I had a choice but to return it. I put it under the bench by the front door while Buster was loading the car. You may have noticed it."

I said, "Yep," and nodded.

Ethan looked up, "Yep, what?"

164

I held the phone away from my ear and said, "I think she wants me to mail a package for her."

He snatched the phone out of my hand and pressed the pause button.

I said, "Hey, I'm not done with that!"

"Yes, you are." He backed away toward the bedroom with the phone held behind him as he fixed me with a level gaze. "Dixie Hemingway, if you don't tell me what happened to you right this very minute, I'm going straight down to the water and your phone is taking a little walk with the fishes."

I grinned. "I think you mean *swim.*"

"Yeah, that."

I shrugged. "Baloney. You wouldn't dare."

"I would. You have no idea what I'm capable of when I'm desperate."

I sighed. "Okay, but you're not gonna like it."

He was still holding my cell phone behind his back, but now the grin on his face fell. "What do you mean?"

"I mean, you better sit down."

"Really?"

I nodded solemnly. "Yep."

He stared at me for a second, trying to figure out how serious I was, and then handed over my phone as he walked past with slumped shoulders into the living room. He lowered himself gently on the couch while I sat down in the armchair opposite him.

Ethan looks like a tough guy. He played football in college, and he was on the wrestling team, too. He can bench-press a million pounds, or something like that, and his biceps are about as big around as my thighs. But one thing most people don't know — he's a bit of a softy.

I put my hands on my knees and took a deep breath. "So . . ."

"Wait!" He grabbed one of the pillows off the couch and hugged it to his chest. "Okay. I'm ready."

I told him the whole story, at least a PG version of it anyway. I did my best to downplay the drama, like how disoriented I was at first, or how terrifying it was when I woke up and realized there might still be an intruder inside the Kellers' house. I didn't want him to get too upset before I got to the part about Levi, especially since I was pretty sure when he heard what I'd found there he'd keel over right in front of me.

The whole time I was talking, he just hugged his pillow. In fact, he seemed to be taking it pretty well — no swooning, no dramatic groaning — he just sat there and listened quietly. Once he realized I'd gone over to Levi's house, though, he looked up and frowned.

"Dixie, why in the world would you do that?"

"I know. It was dumb, but when we found out people didn't get their morning papers, I started getting worried."

He said, "Yeah, maybe. But what if it was Levi that followed you to the Kellers' and attacked you? Did you ever think of that?"

I shook my head. "No. That's not possible. I went to high school with him."

"You know as well as I do that doesn't mean a thing. I'm sorry, but that was a really dumb decision."

I raised an eyebrow. "I know, I just said that. I agreed with you in advance."

"Okay, well, was he there?"

I nodded. "Yeah, he was there."

"And? What did he say?"

I looked around the room and tried to figure out how to tell him, but there just wasn't any other way.

I said, "Ethan, he was dead."

He looked up, his eyes wide. "What?"

"Somebody killed him. When I knocked on his trailer door, it swung open and he was inside . . . in a pool of blood."

His face went pale. "You're telling me that somebody murdered Levi Radcliff?"

"Yeah, but . . . wait, how do you know his last name?"

He leaned back and ran his hands through his hair. "Wow. I know him."

"You mean . . . you were friends?"

"No, I didn't know him personally, but his father was a client. My grandfather represented him in court. He was an in-house accountant for a big management consulting firm, and he got accused of embezzling money."

"Levi's father?"

"It turned out he was moving hundreds of thousands of dollars to offshore accounts in the Virgin Islands, accounts that he'd set up himself with bogus companies. It was big news because he was already a rich guy."

"Wait a minute. Levi's father is rich?"

He nodded, but I noticed there was a faraway look in his eye.

"But Ethan, that's impossible. I saw Levi's house. He lives in a ratty old trailer home."

"I know. After Levi's dad went to prison for embezzling, his mom filed for divorce. Levi was just a kid then, probably five or six years old, and the divorce was nasty. There was a custody battle, which his mom finally won, but then there was a long fight over money and assets, and then the defense attorneys produced a prenup, and even though Levi's mom said she'd never seen it before, her signature was on it and a handwriting analyst testified it was genuine, so the judge ruled against her and she and Levi ended up with nothing."

"Wait. How do you know all this?"

"Huh?"

"I mean, this must have been decades ago . . ."

He looked down and rubbed the palm of his right hand with his left thumb. "I told you, his father was a client."

I narrowed my eyes. "Why do I think there's more to this story than you're saying? Because it doesn't make sense you'd know all this unless you spend all your spare time at work going through your grandfather's old files."

A wry smile formed on his lips. "Why do I think you missed your calling as a trial attorney?"

Ella had hopped up on one of the stools at the kitchen bar, and the entire time we'd been talking she was watching us with sleepy eyes, but now something had caught her attention outside, a bird or a squirrel maybe, and she was focused like a laser beam on the patio window.

I said, "And what did you mean when you

said Levi's dad *was* a rich guy?"

He shook his head. "Okay, but seriously, Dixie, this is just between you and me."

"Of course. Who would I tell?"

He gave me a look.

"Good point. I won't say a word to Judy."

He looked down at his hands. "Levi's dad killed himself three weeks ago."

I gasped. "What! How do you know that?"

"Because I'm the executor of his will."

I just sat there, staring wide-eyed at Ethan while all kinds of questions started bubbling up in my mind, most of which I knew he was probably not in a position to answer ethically.

I said, "He killed himself in prison?"

"No. Here in Sarasota. He only served three years at a minimum-security facility. Then when he got out he just picked up where he left off."

"How involved could his estate be if he was so hard up he was stealing money from his employer?"

"Dixie. Poor people steal. This guy embezzled. He bought a twenty-thousand-square-foot mansion on Bird Key for his second wife, he's got a condo on Miami Beach and another in Santorini, and he's got more Swiss bank accounts than I can keep track of, along with all kinds of offshore companies and tax shelters. The dude was a millionaire ten times over."

For once, I was speechless. And, of course, the first thing I thought was: Did Levi stand to inherit any of his father's millions? Because if he did, I imagined Detective McKenzie would be very interested to know what would happen to those millions if, for example, Levi was unable to accept them.

I whispered, "Ethan . . ."

He nodded slowly. "Yep."

16

Ella had hopped down off her kitchen stool and taken up a position on the windowsill. She was completely motionless except for her tail, which quivered slightly as she scanned the limbs of the trees outside. I was sitting in the chair opposite Ethan, and in the pregnant silence between us, my mind had turned immediately to Sasquatch. I mean, Mona Duffy . . . Levi's fiancée.

Sometimes, when I meet someone new, I know right off the bat what kind of person they are. Whether it's a sixth sense or gut intuition or what, I don't know, but I can tell almost the way a cat instantly knows a friend or a foe.

Naturally, when I was standing on the steps of Levi's trailer and heard the sound of Mona's voice, I knew right away. I turned around and saw her indignant face staring up at me, and a tiny voice in the back of my mind said, *Nice girl.*

Sometimes I'm wrong.

Part of the problem is that I tend to be drawn to loony-birds like a moth to a flame, and vice versa. I've always imagined it's somehow related to that old Hemingway Curse, because it definitely gets me in trouble sometimes.

Mona seemed about as unhinged as an old outhouse, and yet . . . There was something about her, something in her face, her eyes, that made me think she was more than the angry mask she presented to the world.

On the other hand, there's nothing more dangerous than greed. If Mona Duffy was in a position to have access to a lot of money in the not-so-distant future . . . well, I shuddered to think what it might make her capable of.

Ella had given up on whatever creature was taunting her outside and had sidled up next to Ethan on the couch. She was kneading his lap with her two front paws and looking up at his face with an expression of rapturous affection while he absentmindedly ran his hand down her back. I realized he was watching me.

I said, "What?"

He shook his head. "Nothing. I'm just sorry you had to see Levi like that."

I said, "I'm fine. I just feel bad for him, and for Mona, but also . . ."

"Also?"

"Well, there's one more thing. It's stupid, but basically Levi and I had a thing in high school . . . kind of."

He frowned. "Huh? You never told me that."

"Well, you never told me you were the executor of his father's estate."

He got up and came around to my side of the coffee table and sat down on the floor in front of me. "Oh, yeah. Good point." He rested his head on my knee. "Remind me to have my secretary update you daily on all my clients."

I flicked the top of his head with my index finger.

"Ouch!"

"Nobody likes a smart-ass."

He grinned. "Yes, they do. So what do you mean, a *thing*?"

"He's the first guy I ever kissed."

He looked up at me, genuinely surprised. "For real?"

"For real."

"Okay, that's kind of heavy."

"I know, except *not*. It was ninth grade, we were waiting in the hall outside one of our classes. And for the record, I didn't kiss him. He kissed me, and nothing happened after that."

He put one hand on mine and smiled. "I'm not jealous, if that's what you're thinking."

"I know."

"But either way, that just makes it even sadder. It sucks."

I ran my fingers through his hair and said, "I know," again, but inside I thought, *This is why I love you.* Ethan has a talent for zeroing in on the heart of the matter, which I guess is what makes him such a good attorney, but it also makes him a damn good *b*-word.

He shook his head slowly. "That poor guy. Do you know if they have any idea who could have done it?"

I said, "Nope."

He nodded and turned away, but I could still feel his eyes on me.

I said, "I'd like to forget the whole thing as soon as possible."

"I don't blame you."

"And I've got tons of clients this week, plus I've had enough drama today to last a lifetime."

He nodded resolutely. "Oh, for sure. One hundred percent. Yes, ma'am. I couldn't agree more."

I held my hand over his head, ready to flick it again. "Why do I think you're being sarcastic?"

"I didn't say a thing!"

"Yeah, but you're thinking something, I can hear it."

He smiled as he reached up and took my hand in his. "I just have a feeling you won't leave it at that. You may be surprised to hear this, but . . . I know you."

I rolled my eyes. "Fool, you don't know me. First of all, I'm too busy to get involved, and even if I did there'd be nothing for me to do. I'm sure Detective McKenzie doesn't need my help."

"Hmm. Where have I heard this before?"

I ignored him. "But you know what? I bet she'd be very interested to hear what you know about Levi's father. And she was trying to locate Levi's next of kin — apparently his fiancée wasn't much help. Do you think you might have his mother's contact information in your files?"

"I know I do, but more importantly . . . I'd imagine McKenzie would like to see his father's will."

I nodded slowly. "I think you're right."

"When I get back to the office this afternoon I'll give her a call. I can make a copy and have it sent over to her."

I thought for a second. "Or I can take it to her . . . if you want."

"Oh, yeah? I thought you weren't getting involved."

"Delivering a file to Detective McKenzie isn't 'getting involved.' I just think the sooner she sees that stuff, the better. Plus, I have to go back to the Kellers' anyway. I'll be right around the corner from your office."

He sat up. "What? You have to go back there?"

"Of course. The Kellers aren't home for another week. Which reminds me . . ." I reached out and snatched my phone from his hands. "I never listened to the rest of that message."

"Wait a minute, aren't you a little nervous?"

"No. And even if I was, I've got Barney Feldman to protect me. I'm sure if somebody actually did break in, whatever they were after they already got. I don't think they'll be coming back anytime soon."

He nodded firmly. "Yeah, I'll meet you there."

"No, you won't." I pressed the play button on my phone.

"I will."

I held one finger up to his lips. "No. Shut

177

up now."

He kissed the tip of my finger as Mrs. Keller's message continued.

"*. . . so Dixie, about that package, would you mind delivering it? Apparently the actual owner was quite eager to come pick it up, but I said I wouldn't be comfortable sharing my home address with a stranger. I told him I'd have my cat sitter deliver it, and — I hope you won't mind — but I've already gone to the liberty of arranging a meeting for you. It's tomorrow at 3:00 p.m. with a man named Paxton. He's a collector there in town with a small gallery. Hold on, I have the address here somewhere . . .*"

There were shuffling sounds as I held the phone away from my ear. Ethan had gotten up and was standing in front of the open refrigerator, looking for something to eat, which was a shame since there wasn't much more than a jar of mayonnaise, a bottle of OJ, and a few carrot sticks in there.

"*Here it is. 3535 Pineapple. I gave him your phone number . . .*"

She stopped abruptly and then whispered, "*Oh, dear, here's Buster.*"

I heard Mr. Keller say something in the background, and then Mrs. Keller's voice turned bright and cheerful again.

"*Oh, Dixie, Buster just reminded me. My*

neighbor's daughter Lizette — I believe you know her. She'll be stopping by the house every once in a while to keep Barney company, in fact she's going over this afternoon when she gets home from school. She's a very nice young lady and absolutely adores Barney to pieces. Oh, my goodness, I'm so glad I remembered to tell you. It would've been quite a shock to bump into someone in the house without knowing first! Can you imagine?"

"Yeah," I mumbled. "I actually can."

"Please give Mr. Feldman a big kiss from us and thanks so much for taking care of things, and feel free to call if there are any, you know . . . problems. Arrivederci for now!"

I flipped the phone shut as Ethan took a bite off the tip of a carrot stick and handed the rest to me. "What now?"

"Mrs. Keller . . . She bought something at a gallery, but I guess they'd already sold it to somebody else. She wanted to know if I could return it tomorrow. She already set it up."

He picked up his briefcase. "Why can't she just do it when she gets back?"

I shrugged. "It sounds urgent, plus she doesn't want her husband to find out. She promised him she'd stop buying stuff."

He knelt down and kissed the tip of my

179

ear, and a wave of goose bumps rippled across my back. He said, "Well, I'm headed back to work. Are you sure you don't want me to go with you?"

I bit off a piece of carrot and munched it. "No, I'll be fine. And anyway one of my clients lives just up the street from the Kellers. Her daughter's going over to play with Barney after school, so I may be off the hook until morning."

"Good. I think you should give yourself a break and call it a day."

As innocently as possible, I said, "Well, if it'll make you feel better, I'll give you a call if I have to go back over there."

"Really? You'd do that for me?" He opened the door with a mischievous grin. "That would be ever so thoughtful of you."

I narrowed my eyes. "I will ever so thoughtfully throw this carrot at you."

"Ha. You wouldn't dare."

Without even hesitating I chucked it at him, but he caught it midair and grinned. "Wow. Our kids would need some intense therapy." He waved the carrot at me like a lecturer's baton. "Oh, and by the way, you should hang out naked in a sheet more often. It's kinda hot."

I sat there for a few minutes, happy for some time alone as I listened to the sound of Ethan's car roll down the driveway. I knew I should probably have called Mrs. Keller right then. I knew if it were my house and the police had been called in to search through all my stuff, looking for evidence that there'd been some kind of burglary, I'd probably want to know — especially if my house was filled with valuable artwork. Other than my guns, which are well hidden, the next most valuable thing in my place is probably a thirty-count case of two-ply jumbo paper towels from the Costco on Tamiami Trail.

But then I thought, *Would I really?*

The problem was, I didn't know for sure what in the world I would say. It was still anybody's guess what had actually happened, so the idea of calling the Kellers up and worrying them about it seemed pointless. And even if Paco's theory was right and I really had been attacked, there wasn't much they could do about it now . . . and Mrs. Keller already seemed pretty stressed out as it was.

With everything that had happened since that morning, my mind felt about as mushy as a bowl of cold oatmeal, and now, with Ethan's news about Levi's father, a heavy cloud of fog was banking up in my head. All I wanted to do was crawl back under the covers and stay there until nightfall. I hadn't even started my afternoon rounds yet, and the day already felt like it had lasted a century.

I decided for the time being I'd just leave the Kellers alone and let them enjoy their vacation, at least until I knew for certain what had happened. Plus, I figured what they didn't know wouldn't hurt them.

I wish I could have said the same thing for myself.

17

Some folks make the mistake of assuming that because cats in the wild hunt alone, it necessarily follows that all cats are loners, that they couldn't care less about people, and that the only reason they pretend to be even halfway interested in the human race is because of the warmth, comfort, and kibble we provide. Well, anybody who's ever shacked up with a cat knows that's a bunch of baloney. Cats may hunt alone, but in the wild they live in colonies with social hierarchies as complex and intricate as a daytime soap opera. They thrive on attention and love and companionship every bit as much as dogs . . . they're just a little more discreet about it.

Fortunately for me, Lizette had been more than happy to hang out with Barney Feldman and serve him dinner. And even though I was in a complete soporific daze after talking to Ethan (in fact, I was lucky I hadn't walked out of the house with the bedsheet still draped around me like a toga) I managed to move through my afternoon clients at record speed, with a promise to each and every one of them that I'd make it up next time with some special treats and an extra helping of TLC. I was back home and curled up under the covers not long after the sun went down.

When I woke the next morning, I let myself lie there for longer than I normally would and enjoyed a few blissful moments of stupid, watching the stars twinkle in the window. Gradually, though, as the stars faded with the morning light, everything that had happened the day before started trickling back into my consciousness.

I thought of Mona, and the strange look on her face right after she'd woken up outside Levi's trailer. At first I'd thought it was a look of triumph, that flash in her eyes. It made me think of a panhandler who's just discovered gold. Then, when she ran screaming across the yard toward the ambulance, I'd thought exactly what Sergeant Owens had later confirmed: That the poor thing was convinced I was responsible for Levi's death and that she'd caught me red-handed.

But now, seeing her face floating above

me, I wondered . . .

There was something more. It was a darkness, almost as if the pupils of her eyes were
fully dilated even in the bright sunlight —
two bottomless pits of black. It was a look
I'd seen before, and I felt something shift in
my chest, as if my sternum had collapsed
slightly like a house sitting on a sinkhole,
and for a split second a wave of unsteadi-
ness washed over me, a kind of hopeless-
ness I hadn't felt in a very long time.

Without another moment's thought, I
jumped out of bed and rushed into the
bathroom. I splashed my face with water so
cold it made my heart race. Then I ran into
the closet and got dressed as quickly as possible. I wear the same outfit every day: khaki
shorts and a white sleeveless tee. I'm thank-
ful for my measly wardrobe on days like
this, when I feel a little wonky. It just means
getting dressed doesn't involve a whole lot
of thinking. The only decision to make is
which shoes to wear, and even that's
completely streamlined.

Everybody who knows me knows I won't
tolerate ratty shoes, so I keep a rotating sup-
ply of at least seven identical pairs of white
sneakers — all Keds. I'm on my feet all day
long, and my shoes get a lot more mileage
than most, so I don't wear a single pair

more than a couple of days before I throw them in the washer with a little bleach thrown in. Once they get even the slightest bit ragged around the edges they go straight in the "Old Shoes Bag," a cleverly named canvas tote that I keep hanging on the doorknob inside the closet.

When it's filled up, I take the whole thing over to the charity bin in the parking lot outside the post office and start all over with some brand-new ones.

The sun was just coming up over the treetops to the east, and the air was a good ten degrees cooler, which was a good thing, since it meant the drive to town would be more dappled shade than broiling heat wave. I put the windows down and left my sunglasses tucked in the sun visor over the passenger seat, and as I pulled out on Midnight Pass Road, I breathed a sigh of relief.

I felt like I'd just narrowly avoided lying in bed all day with the covers pulled over my head.

I always keep my hair tied back when I'm working, mainly because it's cleaner for mucking out cat boxes or snapping leashes on tongue-wagging dogs, but also because I like to think it makes me look more professional. Usually I tie it up in a ponytail with a scrunchie — that is, if I haven't used all my scrunchies for cat toys — but driving into town I realized I'd been in such a hurry to get out of the house that I'd forgotten. My hair was whipping around like one of those spinning mops in a drive-through car wash.

I didn't care.

My eyes were fixed on the road, and with the cooler air I felt a little more clear-headed. In fact, I felt like Ella on the prowl — fully focused on something up ahead and just beyond my reach . . . something taunting me . . . teasing me.

I knew it couldn't be a coincidence — that three weeks ago Levi's father had committed suicide and now someone had murdered Levi. Even if Levi's dad had been a penniless beach bum, the proximity of their deaths would have raised all sorts of questions and suspicions.

It gave me a sick, nervous feeling in the pit of my stomach to know that somewhere, maybe in the car passing me now, or in any one of these darkened houses with the curtains drawn, was the person who had killed Levi, the person who had decided that, for whatever reason, Levi's life wasn't worth a hill of beans . . .

And then it hit me: a terrible thought, one that might possibly have been subconsciously percolating in my mind all night long.

When I'd left for work the previous morning, if it had indeed been Levi parked outside my driveway, I wondered what would have happened if I'd gotten to him just a little bit earlier . . . if I'd been just a little quicker getting my bike out . . . if I'd caught up with him before he pulled away?

I've never been a big believer in the whole idea of fate or destiny. I like to think we all have control of our lives, that we're more than just puppets, with our every move predetermined by some kind of cosmic string system and our futures all laid out in advance by the powers that be — but unfortunately, if that's true, there's a flip side.

It means every action, every thought, every single decision we make has the potential to utterly change the world. If I had caught up with Levi that morning, if we had talked even for just a minute, who knows what would have happened after? Would that have been enough to interrupt the momentum of his day, enough to break up the chain of events that was ahead, the chain of events that led to his death?

I shook my head, like trying to shake the last penny out of a piggy bank. I told myself there was no point dwelling on what had happened. Levi was gone, and nothing could change that. And now, with Ethan's files and Levi's father's will as a guide, I knew it was only a matter of time before Detective McKenzie tracked down whoever was responsible for his death.

I gave myself a little nod in the rearview mirror. I knew it wouldn't be easy to forget what I'd seen the day before . . . the image of Levi lying there, his face frozen in alarm like one of Mrs. Keller's masks, but all I could do was keep my head down and forge ahead.

No problemo, I thought.

If there was an Olympic event for avoiding unpleasant memories I'd have a whole display case chock-full of gold medals.

And the secret to my success?

Routine . . .

18

Tom Hale lives in an old Art Deco building called the Sea Breeze, which is fitting since it sits right on the edge of the Gulf about a half mile before the center of town. It's painted a light shade of Florida-pink, and all the outward-facing apartments have balconies with curved stucco roofs over them. From a distance, the whole thing looks like a giant pink honeycomb, or maybe one of those old Pueblo villages built into the side of a desert cliff.

In exchange for his handling my taxes and anything else having to do with finances, I give Tom's retired racing greyhound, Billy Elliot, a couple of good outings every day. It works out well for both of us, since I'm terrible with money, and Tom uses a wheelchair so walking Billy isn't easy.

The building was recently given a face-lift. Not only did they put in new revolving glass doors and a security camera, they completely remodeled the lobby. It used to feel a little scruffy around the edges, but now the floor is all polished pebble, and there's a big chandelier in the center dripping with crystals that sparkle like pink rosé. Giant copper urns with baby palms and arcing ficus trees are grouped here and there in lush arrangements, and the walls are all mirrored from floor to ceiling.

The elevator is mirrored, too, with a thick Chinese-red carpet and strips of tiny amber lights in the corners. It sort of feels like a movie star's dressing room. As the doors closed with a quiet whoosh, I came face-to-face with myself in the mirror and whispered, "Oh, dear."

I'm used to being a little surprised. Most days I'm up and out of the house so fast that Tom's elevator is the first chance I get to see myself. If I've taken the time to put on makeup, which I do a little more often now that Ethan's around, nine times out of ten I do it blindly over my closet desk as I check my notes for the day. Usually I'll find a little smeared mascara or a smudge of lip gloss riding up my lip like the remains of a burst chewing-gum bubble, but this was different. I couldn't see the bump on my head at all, but that was because the wind had blown my hair into a complete frenzy. I looked like I'd been given a makeover by a team of juvenile delinquent squirrels with attention deficit disorder.

Just then, the doors slid open to reveal a woman in her late twenties, with beautiful olive skin, brown eyes, and long hair so thick and shiny it looked like a dark river of chocolate spilling over her shoulders. She had an odd look on her face, almost like she was surprised to find anybody else in the elevator, but then I realized she was waiting for me to come out. I was about to tell her this wasn't my floor when I saw the big pink chandelier hanging in the lobby behind her.

I said, "Oh, no! I was so busy admiring myself in the mirror I forgot what I was doing. I'm going up."

The woman nodded curtly and stepped in, pressing the button for the ninth floor as the doors closed. We were standing side by side now, and in the reflection of the mirror I noticed her necklace. It was a small Catholic cross, beautifully carved from luminous sea-green stone, perhaps jade, except it had a soft bluish hue I'd never seen before. It was about an inch tall, set in an exquisitely thin silver bezel and hanging just below her throat on a braided silver chain.

Right about the time I realized I was basically staring at her, she glanced down at her feet and then at me, which I realized was her subtle way of signaling I still hadn't selected a floor.

"Wow. I'm such a dummy."

I leaned forward and pressed the twelfth-floor button. The woman stretched her lips into a thin forgiving smile, narrowing her eyes slightly, as if she could barely stand another moment alone in this tiny space next to me.

She was wearing a silk floor-length skirt, dark navy blue, with a high waist, wide belt, and an open-lapeled silk jacket the color of newly fallen snow. I knew right away it was something nice. It had that kind of polished edge that only fancy clothes have, the kind of expensive ensembles they hang in the windows of the tonier shops downtown, the kind I usually walk by with my gaze fixed straight ahead, like a horse with blinders.

I suppressed the urge to ask where she'd bought it. I had the distinct feeling she wasn't in the mood for small talk. She was standing perfectly erect with her shoulders back and her long neck straight, her cold brown eyes directed forward and focused on nothing, like she was the only person in the universe. I stood up straight and stared at the mirror, copying her icy gaze, and thought, *All right. Two can play this game.*

I think it's fair to say, standing there next to her in my work clothes with a wind-teased squirrel's nest on my head and the occasional cat hair clinging here and there, that I looked not unlike a homeless runaway, or maybe the love child of Donald Trump and a long-haired alpaca.

I reached down into one of the side pockets of my backpack and felt around for a hair band, luckily finding one right away, and forced my hair back in a ponytail. As I snapped it in place, I realized it looked exactly like one of Levi's green rubber bands, the ones he used to tie around the morning paper.

I had decided that when I got to Tom's apartment I wouldn't mention what had happened the day before, especially since McKenzie had asked me not to talk to anyone about it yet. But also, I knew if I did I'd probably break down in a sobbing mess, and even just thinking about Levi made my throat feel hollow.

I glanced over at Ice Princess, but she was still staring straight ahead in her own world. When we got to the ninth floor, I thought, *I'm going to say something nice to her.*

The doors slid open and I blurted, "Hey, I like your necklace."

At first she looked slightly horrified that I'd even had the gall to speak to her again, but as she stepped out she reached up with one hand and touched the green cross with the tips of her fingers. "Oh, thank you."

"Yeah, it's really pretty. Is it jade?"

She held the door open. "No. Peruvian opal. From my homeland."

I said, "Ah," and smiled pleasantly.

She let go of the door and then disappeared down the hallway without so much as a nod good-bye, but for some reason I felt better. And now that she was out of the picture, I looked better, too. Tom and Billy Elliot had been on vacation for almost a week, visiting Tom's oldest son, so I didn't want to look like an emotional wreck when I greeted them.

As soon as I took my keys out, I heard a low-pitched *woof* and then the quick tap-tapping of Billy Elliot's wagging tail on the parquet floor. I like to keep myself on a pretty strict schedule, so over time Billy has learned to anticipate my arrival down to the minute. He was already waiting for me just behind the door.

Greyhound racing is a big deal around here. There's a decades-old track on the outskirts of Sarasota that puts on races weekly, and there are at least fifteen other tracks within a four- or five-hour drive. I guess it's fun for people, and I'm sure it pours tons of money into the local economy, but in my book none of that makes it right.

Whenever I hear the word *retirement,* I think of silver-haired couples driving around in golf carts or touring through town on a bicycle built for two, on their way to a two-dollar matinee at the movie theater or an early-bird dinner at the local diner. But in the world of greyhound racing, *retirement* is all too often a nice word for something . . . well, not very nice.

Tens of thousands of greyhounds are bred every year, but only an elite few ever make it to the racetrack, which means the majority get "retired." Even for the champions, a good racing career doesn't last long. Their bodies can only take so much, and if they're not winning they meet the same end as their less-speedy littermates — unless of course they're lucky enough to become breeders for new stock, or get rescued like Billy Elliot.

You would've thought he hadn't seen me in years. First he ran around in circles, leaping up and down like a rabbit, and then he lavished me with kisses. I found Tom in his wheelchair at the kitchen table, where there were stacks of files and spreadsheets laid out in front of him in a wide semicircle.

Billy Elliot ran over and sat by his side, looking back at me with a wide grin as if to say, *Hey, look what I found!*

I said, "How was your vacation?"

Tom has a boyish round face with a head of curly black hair and a little round belly. He wears steel-rimmed glasses that always make me think he looks a bit like Harry Potter, that is if Harry Potter were forty-two and slightly pudgy. He's one of the most well-read people I've ever met. He knows a little bit about practically everything — art, music, architecture, literature, finance. When I grow up I want to be just like him.

He took off his glasses and rubbed his eyes. "Well, considering my son is a complete maniac, not to mention an immature, binge-drinking wreck, it was fine."

"Uh-oh. That doesn't sound good at all."

He chuckled. "Well, I might be exaggerating a bit. To his credit I think he invited me down just so I'd give him a lecture about how he needs to grow up. The kid is twenty-six years old and has never held a job for longer than a year. But don't get me started. How are you?"

"Well, funny you should ask, I've had an interesting week so far."

He pushed himself back from the table.

"Oh, good, tell me all about it. I need something to divert my attention from these spreadsheets."

I said, "Well, I'm fine now, but look . . ."

I lowered my head and parted my hair to the side.

"Ouch! How'd that happen?"

I considered telling him, but the thought of one more person thinking of me as a delicate fainting flower made me sick, so instead I just very slightly altered the truth.

I said, "Um . . . I slipped on an orange peel. Can you believe that? I was at a client's house. I went straight down and hit my head. But Tom, the weirdest thing happened. While I was lying there catching my breath, I saw an image in my mind, it was a statue, kind of like a Buddha, except it was a woman. Have you ever heard of anything like that?"

Tom frowned. "Wait, you're saying you got knocked out?"

Billy Elliot sighed and stretched out on the floor at Tom's feet. I think he knew from the sound of our voices he wasn't getting a walk anytime soon.

I said, "No, no. Nothing like that. But it hurt like hell and I was definitely a little dizzy for a minute, so I was just lying there waiting for it to go away when that image popped up in my head, and it's just been bugging me ever since. I must have seen something like it somewhere, but for the life of me I can't think where."

"Was it Kuan Yin?"

I said, "Connie who?"

He grinned. "Kuan Yin. She's what they call a bodhisattva, an enlightened being that's reached a state of grace. Some people think when they die, Kuan Yin places their soul in the heart of a lotus flower. She's the most well-known female Buddha figure I know of."

I said, "Huh. She sounds awesome. Does she have big huge bowling-ball-sized breasts?"

He tilted his head to one side. "Um, no."

"Oh. Well, this one did. And her toes were painted red and she was totally naked and big and curvy."

He put his glasses back on. "Ha — that doesn't much sound like the Buddha I know. I think the word you're looking for is *zaftig.* Except for the red toes, it sounds more like an ancient earth goddess, like Gaia or Shala."

"Who?"

"Almost every ancient culture has one. Usually they represent the bounty of nature or fertility, like Venus, the Roman goddess of love."

"You mean Venus on a half shell?"

He chuckled. "You're thinking of how Botticelli envisioned her, but the idea was around long before he came along. Some of them date all the way back to the Paleolithic age . . . Here, I'll show you."

He turned his wheelchair back to the computer and tapped a few keys. The screen filled with pictures of all kinds of small sculptures and figurines. They were mostly made from stone or clay, some crude and jagged, but others carved with exquisite care.

"Are they expensive?"

He smiled. "Some are modern knockoffs, but some, especially an older one, could be worth hundreds of thousands, if not millions."

I said, "Huh."

Something had clicked in my head. It might very well have been my poor skull shifting back in place, but I think it was something more. Unless I was remembering something from my past life as a cave-woman, there was absolutely no way I'd fainted that morning, because those figurines on Tom's computer . . . I'd never seen anything like them before . . . so how could the whole thing have been a dream?

I looked closer at one that had caught my attention. She was made of white stone. Her oval eyes were blank, but her lips were set at a slightly mischievous angle, and her head was as smooth and bald as an egg.

I pointed. "Hey, Tom? Do you think you could print that out for me?"

19

The parking lot at the Sea Breeze is shaped like a racetrack, with a big oval of lush green grass in the middle, and sometimes I wonder if Tom didn't move here for that reason alone. It's the perfect place for Billy Elliot.

In his heyday, Billy was a champion racer, and he had a longer career than most. A lot of greyhounds his age, especially the ones with an illustrious record, have to contend with all kinds of health problems stemming from the abuse their bodies took from racing, but so far Billy is in pretty good shape. Tom gives him daily supplements to help keep his joints limber, and he needs a mild pain reliever now and then, but otherwise he's fit as a fiddle, which is more than I can say for myself.

The order of events is basically the same every day. After Billy does his business and marks a couple of bushes for future reference, we start out at a relatively slow pace around the lot. Then, once we're both warmed up, we increase the speed a bit. Billy's usually the one to make that call, and I know he waits a little longer than he'd prefer for my sake.

I do my best to keep up with him, but I never last much longer than twenty minutes. If he looks like he's still got a little gas in his tank, I'll let him off the leash and he'll shift into greyhound gear and race around the lot a few more laps at breakneck speed. That gives me the opportunity to stand doubled over with my hands on my hips and wheeze like a donkey.

While I did that, I thought about the picture Tom had printed out for me. It was folded up and tucked away in my back pocket, and I'd already told myself what I needed to do next: it was time to call Mr. and Mrs. Keller. All I needed was one look at those little statues on Tom's computer screen to know what had happened to me in the Kellers' house wasn't a dream, nor was it the product of my overactive imagination or low blood sugar. Paco was right. Somebody had attacked me.

I still didn't know where that statue had come from or how it wound up in the hands of my attacker, but I had a feeling Mrs. Keller might be able to shed some light on the subject.

I'd wait until I was back in her house, and since Italy is six hours ahead, it would be around midday there and a perfect time to call. I wasn't looking forward to worrying her about it, and I really didn't feel like getting caught up in whatever web of deceit she'd woven to appease her husband, but I knew I didn't have a choice.

After that I'd call Detective McKenzie. I wanted to tell her the whole story — everything I'd figured out about that morning, including Paco's theory that my bump wasn't consistent with a fall, and I also wanted to show her the picture Tom had printed for me. Given how much that figurine might be worth, it seemed perfectly reasonable that somebody could have broken into the Kellers' house to steal it. Seeing as how it was so early in the morning, they probably thought they could escape without any of the neighbors noticing. Deputy Beane had mentioned she'd canvassed the neighborhood and no one had reported anything suspicious, so all in all it was a perfect plan . . . except for one thing: Levi.

I think it was possible that, in an indirect way, it was Levi's fault I got conked on the head in the first place. After my attacker found what they were looking for, they must have planned on slipping out before I even knew they were there. But something had stopped them, and I'd be willing to wager ten bucks it was the sight of Levi driving by, delivering papers.

They probably figured the risk of a witness was much worse than contending with a 135-pound cat sitter, so they donned one of Mrs. Keller's masks and took me out of the picture with whatever they happened to have handy . . . like a stone earth goddess. I cringed at the idea of me lying there in the laundry room, unconscious, while they waited for the right time to make their escape. Of course, the big question was: If Levi had been there when they finally came out, had he confronted them?

Or worse, had they followed him home?

Once Billy and I were back upstairs, both of us panting like crazy, I hung his leash on the hook by the door and then followed him back into the dining room to say a quick good-bye to Tom. He had laid out a few documents with pink Post-its running down the right-hand side.

Turning to me with a somber look on his face, he said, "Before you go, we need to talk."

I knew by the sound of his voice it had something to do with money. I threw my backpack over my shoulder and whined, "Can it wait till tomorrow?"

"Dixie, sooner or later we have to come up with a plan."

I said, "How about later?"

"Can you at least sign a couple of things?"

"Ugh. Do I have to read them first?"

He slid his glasses down his nose and gave me a disapproving frown. "Of course you do. Does that mean you will?"

"No."

He handed me a pen. "I didn't think so."

There were three separate documents. As I signed one he'd slide it away and replace it with another. "Dixie, you really can't avoid this much longer."

"I know, I know. It's just hard."

"That may be, but the longer you put it off, the harder it's going to get."

I handed his pen back. "Okay, I promise we'll talk next week."

He stared at me as I hurried down the hall.

"I promise!"

One of my very first jobs as a pet sitter was for a cat named Ghost. Awful name, sweet cat. He was a silver-blue Abyssinian, as stunningly beautiful as his owner, Marilee

Doerring. Unfortunately, that beauty had drawn a very bad man to her, and she ended up getting killed.

We weren't exactly close friends, but Marilee and I had a kind of unspoken bond, and her grandmother, Cora Mathers, is still a big part of my life. I go over at least once a week to visit her. These days, she's the closest thing I have to a mother.

Marilee was rich, and when she died, her will stipulated that a sizable amount of her estate go to Cora, enough that she'd never have to worry about who would take care of her in her old age. The rest, to everyone's surprise, went to Ghost. And even more surprising, at least for me, yours truly was named as Ghost's guardian and sole manager of his inheritance, which, to put it mildly, was a boatload of money.

I knew I was the last person on earth to be trusted with that kind of responsibility. For example, I have no idea how much money I have in my bank account, and the last time I balanced my checkbook Ronald Reagan was president. Math is not my strong suit. It's not even my weak suit, plus it just made me sad to think about Marilee, so I asked Tom for help managing everything. He's taken care of all the financial details ever since, and I try to have as little to do with it as possible.

Ghost, on the other hand, I knew exactly how to handle. I found him a good home with a family that runs an orchard just north of Sarasota. They have tons of land, with rows and rows of orange trees teeming with birds and butterflies, and all it took was one visit to know it would be the perfect home for a cat like Ghost. The Griswolds love him and take excellent care of him, and they send me letters and photos every once in a while to keep me up to date on his adventures. In return, they're given a monthly stipend from Marilee's estate to help keep Ghost living in the luxurious style he was accustomed to when she was still alive.

Unfortunately, time goes by and Ghost is only getting older, and now there's the question of what happens to Marilee's estate going forward. You'd think eventually all that money would just dwindle away and I'd never have to think about it again, but the problem is . . . well, the real problem is Tom Hale: He's a financial wizard. Early on, he took a portion of the estate and invested it, and now it's grown into a small fortune. All of it, every last penny, becomes mine when Ghost passes away.

It's a secret. Nobody knows but you, me,

and Tom, so please — try not to blab it all over town.

20

I read an article in the paper recently about all the unrest in the Middle East, and how one of the lesser-known consequences is that museums have become increasingly vulnerable to looting. Thieves break in and take whatever they can get their hands on, like ancient tools, pottery, jewelry, and, most notably, small statues and figurines. Priceless treasures have disappeared across the entire region, from Sudan and Egypt all the way to the northernmost cities in Afghanistan.

I was thinking about that as I made my way across the parking lot at the Sea Breeze. You'd think it would be impossible to get away with selling a hot artifact pilfered right out of a public museum, but when riches are at stake there's always a buyer willing to hazard the risk, plus it can always be passed off to a less knowledgeable (or less virtuous) dealer, then along comes an unsuspecting customer, completely innocent of its questionable provenance. The black market for art and antiquities is a multibillion-dollar business. It extends its long, greedy fingers into every corner of the world . . . even as far as, say, a charming little gallery on the outskirts of Tampa.

As soon as I got back in the Bronco, I reached for my phone and navigated to my saved voice mails. I wanted to hear Mrs. Keller's message again. There was one thing she'd said that had stuck in my mind: *"I promised Buster I wouldn't buy any more masks — but this was different, and I just couldn't stop myself."*

I played that part a few more times. There was definitely something about the way she paused slightly when she said "different," like there was something else . . . something unspoken. Of course, they always say it's a woman's prerogative to change her mind, and I couldn't agree more (I think), but I was beginning to wonder if maybe Mrs. Keller had actually kept her word, at least technically. Just because she'd promised her husband she wouldn't buy any more masks didn't mean she couldn't have turned her attention to some other collectible item . . . say, ancient figurines?

The entire way to the Kellers' house, my

head was buzzing with everything I'd figured out so far, but somewhere in the back of my mind was the lurking suspicion that my whole theory — that there was a connection between what had taken place at the Kellers' and what had happened to Levi — was as flimsy as a house of cards, as if the slightest breeze or tiny tremor in the earth's surface could bring it all crashing down.

But I didn't care. My day hadn't started out so great, and even if there was no connection between the two, just the action of trying to solve the riddle of it made me feel better. There was one more thing, though . . .

Ethan.

It was what he'd said the day before, after I'd told him everything and he was about to leave. I couldn't even remember it exactly, just that it had started with two simple words: *"Our kids."*

At the time I hadn't noticed, at least I don't think I had, but now I realized it was still moving through me — slowly, deliberately — like a virus spreading to every cell in my body.

It's hard to explain without sounding overly theatrical. Trust me, I'm the kind of girl who likes things as drama-free as possible, but there's just no way around it . . .

the moment I lost Todd and Christy, a funny thing happened.

I say "funny" because it's hard to come up with a better word. It was as if I broke apart, like Humpty Dumpty, except there were only three pieces. One piece of me collapsed in a heap, like a bird that's hit a plate-glass window — completely gone, still, hopeless. Another piece of me split away and flailed like a cat caught in a trap. It hissed and cried and fought.

I know now that all of it, the tears and the darkness and the histrionics, it was all for show. I think I knew it even then. It was just a smokescreen, a clever way of diverting the world's attention from the third piece, the piece of me that survived, the piece that looked into the eyes of the emergency room surgeon on duty the night Todd and Christy were brought in. The piece that *knew.* The piece that immediately set about building a wall.

By the time the crying and the fighting, the darkness and the denial and the pain of it all had finally quieted down, that wall was complete. It was layers and layers thick, solid concrete with steel reinforcements, wrapped several times over with razor ribbon and barbed wire. It surrounded my heart, and for all practical purposes it was

213

one hundred percent impenetrable. It was the only thing I knew how to do. I did it because I never wanted to feel that pain again.

Ever.

When I heard the words "our kids" tumble out of Ethan's mouth, it felt like a little piece of that wall had dislodged itself and fallen somewhere inside me. The unsettling thing was, at least so far, I hadn't bothered to put it back in place.

I don't know what the heck I was expecting when I inserted my key in the Kellers' front door. I knew it was safe, and I knew there was no one inside, plus I knew Lizette had already been there. If I'd thought there was even the slightest risk of danger I would never have allowed her to come and take care of Barney Feldman the night before. But as I stepped in, I took a couple of quick glances up and down the road just in case, and then after I closed the door behind me I locked and bolted it.

The house was quiet. All I could hear was the gentle hum of the air conditioner and the quickening thump of my heartbeat. As much as I dreaded breaking the news to the Kellers that they might have been robbed, the prospect of finally getting some answers to what the hell had happened to me sent a surge of adrenaline through my veins.

I pulled my phone out and took a deep breath. Dialing the Kellers' number, I could feel Dick Cheney glaring down at me from his perch on the wall, but I ignored him. The first thing I heard was a couple of electronic clicks, and then silence. I started thinking maybe I'd dialed the number incorrectly, but then there was a short high-pitched buzz, and then a noise that sounded more like a couple of bleating sheep than a telephone ring.

"Baaaaaaa. Baaaaaaa."

They came in pairs, with about a three second pause in between, repeating about five times. Then there was another click and a low hollow hissing.

I said, "Hello?"

The line went dead.

Mrs. Keller hadn't given me a different number to use while they were in Europe, and I had just assumed she'd bought some kind of international plan for her cell phone, but now I wasn't so sure. I carefully dialed the number again and got the same thing, except this time there was no hissing at the end, just dead space.

I snapped the phone shut and held it out in front of me, hoping that somewhere on the other side of the planet Mrs. Keller had seen I was trying to reach her and would call me back. But it was no use. After a minute or so I let out a long sigh. I hadn't considered the possibility that I wouldn't at least get her voice mail. Now my plans were completely derailed.

I realized I was just standing there with my backpack slung over my shoulder, so I dropped it down on the leather bench by the door and muttered, "Good morning, everybody," but my heart wasn't in it.

Dick Cheney was still leering at me, surrounded by his motley crew of mask cronies. His expression had taken on an almost clownlike tone now, and as I dropped my phone down on the bench next to the backpack, I could've sworn he made a face at me, the way a little kid makes a face at his mother when he thinks she's not looking. I decided to take the adult approach (something I do occasionally) and ignore him, but I could totally tell all his little mask friends thought he was the coolest thing ever, so as I went by I flicked the tip of his nose with my finger the way I'd flicked the top of Ethan's head.

At the end of the hall, I could already see the fluffy tip of Barney Feldman's tail peeking out from under the antique credenza, so

I kept a wide berth.

I said, "I see you, so don't even think about it."

Silence. I turned around just shy of the living room and folded my arms over my chest.

"Barney Feldman, I am not in the mood for your shenanigans today, so if you want your breakfast you have to come out and say good morning like a proper gentleman."

He thought for a moment, but then one black-tipped paw shot out and batted the air tentatively.

I shook my head. "No, sir."

The paw withdrew and there was silence again.

"Barney . . ."

One more quick paw swipe.

"All right. I'm counting to three, and if . . ."

But then he came sliding out, chirping like a chipmunk and waving his tail jerkily, as if to say, *Okay, grumpy!*

I reached down and gave him a few scritches between the ears, and then he padded after me into the kitchen. I spooned an extra helping of tuna in his bowl and mixed it into his kibble with a little warm water while he caressed my calves with his cheeks. He's a good boy.

At first I couldn't find his place mat, but then I found it on the island, spread out to dry on a clean dish towel next to a handwritten message on a piece of paper torn from a spiral notebook:

Hi Mrs. Hemingway!

Barney is SUPER frisky today! He played for an hour with one of his Ping-Pong balls while I did my homework. Then we played some more and when I left he was sound asleep. I'll come back after school and I can give him his dinner too. I get so much more work done here cuz I don't have to listen to my two older bothers, I mean brothers, play their lame computer games all afternoon.

PS — Full Disclosure. There was a Teen Wolf marathon on MTV so we watched a little of that too, but don't tell my mom!

Her name was signed in bright blue ink at the bottom with a big curlicue *I* and a plump heart over the *i* instead of a dot, and underneath was a surprisingly skillful drawing of Barney. He had a mischievous twinkle in his eye and bushy whiskers, and his paws sported outrageously long claws that ended in sharp, gleaming points.

I smiled. I knew Lizette, but I hadn't actually seen her in almost a year. I'd taken care of her four-year-old Lhasa Apso while her mom recovered from surgery for a slipped disk. At the time, Lizette was awkward and shy, still struggling to define what kind of woman she wanted to be, but it was clear from her note that she'd blossomed since then. I couldn't wait to tell her how impressed I was with her drawing talent.

After I washed out Barney's bowl and place mat, I took him out back to the garden and gave him a good grooming with a stiff-wired brush. I must have collected a half pound of fur, which helps ward off marauding critters, so I sprinkled it around the garden. While I was doing that, I caught Barney pawing at something near one of the miniature roses. It was a little pile of coarse yellow powder, sort of like cornmeal. I know sometimes people use cornmeal to repel ants, but I didn't want Barney eating it so I shooed him away.

After that we had a nice time chasing bees. There was also a Cape honeysuckle scrambling over one of the garden walls, and for a while we watched with rapt attention as a pair of tiny ruby-throated hummingbirds pirouetted around its neon-orange blossoms. It was better than a movie.

I left Barney stretched out on his side, his arms and legs all akimbo in a square of sunlight by the folding glass doors in the living room. I gave him a kiss on the nose and told him what Lizette's note had said — that she'd be back this afternoon to hang out with him. I knew he hadn't seen it because he's not allowed on the counter-tops.

In the foyer, I leaned against the wall and tried to call Mrs. Keller again, but to no avail. I figured I'd just keep trying for the rest of the day until I got her, so I grabbed my backpack and was almost out the door when I remembered: my meeting with the gallery owner was at three o'clock, and since I didn't think I'd be back before then, I wanted to take Mrs. Keller's package with me.

I knelt down next to the bench and pulled it out, and then when I was reaching for the doorknob I felt a tingle of excitement, like a tiny army of ants racing up the back of my neck.

"No," I whispered out loud. "You *can't.*"

I paused and looked down. It was a brown cardboard box, roughly ten inches square, sealed with clear wrapping tape and several red FRAGILE stickers. It was addressed to

Paxton Fine Art & Antiques in Mrs. Keller's curly handwriting. I weighed it in my hands and jiggled it slightly. There was something heavy inside.

Well, I thought, *you've finally gone right off the deep end.*

With one quick swipe, I ran my fingernail along the taped edge where the flaps met at the top, and it popped open like a jack-in-the-box.

21

When we were little, Michael and I would wake up around four a.m. on Christmas morning, our alarms set to "sneak mode" — a special feature of any child's internal clock — and tiptoe downstairs to inspect all the goods our grandparents had laid out under the tree after we'd gone to bed the night before. I remembered on at least two different occasions Michael went into the kitchen and came back with a spool of wrapping tape and a sharp kitchen knife — a definite violation of my grandmother's strict kitchen rules.

I can still feel the terrible thrill of it. He would already have selected the best present, either the biggest or the heaviest, and with the calm dexterity of a gourmet chef he'd set upon it with confident ease, skillfully carving his way in, taking extra care not to cause any irreparable damage.

I, on the other hand, followed the rules. I

never said a word in protest, though, and I never ratted him out. I just sat there and watched, part appalled, part delighted, while he inspected whatever gift was inside and then expertly wrapped it back up good as new. Then he'd put it back in its place under the tree and we'd slink back upstairs to lie in our beds for a few more restless hours.

Not once did it ever occur to me that I could easily have done the same thing with one of my presents, and strangely enough, I didn't want to. I didn't want to spoil the surprise. When Michael and I finally did come downstairs, sleepy-eyed and innocent as can be, that look of delight on my grandparents' faces was well worth the wait. It's still one of my most treasured memories.

Now, sitting there on the bench just inside the Kellers' front door with Mrs. Keller's package sitting on my lap, I was reminded of that rush of guilty excitement. I also wondered if I might need to call Michael for a little help wrapping it back up.

The box was packed with soft, crumpled tissue paper printed with red and black block-cut shapes, sort of like stylized cave drawings. As gently as possible, I removed some of the tissue from the top and laid it on the bench next to me. Underneath was a shiny silver dome that at first appeared to be some kind of mirror, but after I removed more of the surrounding tissue I realized it was the lid to a squat, glazed clay jar about the size of a cocoa tin and held in place with a piece of thin red twine.

"Dammit," I whispered as I pulled it out of the box and turned it on its side.

It was heavy, probably about ten pounds or so. I removed the twine and lifted the lid, and inside was nothing but sand — except it was bright yellow. The same bright yellow, in fact, as the cornmeal that Barney had found in the garden.

I whispered under my breath. "No way . . ."

As eccentric as Mrs. Keller was, I seriously doubted she would ever have paid, as she put it, a "small fortune" for a jar of cornmeal. It had to be something else. I don't know what frankincense looks like, or myrrh, for that matter, but I figured it had to be something like that, or some kind of ancient incense . . . maybe Cleopatra's eye shadow? Nefertiti's talcum powder?

I shook my head as I tied the lid back down and lowered the jar into the box with a sigh. It didn't much matter anymore, because one thing was certain — it wasn't a stone statue. I looked up to find Barney Feldman sitting like a sphinx in the doorway to the hall and watching me with his eyes narrowed to tiny accusing slits.

I said, "It's not what it looks like."

I doubt he believed me, and I couldn't blame him. It was *exactly* what it looked like: I had opened Mrs. Keller's package and snooped through it. I'd been so certain there was a statue inside. For a split second, I imagined Lizette opening the front door and finding me sitting there like a common thief. I imagined her saying she'd have to report my illicit activities to the Kellers . . . and then I stopped myself.

At that very moment, I realized it was high time I gave myself a good talking-to.

As quickly as possible, I stuffed the tissue paper back in, muttering under my breath the whole time. "Are you out of your cotton-picking mind? This is the about the silliest thing you've ever done in your entire life. Seriously? You're sneaking around in people's houses opening up their things?"

Myself replied, "What was I supposed to do? I needed to know what was inside."

I stood up and marched the box into the kitchen. "And now you know. Feel better?"

Myself shook her head. "Not really."

"Well, let that be a lesson to you."

I frowned. I had no idea what I meant by that or exactly what lesson I thought I was trying to teach myself. All I knew was that I felt like a complete fool.

I found a roll of tape in one of the kitchen drawers and sealed the box back up, and as I passed back through the living room I noticed Barney had returned to his patch of sunlight and was sound asleep. I didn't want to wake him up with another kiss good-bye, so instead I gave Dick Cheney a contrite nod as I set the alarm.

Back in the Bronco, I put the package in the passenger seat next to me and announced out loud, "No more."

I was done trying to figure out what had happened. If I'd found an ancient figurine inside that box, then maybe I would have had a different attitude, but failing that, there was nothing to prove I hadn't fainted and dreamt the whole thing. I told myself I was lucky I hadn't gotten through to Mrs. Keller, because if I'd told her my whole cockamamie story she'd think I was nuts.

At the stop sign, I turned right on Calle Florida and took it all the way to Beach Road. Then I headed north along the coast to my next client. Just as I passed the turnoff to Ocean Boulevard, my phone rang and I nearly jumped out of my seat. I didn't even look at the caller ID before I answered it.

"Mrs. Keller?"

"No, this is Wilfred Paxton. I'm calling for Miss Hemingway."

He sounded younger than what I would have imagined for a man named Wilfred, and there was a slight British clip to his voice.

I said, "I'm so sorry, yes. Mrs. Keller told me you might call."

"Yes, brilliant. I believe she asked you to meet me at the gallery?"

"She did, and I'll be there at three."

"Yes, that's why I called. I'm afraid my flight was canceled and I had to take a plane to Miami. I'm waiting for the connecting flight to Sarasota now."

I pulled over to the side of the road in front of Beach Palms, a tiny bungalow hotel that faces the ocean. In Florida, it's perfectly legal to talk on the phone while you drive, but I'd recently been rear-ended by a young woman who was too busy talking on her phone to be bothered with watching the road. Other than a cut on my lip and some tears, we were both fine, but I interpreted it as a subtle warning from the powers above. Ever since then I've tried to be a little more careful.

I said, "Not a problem at all. I didn't realize you don't live here."

"I do. I'm just returning from a buying trip in the Andes. My plane arrives this afternoon, and I should be at the gallery no later than five."

I said, "It's Pineapple Avenue, right?"

"Yes. 3535 Pineapple, just down the street from the Opera House. It's a hideous pink building. You can't miss it." There was a moment of silence, and then he said, "Miss Hemingway, does anyone know you're meeting me today?"

I blinked. "Well, Mrs. Keller knows, of course, but other than that I don't think so. Why?"

"I'm sure it's nothing to worry about, just . . . the item you're bringing, it's quite valuable."

"Don't worry, Mr. Paxton, it's safe with me." I started to ask him what the yellow powder was in that clay jar, but I decided for now it would be better not to confess that I had opened it. Instead, I said, "I promise I won't let it out of my sight."

"Very good. I'll see you then."

I dropped the phone back down in its cup holder and rested both my hands on the steering wheel. Right in front of the Bronco was a squat palm tree, and there was a small red-crested woodpecker making her way around its fat trunk, hunting for insects. To my left, on the other side of Beach Road, was an open field of sand, filled with sea oats, pencil trees, wild yucca, and patches of prickly pear leading all the way down to the beach, and to my right was the little white picket fence that surrounds the Beach Palms' back patio. There were four blue-and-white-striped lounge chairs lined up in a row, and I considered getting out of the Bronco, hopping the fence, and stretching out in one of them for the rest of the day. I thought if anyone asked what I was doing there, I'd smile pleasantly and order a Corona with a wedge of lime.

I looked down at Mrs. Keller's package on the seat next to me and sighed. There'd been something in Mr. Paxton's voice, a nervousness perhaps, that I didn't like one bit, and I was beginning to wonder what the hell I'd gotten myself involved in. There are all kinds of powders in this world, powders that aren't necessarily valuable because they're rare or ancient or may have come from Cleopatra's makeup kit, but because they can be produced with relative ease and sold to users and dealers for outrageous amounts of money.

Not that I thought for one second that Mrs. Keller's new hobby was dealing in illicit drugs, but it did make me wonder if she herself had the slightest idea what in God's name was inside that jar.

22

As soon as I walked into the Village Diner and saw the look in Tanisha's eyes, I should have known something wasn't right. She was in the kitchen, her big round face framed in the order window, and when I waved to her, instead of waving back and winking like she normally does, she shook her head slowly and frowned.

There was an elderly couple in front of me, standing by the cash register waiting to pay for their breakfast and holding hands. The man was tall and good-looking, his silver hair neatly combed over to one side to cover his bald spot, and the woman was wearing a baby-blue poodle skirt with two pink appliquéd flamingos at the hemline on either side. Her shoulder-length gray hair was held up in the back with a matching pink hair clasp, and I muttered a silent prayer that when I was her age I looked half as fabulous as she did.

Just then Tanisha came through the swinging door of the kitchen, holding both hands up and massaging the air in front of her like she was trying to soothe a rabid dog. She's built like a linebacker, almost as wide as she is tall, and the elderly couple in front of me practically flung themselves into the aisle to let her through.

She said, "Now, Dixie, don't be mad, but I got somethin' to tell you."

"Oh, no. Please don't tell me you're out of biscuits . . ."

"No, nothin' like that. In fact, before you say another word I want you to know I got two big fat cheese biscuits warmin' in the oven especially for you."

Tanisha is a kitchen genius. Usually by the time I slide into my booth she's already got my breakfast started, and without even asking she makes my bacon exactly the way I like it — practically burnt to a crisp with no yucky white spots on it — but the way she was acting made me think she was worried about something more important than my breakfast.

I said, "Tanisha, why do you look so upset?"

She glanced up and down the counter and then lowered her voice. "Okay, you and I both know I got a big mouth, right?"

I narrowed my eyes. "I don't know where you're going with this, but for now let's say I don't disagree."

"It's just that poor child is so bad off, and I can't stand to see her suffer any more than she already has."

My arms went limp at my sides. "Tanisha, what the hell are you talking about?"

With a sigh she closed her eyes and tilted her head slightly toward the back of the diner. There, in the last corner booth normally reserved for me, was Sasquatch.

"Tanisha . . ."

"I know, Dixie, I'm real sorry. It's all my fault."

"What is she doing here?"

"Well, you know she lives right up the street from me, and all this business with her man gettin' killed and all, well those cops told her you and me is friends, and that's how you knew where to find Levi yesterday because I told you where he lives. Or lived . . ."

"Oh, no . . ."

"Oh, yes, and so she comes over last night, she's terrible upset, and she told me how she was so mean to you and says she wants to apologize, and then the next thing I know I tell her you're here every morning and now she shows up out of the blue wantin'

233

to talk to you!"

As discreetly as possible, I glanced again toward the back. Mona was sitting perfectly still, her shoulders pressed squarely against the back of the booth. I couldn't quite tell if she was watching us, or if she was completely lost inside herself.

I pivoted around so my back was to Mona and said, "Tanisha, you don't understand. This is not good."

"I know, I know. I was just as surprised as you when she came through that door, but what could I do? I can't tell the poor thing to go home."

"Look, I'll explain it later, but I think you better call the police."

She took a step back. "Huh? What do you mean?"

"Tanisha, what happened to Levi yesterday . . ."

I couldn't quite figure out how to tell her what I was thinking, but I didn't need to. I saw it register in her eyes.

"No."

I nodded. "It's possible."

She looked as if she might burst into tears. "Oh, Dixie, are you sayin' what I think you're sayin'?"

"I could be wrong, but it's possible she's dangerous, so we need to stay as calm as possible. I'll go talk to her, but I want you to walk back to the kitchen like nothing's wrong and call 911 right away."

She whispered, "Now, hold on a minute. What if she tries to hurt you?"

I tried to sound as confident as possible. "No, if she wanted to do something crazy she wouldn't have come here. But we shouldn't take any chances. Just go on."

She closed her eyes. "Oh, Lord. I knew I should've stayed in bed this morning."

"You and me both. And by the way, you owe me for this. I'll expect a couple of those cheese biscuits every morning from now on."

"Girl, unless you plan on windin' up fat as me you better think of some other options."

She hustled back to the kitchen while I took a deep breath and thought, *Well, this should be interesting.*

For some fool reason, I grabbed the morning newspaper off the end of the counter as I went by. I needed something to do with my hands. When I folded it under my arm I felt a quick jab of pain in the center of my chest, as if someone had poked me with the tip of their index finger, and then I figured out what it was: the *Herald-Tribune* had already found a replacement for Levi.

Sasquatch was sitting with her arms in her lap and her eyes fixed on the back of the head of the man in the next booth. Her gaze didn't waver, even as I came to a stop at the table. Anybody else would have looked up, but she didn't. Her jaw was set like a vise.

I said, "Umm . . ."

Without looking up, she said, "I'm Mona Duffy. We met before."

She was wearing tight black leggings and a large blouse buttoned up to the neck. It was white, with pink and red dots in crisscrossing lines forming a faded plaid pattern, and I noticed the dots were actually tiny cartoon strawberries. Her dyed magenta hair was messed and flattened on one side, and her eyes were bloodshot and puffy.

She extended her hand. "Tanisha told me I could find you here."

For once in my life I couldn't think of anything to say, so I just shook her hand limply and nodded. There was a purple canvas handbag on the bench next to her, with black fringe along the seams, and I noticed it was propped open. The shoulder strap was gathered into a neat coil next to it.

She said, "I need to talk to you."

I laid the newspaper down on the bench

and slid in next to it, glancing at the headline on the front page. It read: "Ringling Circus to Hold Local Clown Auditions!" in big bold letters, and for a few blissful nanoseconds I wondered what my chances were. I glanced around the diner looking for Judy, but luckily she was already headed to the table with a pot of coffee and two menus.

My eyes met Mona's, and for a few surreal seconds I think we both realized how strange it was to be sitting across the table from one another, especially considering how we'd met. Emotions were moving across her face like storms across a continent — fear, grief, anger — and I wouldn't have been surprised if she'd been up all night crying.

I said, "Mona, I can't tell you how sorry I am about Levi."

Her eyes narrowed. "Oh, really?"

Before I could react, Judy interrupted, her voice bright and cheerful. "Coffee?"

I nodded as she laid the menus on the table and flashed us a big toothy smile, as if everything in the world was completely hunky-dory. She filled Mona's cup first and then mine.

"You ladies know what you want or do you need some time to think?"

I said, "Maybe just a few minutes, thanks."

Judy nodded pleasantly, but as she turned to leave I could tell she was watching me out of the corner of her eye. As soon as she was out of hearing range, I said, "Look, I know we didn't get off to a very good start, and I don't blame you for being suspicious, but you have to trust me. I had absolutely nothing to do with what happened to Levi."

She was quiet for a moment. "Then what were you doing there?"

"I told you. I was just checking on him."

"Why? What did he tell you?"

I could hear a note of desperation in her voice, and it occurred to me that she wasn't here for revenge or a confrontation or anything like that. Just like me, she was looking for answers.

I said, "He didn't say anything. I didn't even talk to him that morning. I was just worried something was wrong."

A blush of scarlet appeared on her neck. "I don't get it. What do you care?"

"Well, I've known Levi for a long time. We went to high school together, and —"

Her lips curled, "Oh, I get it."

"No, it's nothing like that. We were just friends, and we weren't even that close."

"Then how'd you know something was wrong?"

I sighed. "That morning, I was at a client's house and somebody attacked me, at least I thought they did, and I was worried Levi might have seen something. I was worried that whoever attacked me might have followed him home, and . . ."

Tears suddenly welled up in her eyes and her lips began to quiver.

"Oh, honey, I'm sorry. I know how hard this must be . . ."

She squeezed her eyes shut. "You don't know."

I took a breath. "I do. I was married once . . . I know what it's like to lose someone you love."

She shook her head and her voice dropped to a whisper. "It ain't like that . . . and anyway, it don't matter now . . ."

She put her elbows on the table and buried her face in her hands just as Judy went past the booth to the back corner. There was a wooden high chair and a couple of folding trays leaned up against the wall, and as she clattered the trays around pretending to organize them, she caught my eye and mouthed, *You okay?*

I gave her a quick nod and said, "Judy, can you do me a favor and tell Tanisha I said never mind?"

She came around the corner of the booth

with one of the trays. "Never mind?"

"Yeah, when I came in I gave her . . . my order. Can you just tell her I don't need it anymore?"

She glanced at Mona and then back at me. "Are you sure?"

"Yeah, it's fine."

"Okay, I'll tell her."

As she headed back for the kitchen, I looked back at Mona. She'd taken her hands away from her face and put them on the table in front of her. There were red stripes running down her cheeks where her fingers had pressed into them.

I said, "You told me someone came home with Levi the night before . . ."

She nodded slowly. "Yeah, he always had different girls. Always out drinking with his friends and partying. I tried to ignore it, but . . ."

"Do you know who she was?"

Her eyes narrowed. "I don't know. Maybe. He was going through a rough time."

"Was it about his father?"

Her face darkened. "What do you know about it?"

"I have a friend who's an attorney. He represents Levi's father with some stuff."

She didn't look completely convinced. "Well, I don't trust lawyers any more than I trust cops."

"I trust this one. He's a very good friend."

Her voice flat, she said, "I lied to that detective."

I said, "I know you told them it was me, but there's no need to apologize. I probably would have thought the exact same thing. And anyway, I used to be a sheriff's deputy. I promise you no one thinks I had anything to do with —"

"No . . . I mean I lied about me and Levi."

The blush of pink on her neck had spread across her face, and now her entire body started to tremble like a volcano about to explode. It took me a second to comprehend the weight of what she was trying to tell me, but then I felt my heart kick into high gear as a rush of adrenaline shot through my bloodstream. I looked over my shoulder to see if I could still catch Judy, but she'd already disappeared into the kitchen. I was beginning to think maybe I'd called off the cops too soon.

Mona was staring straight ahead, unblinking. I noted her hands were under the table and her purse was standing open on the seat next to her, and as I glanced around the diner I heard Tanisha's voice in my head, *What if she tries to hurt you?* If Mona was about to confess what she'd done, there was no telling what she might do next. At this point, she seemed completely, utterly capable of anything.

Time seemed to slow down to a crawl, and suddenly I was aware of everything around me. There were two young men having an animated conversation in the booth directly behind me, completely oblivious to the drama unfolding right next to them, and I remembered noticing they were sharing a tall stack of pancakes. In the booth directly across the aisle from us were two middle-aged women, business types, one black and one white, both in smart suits and polished high heels, and they were arguing over who was picking up the tab for breakfast.

I tried to keep my voice as steady as possible. I had decided if Mona made a move for her purse, I'd have no choice but to lunge across the table to stop her.

I said, "Mona . . . *what did you do?*"

23

Love is a funny thing. Of all the emotions, it's the most profound, the strongest, the deepest, and last but not least — the *weirdest*. It makes people do things they wouldn't believe for one second in a book or a TV show, and it can transform the purest soul into the most hideous green-eyed monster. The history of the human race is liberally sprinkled with love-crazed fools. Think Napolean and Josephine, Edward VIII and Wallis Simpson, Sid and Nancy, Jon and Kate.

Sitting there in the diner across the table from Mona, I wondered how in the world she and Levi had ever found each other. In high school, Levi had been a star athlete, and there was a never-ending line of girls who would have jumped for joy if he'd so much as looked at them. But Mona . . . she was clearly a mess. Angry, bitter, afraid, and — I was pretty sure — homicidal, too. Luckily, I couldn't have been more wrong about what she was about to tell me.

She'd been silent for a while, concentrating on a spot in the middle of the table. I said, "Mona, if you've done something wrong, for whatever reason, the only way out is the truth."

She nodded slowly, almost like she was coming out of a coma, and said, "It's about Levi. We wasn't engaged."

I said, "Huh?"

She shrugged slightly. "I just made it up."

I took a deep breath. I guess I should have been happy she hadn't just confessed to murdering Levi, which I was . . . but I'm ashamed to admit I was also thinking: *Why me?*

For as long as I can remember, people have felt compelled to tell me their deepest, darkest secrets. Only last week, I was in the frozen food section at the grocery store, and a man standing next to me turned and said, "My daughter hates me." Sometimes I wonder if I shouldn't get one of those T-shirts that says ASK ME IF I GIVE A DAMN.

I said, "Mona, I'm not sure I understand . . . Why would you lie?"

She looked out the window. "When I was little, my parents run off because they couldn't handle me. So my grandma, she took me in, even though things was tough for her, and she took care of me ever since. It ain't been easy for her, due to problems I got . . . health problems and such, and sometimes I get in trouble. Even when I had my baby, I thought she'd kick me out, but she didn't."

Trying my best not to sound shocked, I said, "You have a baby?"

She nodded. "Yeah. Only he ain't a baby no more. He's seven. His name's Ricky. After Ricky Nolasco. He was a baseball player with the Miami Marlins."

I nodded mutely.

She said, "Yeah, I know. You're thinking I'm too young to have a seven-year-old kid."

I said, "No, I wasn't thinking that at all."

"I don't blame you. It's true. And now that I got Ricky, Grandma's been torn up worried about what's gonna happen when . . ."

She stopped abruptly and balled her hands into tight fists. I could tell it was taking all of her strength to keep from completely breaking down.

"Two months ago, the doctor told her she don't have much longer to live, and I know she wishes I had my life more together, but I been fired from every job I ever had. She's scared . . . for me, and for Ricky, too, because when her disability checks stop, it's gonna be bad news. And everybody knows Levi's dad is filthy rich."

I sighed. "And you thought if you told her you and Levi were engaged . . ."

She nodded slowly. "Yeah. And I was right. When I told her, she said she could finally rest. She said she could die happy."

"And your grandmother . . . she's sick?"

"Yeah. She's diabetic."

I nodded. I had a client whose father was diabetic, so I knew a little bit about how hard it can be on the elderly. I said, "Oh, gosh, yeah, that's —"

"But that ain't all. She's allergic to insulin."

At first I wasn't sure I'd heard her correctly. I said, "She's allergic . . . to insulin?"

"Yeah. It makes her so sick she can't get out of bed, like she got hit by a bus, but she has to take it or she'll die. It's a rare condition, like one in a million or something, and they tried all kinds of different drugs but nothing helps. It used to be she had a few good days a week, but as she gets older it just gets worse and worse. We're lucky if she has one good day a month, and now she has to use a walker to get around."

I sat back against the booth. "Mona, I'm really sorry, but I don't know if I'm the person you should be talking to."

"I got nobody else."

"Okay, well, first of all. I don't want to upset you, but as long as Detective McKenzie thinks you and Levi were engaged, you're probably her number one suspect. She needs to know that you lied."

She shook her head. "No. I don't talk to cops. They can all rot in hell." She looked out the window and then back at me. "Sorry. Nothin' personal."

I sighed. "I'm not a cop anymore."

"I know. I wouldn't be here if you was. Tanisha told me."

I was beginning to think Tanisha was right about her big mouth, but I figured I'd deal with that later. I said, "Look, I know it seems like there's no way out, but it's not that bad. You'll just have to tell your grandmother the truth."

"You don't get it." She looked down at her hands, and I noticed her fingernails were chewed to the quick. "I can't. My grandma . . ."

Tears began streaming down her cheeks, and I felt a knot form at the base of my throat. Tanisha was right. This poor girl was truly suffering.

I said, "Mona, I think if you sit down with your grandmother and explain everything the way you've explained it to me, she'll understand. You just have to be brave and tell her the truth. You have to promise her that with or without Levi you'll be okay, that you're strong, and that she doesn't need to worry about you. I know it seems really overwhelming right now, believe me, but maybe there's someone who could be there with you when you tell her. Maybe a friend?"

She shook her head slowly.

"How about a relative . . . ?"

She didn't answer, just stared at her coffee cup on the table. "Tanisha said you're good with problems."

I said, "Umm, yeah, I suppose you could say that."

She looked up at me, her eyes as pleading as a lost kitten's. "Levi was my only friend."

Right away I knew I was done for. I still wasn't quite sure what Mona had hoped to accomplish by coming to meet me at the diner, but I knew one thing for certain: she needed help. I also knew I didn't have the heart to say no. In a strange way, I felt I owed it to Levi.

I said, "Okay, look. I can't believe I'm saying this, but if you want me to be there when you tell her, I will."

She looked completely shocked. "You will?"

"Yeah, I will. But listen, if you won't talk to Detective McKenzie, then I have to. The more she knows about Levi's life, the sooner she can figure out what happened to him, and it would be wrong of me not to tell her everything I know."

She nodded slightly and looked out the window. I had a strange feeling there was something more. It wasn't that I thought everything she'd said about Levi and her grandmother was a lie, or even that I thought she could have been responsible for his death — now that I knew more about her, that seemed unlikely — but I could still hear that voice in the back of my head saying, *Why me?*

I said, "Mona, Tanisha said you came here because you wanted to apologize, but I don't think that's it . . . and I don't think you came here to ask me for help with your grandmother, either."

She shrugged defensively. "It's a free country. I can do what I want."

I lowered my chin slightly and gave her my best *no-more-bullshit* look. "I can't help you if you're not going to be honest with me."

She looked down and was quiet for a moment. I wasn't sure how old she was, probably in her mid-twenties, but it suddenly occurred to me that she was about as emotionally mature as an eight-year-old girl.

I said, "Mona . . . what is it?"

Her eyes started to fill with tears again, and she reached up and wiped them away with her sleeve. "I don't know. Tanisha said you're the smartest person she's ever known . . . and then, you said something that hit me, you know? Kind of like a bullet in my heart, and then I thought Levi must have said something to you . . . I thought that was why you went to his place."

I frowned. "I don't understand. What did I say?"

She turned to me, and I suddenly felt like I had a view all the way down to the bottom of her soul. "It was outside Levi's trailer, you said . . . 'I'm sorry you're so tortured.' "

I put my hands on top of hers. "Oh, Mona. I'm sorry. I was upset, and you have to admit you weren't being very nice."

She shook her head. "No. It's not that. I mean . . . how did you know?"

"How did I know . . . what?"

She took a deep breath and slowly pulled her hands out from under mine. Then she carefully opened the top few buttons of her blouse and parted it to the side.

I gasped.

There on her chest, what I'd originally thought was a tattoo was a field of bruised skin, deep purple, and scattered across it were small dark spots, almost black, each about the width of a pencil eraser . . . or, I realized with a sinking feeling, the lit end of a cigarette.

I whispered, "Mona . . . who did this to you?"

She looked up, her black eyes completely still.

"I did."

I must have been in a complete fog after I left the diner, because I barely remembered talking to Judy or Tanisha except to say that I was fine and that I'd have to explain everything later. As I got behind the wheel of the Bronco, I glanced under the seat where I'd hidden Mrs. Keller's package and then pulled my cell phone out of my backpack. I had already dialed Ethan's number before I even realized what I was doing.

"Hey, babe. What's up?"

I gulped. "Well, I guess this is one of those phone calls where I'm supposed to let you know if something unusual happened."

"Uh-oh. Should I be sitting down?"

"Well, it's not that big a deal . . . I don't

251

think . . . but I just had a little chat with Levi's fiancée. She was waiting for me at the diner."

"What? How did she know you'd be there? And what the hell did she want?"

"Tanisha told her, and to be honest, at first I thought she wanted to hurt me, but it turns out she needs help, like really bad. The whole thing about them being engaged? It's a lie. She made it up so her grandmother wouldn't worry about her."

"Dixie, you do realize what you're dealing with there, right?"

"Yeah, I know . . ."

"I mean, that woman could be danger-ous."

"I know, but Ethan, the thing is . . . she hurts herself."

"What do you mean?"

"She showed me on her chest. She has all these places where she's burned herself with a cigarette, and the skin is all black and blue."

"Oh, man, Dixie . . . I don't like this one bit. Why did she show you?"

"I don't know, except when she came up to me outside Levi's trailer, I said something to her that must have stuck. She was being so nasty, and it just came out of me. I said I was sorry she was so tortured . . . I didn't mean anything by it, but apparently she thought it meant Levi had talked to me about her."

"Okay, first of all, I'm really glad you called . . ."

"I know. I wanted to hear your voice. It was terrible."

". . . but you need to call Detective McKenzie right away."

I paused. From his tone, I knew exactly what he was thinking.

"Dixie, I could be wrong, but a person capable of that kind of violence to herself . . ."

I wanted to say no. I wanted to argue with him and tell him if he'd seen what I'd seen, if he'd looked into Mona's eyes and seen the fear and sadness there, he'd never think for one minute that she was capable of hurting a fly, much less Levi, a man she clearly loved. But of course he was right. I think I was so convinced there was some connection between what had happened to me at the Kellers' house and what had happened to Levi that I was blind to reality.

"Okay. You're right. I'll call McKenzie right now."

"And Dixie, I don't think you should talk to Mona again."

I sighed. I figured this wasn't exactly a

good time to let him know I'd promised to help her. I said, "Duh. What do you think I am, a complete idiot?"

"Ha . . . well, not a *complete* idiot, no."

"Thanks."

"Hey . . . speaking of complete idiots . . . I'm sorry about yesterday."

My throat tightened. "What about it?"

He sighed. "You know, about what I said . . . I was just making a joke. I don't want you to think having kids is on my agenda right away, because it's not. It was thoughtless on my part, I really didn't mean to . . ."

I pulled the phone away from my ear and glanced down at the screen. I said, "Hey, Ethan, this is Detective McKenzie calling me now."

"Oh, okay, yeah."

"I'll call you back."

He said, "Yeah, yeah, no problem."

I flipped the phone shut and dropped it down in the cup holder like a hot potato.

I had agreed to give Mona moral support when she told her grandmother the truth about Levi, but only on one condition: that she have a doctor look at the burns on her chest. She had balked at first, saying there was no way she could afford a doctor since she didn't have health insurance, but I told her I'd pay for it myself. I gave her a lecture on a topic with which I am well familiar — how avoiding a doctor when there's a clear medical risk is totally irresponsible, completely risky, and one hundred percent immature. Of course, I had fully expected her to flat-out refuse, but to my utter surprise she agreed.

I told her I had a friend on the staff at Sarasota Memorial, Dr. Philip Dunlop, and that I would ask him to give her a call. How I came to know Dr. Dunlop is a whole other story, but let's just say he owed me one. I wanted to call him right away, because I knew the sooner Mona got some medical help, the better off she'd be.

In other words, I didn't have time for chitchat with Ethan. I don't usually just flat-out lie to him like that, but I had no idea what he was talking about, and frankly, I didn't want to talk about it.

24

There's a secret club, a sort of underground society, that only people who've lost a loved one know about. There are no membership cards or annual dues or quarterly conference calls or anything like that. The only way to recognize another member is by a particular look in their eye. It's a mix of things — sadness, joy, longing, wisdom — but when you become a member yourself, you gradually develop a talent for recognizing it, sort of the way a sommelier learns to recognize a fine wine with just one sip. When Mona looked up at me, her blouse parted slightly to reveal the damage on her chest, I knew.

It was probably naive of me, but I just didn't think Ethan could be right — that because Mona was capable of such violence to herself, it naturally followed she was capable of murder. In fact, if anything I wondered if it wasn't the exact opposite:

Instead of directing that rage at someone else, she'd pointed it inward.

There was a time — it probably didn't last more than a few hours — when I felt that kind of passionate rage myself. I don't like to think about it because deep down inside I know it was wrong, but more than that, I don't like to think about it because I'm not ashamed.

It was after I left the hospital, after Todd and Christy were taken to the county coroner. I was on my way home. I had driven my department cruiser instead of the Bronco to the hospital. I wanted to get there fast, so I had my lights and sirens going full-blast the whole way. Afterward, once I pulled out of the parking lot of the hospital, after it was over, I kept them off. I wanted to draw as little attention to myself as possible.

I'd gotten info on the man who was driving the car from the responding deputy, and I'd run it through the mobile laptop in my cruiser. I've forgotten it now, or I've pushed it down so far I can't remember it, but I knew his name. I also knew where he lived, and I had a screen-capture of his driver's license.

That night, I drove to his house.

He was ninety years old. It happened in

the parking lot at the Publix grocery store. He said he'd accidentally hit the gas instead of the brake, and that he felt terrible about it. At the funeral later, his son told me his father had cried every day since, but sitting outside his house I didn't know any of that yet, and if I had I'm not sure it would have mattered.

The last words I said to Todd were just before he'd gone to pick up Christy at day care. I said, "We need some milk and Cheerios, and I think we're out of orange juice, too."

The last thing he said to me was, "See you a little after six."

I don't pretend to know how I got there, but I do know what I was doing outside that old man's house at three in the morning.

I was going to kill him.

I feel guilty about a lot of things. I wish I hadn't asked Todd to stop and get stuff for breakfast. I wish I'd gotten it myself earlier in the day. Or, I wish I'd gone to pick up Christy from day care instead of Todd, but I had a headache and I didn't feel like it. I wish I'd told Todd I loved him after he said, "See you a little after six." I wish I had kissed Christy on both cheeks instead of just one when she left for school that morning . . . I could go on and on and on.

But I don't feel guilty about what I wanted to do to that man.

I don't.

As soon as I swung around the dogleg on Higel Avenue toward the bridge to the mainland, I let up on the gas a little bit. I love this stretch of road, mainly because it's festooned with blooming jacarandas and big giant palms that sway in the breeze, their fronds splayed out like fingers. They look like they're handing out high fives to everyone who enters the island, or maybe waving farewell to everyone who leaves it. I always have the urge to stick my arm out the car and wave back, but I know I'd look crazy if I did that, so I keep it inside and wave with my hand below the windows where no one can see.

The homes on either side of the road along here are mostly bungalows and modest shore houses (with a few mansions sprinkled here and there just to remind you where you are) and they're all painted in the powdery palette of the beach — sky-blue, shell-pink, sandy yellow — like the baubles hanging from a baby's nursery mobile or a box of colored chalks.

About the time I got even with Bay Island Park, I heard the distant clang of a bell and sighed. When tourists hear that bell for the first time, they probably look around for the train that's about to cross the tracks up ahead, but the closest thing we have to a train around here is the old "Cherry the Choo Choo" kiddie ride bolted to the sidewalk outside the Village Ice Cream Shop. The bell is the signal the bridge-keeper uses to let everybody know he's about to raise the drawbridge.

There were a few cars in front of me that had already rolled to a stop, so I pulled in behind them and switched off the ignition as the bridge began its slow salute. To my right were five or six sailboats in the bay, lumbering around in a wide circle with their sails furled, waiting to pass through to the Gulf. Luckily, the whole process is surprisingly quick, but it still meant I'd have a good ten to fifteen minutes before I'd be moving again.

I tilted my seat back and considered taking a quick catnap, but I figured now was as good a time as any to call Detective McKenzie. I'm not sure why, but I'd been avoiding it . . . probably because every time I talked to her I felt like a six-year-old on her first day of kindergarten.

She answered on the second ring with a curt, "McKenzie."

I said, "Detective, it's Dixie Hemingway."

"You must have read my mind, Dixie, I was just about to call you. There's something I want to show you. I'm wondering if you're able to meet me at Levi Radcliff's trailer first thing in the morning."

The thought of going back to that trailer made me sick to my stomach, but I said, "Sure, I'd be happy to."

"Excellent. 5:15 alright?"

"Umm, 5:15 . . . a.m.?"

"No. 5:15 p.m. When I use the term 'first thing in the morning' I generally mean at the end of the day."

I stammered, "No, it's fine I . . ."

"Considering your hours, I just assumed —"

I said, "No, no. Of course, it's not a problem. I forget I'm not the only person who's up that early."

"Great. See you there."

I think I managed to say, "Uh," before the line went dead, but that was about it. I sat there staring at my phone in disbelief. Sometimes I wonder how McKenzie ever manages to solve a single case, and not just because she has the social skills of a skunk with OCD, but because she seems entirely incapable of paying attention to anything in the world except what goes on inside her own damn head.

Just then the phone rang again. It was McKenzie.

"Dixie, I believe you called me?"

I rolled my eyes. "Yes. I did."

"Was there something you wanted?"

I thought for a second. "No, I just wanted to hear the sound of your voice."

I heard her laugh, which I think may have been a first for me, and then she sighed. "You'll have to forgive me. It's been a very busy week. What can I do for you?"

"Well, it may not be very useful, but something happened this morning that I think you should know about . . . Mona Duffy was waiting for me at the Village Diner."

I paused for dramatic effect, thinking McKenzie would interject with a *Wow!* or a *Gosh!* to show her surprise, but apparently she wasn't playing along.

I said, "So, I have breakfast there every morning, and Tanisha, the cook, told her what time I'm usually there. Of course, when I walked in and saw her, I was terrified. I thought maybe she was still thinking I was somehow involved with Levi's death in some way, but I was wrong. She just wanted to apologize, sort of . . . Well, to be honest I think she just needed somebody to talk to. But she told me something you should know. She loved Levi, but I'm not sure he felt the same way. They weren't engaged."

I paused again and tried to catch my breath. I realized I was rambling a little, but surely that little tidbit of information warranted some kind of acknowledgment on her part. Finally, I said, "Hello?"

"Yes, Dixie, sorry. I was just thinking. I had difficulty getting Ms. Duffy to talk at all, except to remind me that she has free speech and we live in a free country, so I wasn't expecting this. I was certain you were going to tell me she said something about about Levi's stepbrothers."

"Stepbrothers?"

"Oh. I assumed your friend Mr. Crane would have told you."

I shook my head. I remembered Ethan had been a little reluctant to tell me he was the executor of Levi's father's estate, so I don't know why it surprised me he might have withheld other facts about the case.

I said, "Actually, no, he didn't. Maybe he thought it would be a violation of attorney-client privilege or something like that."

"Well, I suppose that disproves the theory that in the bedchamber there are no secrets."

I felt my cheeks flush. I didn't know whether to be embarrassed or proud, but mainly I didn't know how in the world she knew Ethan and I were, for lack of a better word, "together." But then again, it's a tiny island. Word gets around. Why it wasn't getting around in my bedchamber I had no idea — I'd have to take that up with my friend Mr. Crane later.

McKenzie continued, "It's commendable on Mr. Crane's part that he didn't tell you, but I can't imagine why it would matter at this point. Levi does indeed have two stepbrothers, both from his father's second marriage. It's all laid out in the will. Mona doesn't seem to know anything about them except their names, and considering what you've just told me, that makes a little more sense now. She's convinced they had something to do with Levi's death. He apparently hated them both . . ."

While McKenzie spoke, I looked out the window to my left. There was a man with a bushy white beard leaning over the railing of the bridge. He was dressed in traditional Amish garb — dark blue trousers, light blue dress shirt, suspenders, and a wide-brimmed straw hat with a black grosgrain hatband. Lined up along the railing next to him were four bamboo fishing rods, and he was gently tugging on each of the lines that ran down into the water below.

I closed my eyes and shook my head slowly.

Most of the time I go around thinking the entire world and everything in it revolves around me, but now I was beginning to think I'd let my imagination run right off the tracks. It was obvious. Levi's death had absolutely nothing to do with me or my masked attacker or stolen figurines or anything else that had happened in the Kellers' house. Levi's death had been nothing more than the result of coldhearted sibling rivalry — pure and simple.

I said, "So . . . these stepbrothers, let me guess — they're named in Levi's father's will."

"You don't know them, do you?"

I thought, *I sure as hell hope not.* "Who are they?"

"Paul Radcliff. He lives just outside Bradenton with his girlfriend, I don't know much more about him yet, but I'm meeting him today. The other man's name is Ruben. He lives here in Sarasota. I believe he's a student at State College."

I let out a sigh of relief. "No. I've never heard of them."

"And their mother, Abina Radcliff?"

"Sorry, no. I don't know her, either."

"I'm curious. Did Mona tell you *why* she lied about Levi?"

I nodded. "Yeah. It was so her grandmother wouldn't worry about her. She's apparently quite ill and she's afraid Mona won't be able to take care of herself after she passes away. Frankly, after spending a little time with Mona this morning, I can't really blame her."

McKenzie sighed. "I believe I'd better have a talk with Mona's grandmother. Dixie, you seem to have a talent for drawing things out of people."

I said, "Tell me about it. Plus, Mona's not very fond of cops."

"Yes. I got that impression. Do you know if she's aware that Levi's father killed himself?"

"I'm not sure, but she definitely knew about his money. That was the main reason she lied. She wanted her grandmother to think she'd be rich one day."

There was a long pause. I could almost hear McKenzie thinking over the phone, and I wondered if she was considering the same thing I was. This whole time, I'd thought the only person who might have been in a position to get Levi's inheritance was Mona, but now with Levi's stepbrothers in the mix . . .

McKenzie said, "Dixie . . . if Ms. Duffy contacts you again, I want you to call me right away."

I said, "Um, okay, of course . . ."

"I don't want to alarm you, but I don't think she should be trusted."

"You don't think she's a suspect, do you?"

She sighed. "Before your call, no. But now . . ."

"Wait, I don't understand."

"I would hope you wouldn't. Unfortunately, it's my job to think like a murderer. Levi's stepbrothers are indeed named in their father's will, but only as contingent beneficiaries."

Now it was her turn to pause for dramatic effect, but unfortunately my legalese is a bit rusty. I said, "I have no idea what that means."

"Their mother comes from a very wealthy family herself, so it means they were set for life with or without their father's riches. Levi, on the other hand . . ."

My jaw dropped open. "Wait. You mean Levi was the sole inheritor?"

"He was. But now it all goes to his stepbrothers. It's to be divided among them equally."

"So Mona was right to suspect them."

"Perhaps, except until now I hadn't considered . . . well, I don't know about you, but if I was going to kill a man who stood to inherit his father's fortune, I think I might wait until after I was married to him. When I thought she and Levi were engaged, I considered his murder to be counterproductive to her motives."

I felt my heart sink. "But if she wasn't after his money, why would you suspect her at all?"

There was a pause. "You said it yourself. She loved him."

Just then I heard the familiar clang of the bridge-keeper's bell up ahead as the bridge began its slow descent down.

"Dixie, I'm sure I don't need to tell you that, in the heat of passion, people can be moved to consider all kinds of terrible things . . . things they'd never dream of doing in their right mind."

I turned the key in the ignition of the Bronco and nodded slowly as I raised my seat back in place.

I said, "Good point."

25

When I turned off Old Wharf Way down the main drag of Grand Pelican Commons, the first thing I noticed was the dirt road leading to Levi's trailer. It was blocked off. Before, there'd been a whole line of emergency response vehicles, but now there were only two — a department cruiser and the new mobile forensics unit. They were parked side by side at the front of the road, and just behind them was a string of black and yellow police tape hung between two trees on either side of the entrance.

The fact that Levi's road was now off limits to anyone other than authorized personnel meant that somebody, probably McKenzie, had decided it was a potential source of evidence, although I wondered what in the world she hoped to find there after so many vehicles (including my own) had rolled over it.

The second thing I noticed was a gray

Nissan coupe at the end of the street on the left, right in front of the trailer I'd originally thought might be Tanisha's. Its round tail-lights were glowing red, but then they went out and Mona rose up from the driver's side. She went around to the back of the car and pulled a grocery bag out of the trunk, and then hurried up the narrow path to the front door.

I slowed down a bit, hoping she'd go inside before she saw me. Not that I wasn't expected, but I needed some time to think. For one, when Detective McKenzie had asked me to call her if I heard from Mona again, I had conveniently neglected to mention that I was on my way to Mona's house that very minute. I know it wasn't the most honest decision on my part, but I knew she'd try to talk me out of it, and I didn't think I'd be able to stop her.

I had warned Mona the authorities would have to be told about the true nature of her relationship with Levi, but I couldn't in good conscience tell McKenzie about the wounds on Mona's chest. I just couldn't. For one, I wanted Mona to get help, and I knew if I betrayed her confidence she'd never listen to me again. And two, I think somewhere in the back of my mind I knew if McKenzie had seen what I had seen —

that terrible field of bruised flesh on Mona's chest, pocked with all those cigarette burns — well, I think she would have very wisely jumped to the exact same conclusion that Ethan had: that Mona was a dangerous person, not just to herself, but to everyone around her.

Luckily for me, unlike McKenzie I don't have to think like a murderer. I can go by my gut, and my gut was telling me that Mona needed help — end of story. If McKenzie happened to see me paying a visit to the Duffy residence, then I'd just have to tell her I thought it was the right thing to do.

I pulled in alongside the grass in front of Mona's car and stepped out of the Bronco. There was a deputy sitting in the driver's seat of the department cruiser, the same deputy who'd been assigned to keep an eye on me that first day outside Levi's trailer. More than likely he was stationed there to keep gawkers and reporters away while the crime technicians did their job, not to mention prevent anybody from sneaking in and tampering with evidence. He had his mirrored sunglasses on, so I couldn't tell if he was looking at me or not, but I gave him a little wave as I made my way up the path to Mona's front door.

The path was red brick, lined on either side with alternating clumps of red and white begonias, and I noticed most of them looked a little peaked in the hot afternoon sun, but the lawn was a deep emerald-green. Somebody obviously took a lot of pride in it, and I had a feeling it was probably not Mona. She didn't strike me as the gardening type at all.

The trailer itself was painted a fresh off-white, like clotted cream, with accents of teal-blue around the window frames and along the roof line, and there was a small porch built onto the front, about five feet wide and just as deep, with rows of potted herbs and chrysanthemums around its perimeter. To the right of the front door, hanging from a brass chain, was a carved wooden plaque painted with orange and yellow daisies. They spelled out a greeting that I couldn't imagine Mona uttering if her very life depended on it: WELCOME STRANGER!

I was just about to knock when I heard a little boy crying inside, and then the door swung open and Mona stepped out. She'd put lipstick on that was almost the same Popsicle-red as her hair, and there were dabs of dusky lavender eye shadow under her thin brows and across her eyelids, all of which only made her pasty skin look even paler. I noticed there were beads of sweat on her forehead, and she seemed slightly out of breath as she looked up and down the street.

"Dixie . . . I'm scared."

"I know, but don't be. Everything's gonna be fine. I promise, you can never go wrong with the truth."

"Yeah, maybe. But she's so weak, worse than ever. Maybe this isn't the right time."

I sighed. "Okay, except the problem is I've already told Detective McKenzie about you and Levi."

"Yeah, I figured . . ."

"So you need to tell her now, because if you don't, McKenzie will."

She ran her fingers nervously through her hair and smoothed it down the back of her neck. "That's why I ain't lettin' that detective in this house again."

I reached out and put my hand on her arm to calm her. "Mona, the only thing that'll accomplish is make her suspect you have something to hide. Look, I know this is upsetting, but you have to do whatever you can to help this investigation. The more McKenzie knows, the quicker she'll catch the person who did this."

Her cheeks flushed. "I told her who did it but she don't believe me."

"You mean Levi's stepbrothers . . ."

She frowned. "How do you know about them?"

"Detective McKenzie told me, but she said those kids are rich already. It's hard to imagine why they'd risk everything for whatever money Levi was going to inherit."

She shook her head. "Well, all I know is Levi hated both of 'em . . ."

"Mona, is there anyone else . . . anyone else who might have wanted to hurt him?"

She sighed and looked up at the sky. "Oh, man, where do I start? Yeah, probably . . ."

"Like who?"

"Like every girl he ever screwed over, or maybe every boyfriend and every husband of every girl he ever screwed over. And I know he was hangin' out with some real lowlifes the last couple months, too."

"What do you mean, lowlifes?"

"Sketchy people, comin' and goin' at all hours. He said he wasn't into drugs but it sure looked like he was selling something." She raised one eyebrow and gave me a knowing look. "One of 'em was Mexican. I'm a heavy sleeper, but sometimes I'd hear his Harley go by in the middle of the night."

I figured this wasn't the time to give her a lecture on racism, so I decided to let that go for now. "And did you tell McKenzie about any of these people?"

Just then a voice came from inside the trailer and Mona shouted over her shoulder.

"Yeah, Grandma, I'll be right there!"

Her hand went to the top button of her blouse, as if to protect it. "Dixie, you didn't tell nobody . . . about me, did you?"

I shook my head. "Of course not. That's entirely between us, but you still have to keep your end of the bargain."

"You mean the doctor . . ."

"Yes, and I'm serious. I want you to make an appointment to see him as soon as possible."

She pulled the screen door open and whispered, "I did already."

I nearly gasped as she motioned me in. The fact that she already had an appointment with Dr. Dunlop was a huge step in the right direction. Then once we were inside, I actually did gasp.

Mona looked around the room and nodded. "Yeah. Grandma really likes Christmas."

We were standing in the living room, which was surprisingly nice, but that's not why I was so surprised.

I said, "Oh, my gosh. This is . . . stunning."

Everywhere I looked there were Christmas

decorations, and I mean *everywhere.* There were multicolored glass ornaments hanging from the arms and backs of all the furniture, and there were ropes of tinsel garland wrapped around practically everything, even the legs of the coffee table. Every surface, every shelf, was filled with little porcelain Santas and glittering snow globes and reindeer and elves.

Mona tipped her chin at the couch. "I'd ask you to have a seat, but . . ."

The couch was green-and-white-striped, and sitting shoulder to shoulder from one end to the other were about two hundred snowmen, all different sizes with different-colored hats, and the back cushions of the couch were fringed with row upon row of sparkling glass ornaments. There were even silver and blue stars hanging from the lamp-shades.

I said, "Wow."

Mona rolled her eyes as she made a motion for me to follow her. "Yeah, tell me about it. Christmas and gardening — it's all she cares about."

We went down a short hallway that led off the to the right. The walls on both sides were covered in dark faux-walnut paneling and hung with family portraits, most of them photographs of Mona in pigtails and braces, and mostly when she was a young girl, perhaps nine or ten. There was only one when she was older. In it she was wearing a bright red gown with a scooping neckline, and there was a corsage of white roses perched like a parrot on her left shoulder. She looked happy and glowing, standing all by herself next to a giant urn of cascading yellow gladiolas.

At the end of the hallway was an open door, beyond which was a darkened bedroom with a queen-sized bed next to a small dresser and a lamp made out of an old milk can. There was a single window over the bed, and two layers of lace curtains drawn across it. At first I thought there was nothing in the bed but a jumble of dark blue sheets and blankets, but as my eyes adjusted to the light, I realized there was an old woman leaning against the headboard, propped up with pillows on either side and blankets pulled around her.

Mona switched the lamp on, and the old woman opened her eyes. She was alarmingly thin, her skin almost translucent, and she was wearing what looked like a thick camel-brown winter coat with black woolen mittens on her hands and a red plaid scarf wrapped snugly around her neck.

Mona whispered, "Gran, my friend is here."

She didn't move, but her eyes turned from Mona to me, and at the same moment I realized there was a little boy lying across the foot of the bed with his arms stretched out over the old woman's legs. He raised his head up and squinted at me, his eyes puffy and red from crying.

Mona said, "And this is Ricky."

He immediately buried his face back down in the blankets. I stepped forward and said, "Hi, I'm Dixie."

The old woman's thinning hair was almost entirely white save for a few strands of gray here and there, but it was surprisingly long, almost down to her lap. She nodded slowly and smiled.

Mona said, "Ricky, say hi to Dixie," but he didn't respond.

"He's mad at me."

I put my hands on my hips and said, "Hi, Ricky. I saw you playing on your pogo stick. You're pretty good. I think I'd break my neck if I got up on that thing."

He looked up and smiled sheepishly. "I'm seven. I can teach you."

Mona said, "Yeah, except you ain't allowed to play on it now, are you?"

She gave me a knowing look and then

pointed at the floor. The shag carpet was a plain, off-white beige. It looked relatively new, except when I saw what Mona was pointing at I had to cover my mouth so Ricky wouldn't see me smile.

I said, "Uh-oh."

There was a trail of brown spots, spaced about a foot or two apart. They came all the way up the hallway and around the bed, then went right back down the hall and out the front door. Each spot was perfectly round and slightly bigger than a silver dollar, like the size of, say, the business end of a pogo stick.

Mona said, "Yep. Brand-new carpet. And he knows he ain't supposed to play on that damn thing inside the house. Right?"

Ricky's face was still buried in the blankets, but I heard a muffled, "Yes, ma'am."

"And what happens when you break Gramma's rules?"

He raised his head up, glancing at his grandmother with narrowed eyes. "No TV for a whole day."

"That's right. For a whole day. Now go outside and play, we got adult stuff to talk about."

He sat up. "I can go outside?"

Mona folded her arms over her chest and

sighed. "Yeah, but you gotta come back in when we're done talkin'."

He jumped off the bed and ran to the door.

"Ricky!"

He stopped on a dime and turned around.

"You know the rules. Stay in the yard. And leave that pogo stick where it is."

His face went from utter delight to pure disgust in the blink of an eye. He glanced accusingly at his grandmother, and then stomped down the hallway, slamming the screen door as he went out.

I said, "Aw, poor thing. You know, they make a really good spray-cleaner for carpets. I use it for pet stains. I'm sure it would get these spots right up."

Mona said, "Well, I hope for that boy's sake you're right." Then she looked around the room and nodded, like she was wrapping up a business meeting. "Okay, then, I'll leave you to it. Gran, Dixie has something she wants to talk to you about."

I turned to the old woman and said, "Yeah, Mrs. . . ."

I stopped. Mona had slipped past me quicker than I would've thought possible. I said, "Hold on," but she was already closing the bedroom door behind her.

I turned to Mrs. Duffy, whose expression

hadn't changed, and said, "Wait right here."

I ran down the hall and found Mona throwing her big purple purse over her shoulder as she headed out the front door.

"Mona! No, ma'am. You need to come right back in here . . ."

She turned around and leveled a look at me with determined eyes. "Dixie, I can't."

"Yes, you can. Trust me, everything's gonna be just fine."

She shook her head and lowered her voice. "No, I mean, I *can't*. I got that appointment with your doctor friend. If I don't leave now I'll be late."

My jaw dropped wide open. "Are you kidding me? It's today?"

She nodded.

I sighed. "Okay, great. Except what the heck am I supposed to say? You need to be here when I tell her."

Her lower lip began to quiver, and her eyes suddenly took on that lost-kitten look she'd given me at the diner. It probably wouldn't have worked this time, except now there was a little lost-puppy mixed in as well.

She said, "Dixie . . . please?"

26

I watched through the screen door as Mona got in her car, and after she drove away I folded my arms over my chest and looked around me. There I was, standing in the middle of a veritable stranger's mobile home, in what looked like one of those pop-up Christmas stores that magically appear overnight just after Halloween, and I thought to myself, *How the hell did this happen?*

When I agreed to help Mona, I had pictured myself standing quietly in the corner with a beatific smile on my face while she broke the news about Levi, and then, while they hugged and held hands and dabbed their eyes with the tissues I'd given them, I'd be in the kitchen preparing a nice tray with two cups of chamomile tea and maybe some ginger snaps. I didn't think for one second I'd end up doing all the talking myself.

Part of me was a little relieved, though. I wanted it to be over as quickly as possible. I still had my afternoon rounds to get to, not to mention my appointment with Mr. Paxton at the gallery downtown, and I knew Mona would only have made things more complicated.

When I came back into the bedroom, Mrs. Duffy had rearranged her pillows and was sitting up a little straighter now. She'd taken off her mittens, but her eyes were closed and her hands were folded one on top of the other, as if they were trying to keep each other warm. As I lowered myself down on the edge of the bed, I wondered if hypothermia was a side effect of all the medications she was taking.

I had assumed Mrs. Duffy's room would've been packed to the ceiling with more glass ornaments and Santas and snow globes, but it wasn't. In fact, it was quite spare. Apart from the bed and the side table, there was only one other piece of furniture — a white four-drawer dresser opposite the bed, with nothing on it but a round, hand-embroidered doily and a couple of near-empty perfume bottles.

To the right of the bed was a louvered door, probably a closet, and next to that was the only thing hanging on the wall in the entire room — an antique black-and-white photograph set in a gilded oval frame. It was a portrait of an elderly woman in a high-necked blouse and pointed stock collar. She had deep-set black eyes behind tiny wire-rimmed spectacles, with white hair pulled back in a tight bun. Her expression was somber and grim, but also a tad anxious, which, as I turned to Mrs. Duffy, was exactly the way I was feeling that very moment.

Without even opening her eyes, Mrs. Duffy said, "What is it you want, child?"

I realized until now I hadn't yet heard her speak. I should probably have expected it, but there was a deep sadness in her voice that crushed me. I couldn't imagine what it must have been like to live in constant pain the way she had her entire life, and now to have to deal with all this on top of it.

I said, "So, Mona asked me to talk to you about something."

Her eyebrows raised slightly. "It's about the boy, ain't it?"

I blinked. "You mean Levi?"

"I wasn't sure, but I guessed as much."

I nodded. "Mrs. Duffy, I'm sure you know this already, but Mona loves you with all her heart . . ."

"Ain't no need to sugarcoat it."

"Huh?"

She turned to me and opened her eyes. They were the palest gray, almost like dust on a pane of glass. "I know why you're here, Detective. I may be old, but I ain't dumb. Just tell me straight. Do they think she killed him?"

I said, "No, Mrs. Duffy, it's nothing like that."

For a moment she just stared, perfectly still, and then when she finally looked away I could see tears seeping into the wrinkles around her eyes.

"And I'm not a detective, I'm just a . . . a friend, sort of. Mona asked me to talk to you because she was scared to do it herself."

She dabbed the edge of her sleeve at the corners of her eyes. "I know she's scared. I can see it. And what with her past and all, I just thought . . ."

I said, "No, I promise you it's nothing as bad as that."

"Then what is it?"

"Mrs. Duffy, Mona told me about your . . . situation, and your illness. And she knows you're worried about her, about what will happen to her when you can't take care of her anymore. She didn't want you to think she'd be all alone, so she lied to you . . . about Levi."

She turned to me. "That they ain't engaged? Is that what you come here to tell me?"

"You knew . . . ?"

She nodded. "I known it right away. It ain't the first time she lied, and I'm sure it ain't the last, either. And besides, what would a boy like that want with a girl like Mona?"

I sat back. I couldn't deny I'd had similar thoughts myself, but I wasn't sure how to respond. It sounded horribly cold coming from Mona's own grandmother.

She shrugged her bony shoulders and looked down at her frail hands. "Sounds mean, don't it? But you know I'm right. That poor child fell in love with Levi the moment he moved in. A handsome boy like that, who could blame her? From the minute she told me they was gettin' married, I went along with it, because I knew Mona thought it would give me some peace. And she told me Levi's daddy was rich and they was gonna live in a mansion and all." She shook her head and sighed. "That boy was just using her. Believe me, her life ain't been easy. I wish it was true just as bad as she does."

I shook my head. "She told me all about the sacrifices you've made, how you took her in after her parents ran off."

"That's what she told you, huh?"

I decided to ignore the tone in her voice. I couldn't exactly blame her for being so fatalistic about Mona's lot in life — especially considering the lousy hand she'd been dealt herself — but I wasn't sure I wanted to know more. Instead, I nodded matter-of-factly and tried to figure out a way to politely say my good-byes. I'd fulfilled my promise to Mona, and now I just wanted to get on with my day.

Mrs. Duffy was quiet for a moment. She was staring at the portrait of the old woman on the wall. Finally she turned to me, her eyes narrowed. "I don't know who you are. You say you ain't a cop, but if you really is Mona's friend, you oughta know. Her folks didn't run off. They was taken."

"Taken?"

She nodded. "See that bedside table? I keep a gun in that drawer there. Saturday Night Special. Loaded. That's for the day they come back."

I closed my eyes and took a deep breath. Now I was one hundred percent certain I didn't want to know more, but I was beginning to think it was too late.

"Her folks is both down at Florida State Prison in Bradford. They was supposed to get locked up for life, but I ain't takin' any chances. They're bad."

I felt my heart begin to quicken. I said, "What do you mean, bad?"

"It was Christmas morning. Fifteen years ago now. My daughter, Mona's mother . . . she never liked me much. And that boyfriend of hers, he hated me. It was goin' on three years they wouldn't let me see Mona — my own granddaughter. That ain't right. This is America. I got a right to see my own grandchild. So I got the neighbor boy to drive me over there. They only lived twenty minutes away, down Tamiami Trail the other side of Nokomis. I had a little Mickey Mouse toy all wrapped up nice with a bow and all. I just wanted to see her with my own eyes, but they said no. They said Mona was at a birthday party . . . a birthday party, mind you, on Christmas. They wouldn't let me in."

The sun had dipped lower in the sky. It was streaming through the lace curtains in the window and sending little shimmering flecks of gold all over the room. I could almost see them moving in slow motion across the dark blue bedspread.

"I made the boy drive me around the block. I got out and called from the pay phone at the Shop Mart. Then we went

288

back and watched." Her voice had dropped to a whisper. "It was a lot of cops that come, and it took a while, but they finally found Mona."

I shook my head. I didn't want to know, but I knew I had to ask. I said, "Where was she?"

She closed her eyes and her mouth fell slightly open, almost as if she could see it all in front of her now.

"She was down in the crawl space under the kitchen . . . in a cage."

While I'd been inside Mona's trailer, three towering clouds had appeared in the distance over the Gulf, a trio of lumbering giants as wide and tall as a range of mountains, pitch-black against the brilliant blue sky. Where they floated just above the horizon were vertical bands of undulating color — violet, silver, cerise, charcoal — and even though the sun was still sending long yellow streaks of light across the sky, the air smelled of rain.

It felt like a dream.

What Mrs. Duffy had told me . . . I couldn't even begin to fathom what kind of world Mona had grown up in. My own childhood, at least on paper, was a tragedy. My father died in the line of duty fighting a fire when I was nine years old, my alcoholic mother abandoned Michael and me barely two years later, and I can count on one hand the number of times I've seen her since. As I started up the Bronco and headed for Tamiami Trail, I realized that, surprisingly, Mona and I had a lot in common. No wonder I'd felt such a strange and sudden sympathy for her.

Except . . . in reality, my childhood had been very different. For one, I always had Michael by my side watching over me, and our grandparents gave us everything we could ever have wanted and more. Never, not for one second, did I ever doubt I was loved.

My afternoon rounds were a blur. I know I stopped by the Piker sisters' place, and considering the fact they have nine cats, you'd think I would have at least remembered something from that visit but I didn't. At Joyce Metzger's, I'm sure I took her miniature dachshund, Henry the VIII, for his regular walk around Glebe Park, but I couldn't remember a single thing about it.

All I could think about was the moment I'd first met Mona, outside Levi's trailer, how utterly nasty and angry she'd been. It was as if she moved through the world like a shark, always on the attack, always out for blood . . . and now I understood why. When I told her I was sorry she was so tortured, I had no idea the depth of the troubled waters I was wading into. She was indeed tortured, and from a very early age, and now her self-mutilation took on a whole new meaning: it was all she had ever known.

Now, as silly and potentially dangerous as it was, no matter what Ethan or Detective McKenzie or anybody else might have thought, I was happy I had helped her, even with something as simple as talking to her grandmother. She needed to know that the world isn't a shark tank and that she didn't need to be on the attack all the time.

At some point — it may have been when I was checking on the cats at the Silverthorn mansion — Ethan had called, and later I reminded myself I needed to listen to my voice mail. Then, after I crossed the bridge at Stickney Point and headed up Tamiami Trail, he called again, but he didn't leave a message that time.

I felt bad for not picking up, but I told myself I just had too much on my mind. Plus, I was driving. And I knew I wouldn't be able to give him my full attention. And I had to get a move on or I'd be late for my meeting at the Paxton Gallery. And . . .

I couldn't come up with any more excuses.

To be honest, I just didn't want to talk to him.

Not yet.

I knew it was silly, but I was having trouble. I couldn't get over what he'd said . . . about *our kids.* I'm normally an expert on avoiding things I don't feel like dealing with, but I knew this time it wouldn't be so easy, and the fact that he felt the need to apologize was all the proof I needed. Before, it had been a nonissue — or at the very least an unspoken one — but now it was hanging out there in the open between us, like an unresolved note at the end of a song.

Ethan's a straight shooter. I know that from firsthand experience. He says what he means, he doesn't play games, and he certainly doesn't shy away from the truth, so when he said having children wasn't on his agenda, I believed him. But the problem is, I had an agenda once, too, and I can now say without a doubt in my mind that my so-called "agenda" didn't exactly line up with reality, or, for that matter, with what was really in my heart.

Life isn't that simple. Lived at its fullest, life is full of blind turns and unexpected twists and unlimited possibilities. That's what makes it fun. We should all live our lives not knowing exactly what's around the corner.

But not me. I'm done with surprises. I see my life laid out before me, and it's just one straight, narrow road right to the horizon line.

I don't know if I can do that to Ethan.

He deserves better.

27

You'd think a town as small as Sarasota wouldn't exactly be a hotbed of culture, but it's impossible to overestimate the seductive power of our perfect azure skies and crystalline white sand, not to mention our winter temperatures that hover in the mid-seventies. Artists of every shape, size, and color flock here from all over the world. Writers, dancers, painters, singers, musicians . . . and then there's the clowns.

Ever since John Ringling set up his winter quarters here in the late twenties, the Ringling Brothers and Barnum & Bailey Circus has been as much a symbol of local life as the dolphins that frolic in the waves off Siesta Key Beach. Famous clowns like Emmett Kelly and Lou Jacobs lived and died here, and descendants of the famous Flying Wallendas still call it home (and some are still flying). It's not unusual to roll up to a stoplight and find a clown in full makeup at the wheel of the car next to you.

Plus, all that circus money went right into the local economy, which means we can afford to keep all those artists hanging around. Our museum is top-notch, our world-class orchestra is in its sixty-fifth season, and our Opera House just got a twenty-million-dollar makeover. It usually makes me feel classy just knowing it's there, but as I walked along the Opera House on Pineapple Avenue with Mrs. Keller's package tucked securely under my arm, the only thing I was feeling was . . . well, I think *numb* is a good word for it.

The Opera House is a beautiful old hacienda-style building, with rough stucco walls painted the palest shade of pink, topped with a red barrel-tile roof and guarded by three stately palm trees along the curb in front of it. As I walked by the front entrance, I tried to catch a glimpse inside. Supposedly, the big chandelier from *Gone with the Wind* hangs in the middle of the lobby, but since a ticket to the opera is a little outside my budget, I've never actually been inside to confirm it.

Just next door, dwarfed by comparison, is a beautiful old row house that's been divided into three shops, two stories high and covered in a neatly trimmed blanket of climbing hydrangeas. With its three arched doorways and thick-paneled wooden doors, it looks like something a family of hobbits might live in, or perhaps an illustration from the story of Goldilocks and the Three Bears.

On the left side is a quaint little bistro. It sells the most delicious panini sandwiches — so delicious that I sometimes dream about them — and as I navigated through the iron café tables on the sidewalk, the smell of fresh-baked bread and grilled cheese tried to lure me in. The middle shop is a boutique real estate office, with photos of fancy homes in the window that normally I stop and drool over, but I knew I'd be late if I didn't concentrate on the task at hand.

The last door had an oval lead-glass window in the middle, etched with gold lettering that read PAXTON FINE ART & ANTIQUES, and then in smaller letters underneath, MESSRS. A AND R PAXTON, DEALERS. The doorknob was one of those big brass numbers, polished with age, and when I pushed down on its paddle-shaped handle and gave it a nudge, I nearly banged my head on the door. It was locked.

Inside I could see a black metal music stand holding a framed placard that read BY APPOINTMENT ONLY, but then a woman appeared with a ring of keys in her hand. She was wearing a black long-sleeved silk blouse and linen pants with shiny black stiletto heels and a white leather belt around her tiny waist. I stepped back as she opened the door and smiled.

"Miss Hemingway?"

Her hair was pulled into a neat ponytail, and there was a tiny dried flower tucked over her ear, a pale pink rose. Her big brown eyes were partly hidden behind a pair of black horn-rimmed glasses, but I recognized her right away. I said, "Oh, I think we met before — at the Sea Breeze?"

She shook her head. "The Sea Breeze?"

"We rode up together in the elevator . . . remember? I'd forgotten to pick my floor?"

She smiled and shook her head slightly. "I have no idea what you mean."

I blinked. "Oh. Sorry. I guess I'm mistaken. You look exactly like someone I met there."

She looked up and down the street and then motioned me in. "No need to apologize. Mr. Paxton's just upstairs."

I followed her to a reception desk set inside an alcove on the right, with a low counter and a row of white filing cabinets along the back. As she slipped around the counter, she glanced down at Mrs. Keller's package in my hands and said, "I'm Daniela, by the way. I'm Mr. Paxton's assistant."

I nodded and smiled, trying to look as dumb and agreeable as possible. "It's so nice to meet you, and what a beautiful gallery."

There wasn't a doubt in my mind. She was the same woman — the woman whose necklace I had complimented in Tom Hale's elevator. It was true she looked different in a ponytail and glasses, but her beauty was unmistakable. I was absolutely certain of it, but I couldn't very well argue with her. For whatever reason, she didn't want to admit she'd been there.

Of course, my mind immediately started tossing out all kinds of possible explanations. Maybe she didn't want her boss to know she'd been away from the gallery in the middle of the day, or perhaps she was having an affair with someone in the building, or perhaps she was embarrassed to admit on her days off she earned extra money at the Sea Breeze as a housemaid . . . an impeccably beautiful, luxuriously dressed housemaid.

She lifted up a green leather handbag from under her chair, and as she swung it onto the desk it fell open slightly and out slipped a piece of paper printed with what looked like an airline itinerary or maybe a boarding pass. I remembered she'd said the Catholic cross on her necklace was from Peru, her homeland, and I wondered if maybe she was planning a trip home, but I certainly couldn't ask her about it — especially when she was pretending she'd never met me.

She folded the piece of paper back into her bag and pulled out a cell phone, glancing up with a tight-lipped smile. "Make yourself comfortable. I'll let Mr. Paxton know you've arrived."

I wrinkled my nose and resisted the urge to give her a *your-secret's-safe-with-me* wink. Instead, I just nodded and smiled some more as I looked around the gallery.

The walls and floors were all bright white, and arranged around the room were a dozen or so glass cases on white pedestals, each about my height, with only one or two items inside and lit from above with tiny spotlights. The closest held two identical clay vases, both about the size and color of an avocado, with tiny looped handles on either side. They were pretty enough, but in another case farther back was something a little more my style. It was a threaded gold chain necklace with an oval-cut yellow sapphire pendant, set in a diamond scroll, like a cartouche, with a pair of matching sapphire earrings.

Or, I guess I should say, *not* my style — I'm not one to gush over expensive jewelry — but it was drop-dead, tail-wagging exquisite. The sapphire at the end of the pendant was as big as a peach pit, and I could feel myself swaying slightly in my Keds as I gazed longingly into its glittering abyss.

"For a hundred thousand dollars, it's yours."

I turned to find a rugged-looking man in a gray pinstriped three-piece suit, an open collar, and gold chains nestled in the dark hair on his chest. He was handsome, with a small mustache and a five-o'clock shadow, but there was something curiously unsexy about him, like he might make a good villain in a cheesy TV movie.

I probably blushed, because I could feel my cheeks turn warm as I shifted Mrs. Keller's package to my left side and held out my hand. I said, "Great. I'll take two."

He held his hand up and waved it sheepishly. "I'm sorry. You'll have to excuse me. I'm afraid I may have caught a cold on the plane and I'd hate to give it to you. I'm Wilfred Paxton. Thanks so much for your help with this."

I said, "Of course, it's my pleasure."

He looked down. "Is this . . . ?"

I nodded self-consciously, certain he could

tell I had opened it, which of course was ridiculous, but as I passed it to him, I literally felt the smile on my face reshape itself into a kind of nervous, guilty grimace.

"Miss Hemingway, is anything the matter?"

"Who, me?" I shrugged and flashed him my best smile. "No, no, I'm totally fine. It's just been a long day, that's all."

"Yes, I completely understand. Well, don't let me keep you." He nodded at the sapphire pendant in the case behind me. "Shall I wrap that up for you?"

I laughed. "I'm afraid I'd never have an occasion to wear it, but I think Mrs. Keller would probably love it. Why don't you go ahead and send it to her and I promise I'll pay you back later."

He grinned, and I noticed his teeth were the same stark white as all the walls and floors. "She seemed rather reluctant to give me her address, so I'm afraid you may have to act as courier again, speaking of which, please do convey my sincere thanks to Mrs. Keller. She's been very patient about this entire debacle. As you may know, she bought this piece at an antique store outside Tampa, but it had already been promised to a client of mine."

I shrugged. "Well, these things happen, I guess."

He smiled. "Yes, it's difficult to find competent help these days."

Over his shoulder, I could see Daniela sitting at her desk. She looked up and raised an eyebrow. Mr. Paxton led me over to her, and at one point he placed his hand in the middle of my back, which made the muscles in my neck and shoulders tighten, but I tried not to let it show.

"Daniela, give Miss Hemingway a receipt of delivery, please."

He turned and flashed that toothy smile again. "And thank you so much for your help. My client will be very relieved."

I nodded. "Of course, I'm more than happy to help. And as soon as I have a hundred thousand dollars I'll come back and pick up that necklace."

He glanced at Daniela and then nodded at me, and then disappeared through a door in the back of the gallery. I almost stopped him. I actually took a breath and started to say, *Wait.* I was dying to ask what the heck that yellow powder was inside that jar, even though I knew if I did it might create more questions than answers.

Daniela pulled a piece of paper from the printer on the corner of her desk, folded it into thirds, and handed it to me. I tried to catch her eye but she avoided me. I was still thinking I might get her to acknowledge that we'd met before, but she was absentmind-edly straightening the papers on her desk. As I said good-bye, she glanced at the door Mr. Paxton had gone through.

All the way to the Bronco, I could still feel his hand on my back, and then I had the strangest feeling I was being watched. Sure enough, as I pulled out of the parking lot, I noticed two men crossing the street opposite me. One was pale and thin, in a dark suit, and the other was squat and bald, in jeans and a sweatshirt, and they were headed for the gallery. Mr. Paxton was standing in the doorway, his face framed in the oval window, his expression completely blank, almost like he was sleepwalking.

I think on any other day, under different circumstances, I would probably have mulled it over for the rest of the evening, trying to come up with some scenario that explained the oddness of the whole meet-ing, starting with Daniela's strange denial that we'd met and ending with Mr. Paxton's odd expression as I drove away.

But thoughts of Mona's awful childhood were still in the back of my mind, and I was starting to feel bad that I hadn't called

Ethan back . . . and not only that, but I didn't think I was going to anytime soon. It was like a quiet panic building in the pit of my stomach.

The only thing keeping me from pulling over to the side of the road and curling up in a fetal position in the back of the Bronco was the thought of Michael and Paco scurrying around in their kitchen preparing dinner. I could see myself taking a seat on the deck our grandfather built, and I could see Paco handing me an ice-cold beer while Michael spooned something yummy onto my plate. I was thinking maybe hushpuppies and fried catfish would fit the bill perfectly.

With that image in my head, I put myself on autopilot. I've crisscrossed this island so many times I could practically do it blindfolded, so all I had to do was keep my hands on the wheel. I barely had to think about where I was going.

Sometimes that's the best way to get where you need to be.

28

Sarasota has a slew of assisted-living homes and retirement communities, and Bayfront Village is the grande dame of them all, even though its main building is about the ugliest architectural monstrosity this side of the Mason-Dixon Line. The outside walls are pink brick and the roof is red terra-cotta tile, which look pretty nice together, except there are Art Deco sunburst patterns painted in a garish turquoise all along the roof, and that's topped with rows of Mediterranean arches and faux-gold Gothic spires.

The fake cobblestone driveway rolls up to a Spanish-style covered portico, held aloft by four Greek columns, and standing guard on either side are two fat-cheeked cherubs, each peeing into his own sparkling fountain shaped like a giant clamshell. Let's just say if Dr. Frankenstein had been an architect, Bayfront Village would be his best-known creation.

But its residents don't give a hoot about the architecture or the similarly jumbled interior decor, because the services at Bayfront are top-notch. A uniformed valet whisks your car away to some climate-controlled location, the glass doors whisper open like magic as you approach, and Vickie, the concierge stationed at a little gold-leaf desk in the middle of the cavernous lobby, phones up to announce your arrival.

I think it didn't fully dawn on me what I'd done until the elevator spilled me out onto the sixth floor and I looked down the hall. My autopilot had apparently thought a visit to Cora Mathers was in order.

Normally she's standing in front of her apartment, waving her skinny arms over her head like an air traffic controller. Right before I knocked, there was a volley of laughter like two tinkling bells from inside.

Cora opened the door and beamed at me. "Oh, my goodness, what a wonderful surprise!"

Cora's in her mid-eighties, but she's the youngest person I know, in spirit at least. She's just shy of five feet tall on her tiptoes, her skin is the color of fine talcum powder, and her white hair hovers above her head like a fluffy puff of smoke. She was wearing white cotton clamdiggers and a silk blouse covered with blue and pink parrots on a bright field of green palm fronds.

"Is it a bad time? I was just in the neighborhood and thought —"

"Oh, of course not, Dixie. It's never a bad time. You can meet my friend Kate!" She tilted forward and whispered conspiratorially, "She's dumb as a fruitcake and just as sweet."

I followed her in, being careful not to rear-end her as she tottered into the apartment like a penguin. I was already wishing I'd called first — I didn't feel like sharing Cora with anybody — but it was too late now.

Cora's apartment always makes me feel like I'm being cradled. It's airy and cheerful, all wicker and ferns and lace, and the floors are pink tile, with walls a slightly deeper shade of coral. To the left is a breakfast bar with shutters to hide the kitchen, and to the right is an arched doorway to Cora's bedroom.

She looked down at my hands. "Did you forget something? You usually have a few goodies for me, don't you? Some yummy soup from that organic shop or maybe a few juicy peaches?"

I sighed. "I know, but I really wasn't plan-

307

ning on stopping by. I was on my way home and then the next thing I knew . . ."

She shook her head sadly and made a clucking sound.

"What?"

"I just this minute put out a fresh-baked loaf of chocolate bread to cool, but it hardly seems fair to offer any when you're arriving so empty-handed."

As far as I'm concerned, Chicago has its pizza, New Orleans has its gumbo, and Siesta Key has Cora's chocolate bread. She makes it in a bread machine that's probably as old as I am, and the recipe is top secret. I'm completely addicted to it.

I jutted my jaw forward and raised my hand up in a tight fist under her chin. "Listen, old woman, I ain't leavin' this building without some of that damn bread."

She giggled. "Oh, dear. Such violence. All right, then, go on in and introduce yourself to Kate. I'll fetch an extra teacup."

There was a tan elderly woman in a yellow pantsuit perched on the tuxedo sofa at the other side of Cora's glass-topped coffee table. She wore her jet-black hair in a short bob, with a necklace of white beads and two white disk earrings the size of sand dollars. Despite the fact that she looked every bit as old as Cora, when I entered the room she stood up with surprising vigor. Her lips were bright vermilion, her eyelids pale blue, and her arching eyebrows were drawn in with a thin black pencil.

She thrust her hand out and flashed a set of perfectly straight white teeth, and for a second I thought she could probably do a mean impersonation of Liza Minnelli if she put her mind to it. "Charmed to meet you, I'm Kate Spencer."

She had a firm grip. "Hi, I'm Dixie. Cora always speaks very highly of you."

She looked me up and down, appraising me like a steer at market. "Well, the ol' girl is right — she always says you're a right pretty one."

She had a thick Texas drawl. I said, "Aw, that's nice. I actually pay her to say that, but thanks anyway."

She blinked. "You pay her?"

I waved my hand in the air as I sat down in one of the chintz armchairs opposite her. "No, no! I'm just joking."

She was holding her mouth open in a half smile, almost like she was waiting for the joke, and then nodded. "Honey, how old do you think I am?"

I pulled a couple of errant hairs that had fallen across my face and tucked them behind my ear. "Oh, gosh, I'm so terrible at guessing ages, I have no idea."

"Guess! I bet you'll be surprised."

Cora came shuffling in carrying a tray with a teacup and a fresh loaf of chocolate bread. "Dixie, she's a hundred and ten."

Kate fluttered her fingers in the air like she was shooing a fly. "Oh, now, shush, Cora, be quiet."

"Kate, Dixie doesn't want to guess how old you are."

Kate clapped her hands together and interlaced her fingers. "I'm ninety-three!"

I figured I'd play along and act surprised, which wasn't too hard because the woman looked easily ten years younger. I shook my head, "That's amazing. I would've been way off."

She grinned from ear to ear. "I know it. Cora's just jealous."

Cora nodded as she filled my cup. "You're right about that."

I laughed. "Oh, stop. I say every woman in this room is a total knockout."

Cora shook her head as she lowered herself down in the chair next to me. "Well, one out of three ain't bad. Dixie, tell Kate about your hunka-hunka."

"My what?"

She made a *speed-up* motion with her

hand. "You know . . . your man, your hunka-hunka."

"Cora, please tell me you did not just call Ethan my hunka-hunka."

"Well, you won't let me call him your boyfriend, and I believe I recall you told me not to refer to him as your beau."

I said, "Well, that may be, but hunka-hunka is worse!"

She rolled her eyes at Kate. "Oh, Lord, such a preoccupation with labels. What do you want me to call him?"

"I don't know. My . . ."

I looked down. Suddenly there was an awkward silence and I felt a muscle in my cheek twitch slightly. Cora's smile faded. That's the problem with having a friend like Cora. She sees right through me.

"Dixie, what's the matter?"

I looked down and smoothed the wrinkles out of my shorts. "It's nothing. I've had a rough week, but I'm sure you girls have better things to do than sit around and talk about my dumb problems."

Cora wrinkled her nose. "Dixie, we're two old dames having tea. We've got nothing better to do."

"Well, it's completely stupid. I wasn't even thinking about it, but since you ask . . . the topic of children has reared its ugly head."

I turned to Kate, thinking perhaps I needed to offer some sort of explanation, but she had already pivoted toward the window and was staring intently out at the bay with her teacup poised just inches from her lips. I got the distinct impression Cora had already told her all about my sordid past.

I was waiting for Cora to say something like, *Oh, poppycock!* or *You're thinking too much,* but she didn't. She was just sitting there watching me, her pale blue eyes reflecting the light from the windows. Finally, she nodded slowly and sat back in her chair with a sad sigh.

"I see."

I gave her a kind of hopeless smile. "Yeah, that's exactly how I feel about it."

"Tell me what happened."

I shrugged. "I think I'm actually making a mountain out of a molehill, because really when you get right down to it, *nothing* happened. We were just talking, and I threw a carrot at him — don't ask why, I was just being silly — and he made a joke about kids . . . *our kids.* He didn't mean anything by it, I don't think, but just . . . the words *our kids* . . . I don't know. It's ridiculous, but it really got to me."

Cora frowned. "You threw a carrot at him?"

"I told you not to ask why."

She reached out and tore a piece off the loaf of chocolate bread and laid it on the plate next to me. Immediately the room filled with the luscious scent of melted chocolate and butter.

She said, "All right, first of all. It's not ridiculous. It makes perfect sense. You're protecting yourself, and no one can tell you that's not the right thing to do. Dixie, did I ever tell you about my little Buddy?"

I glanced at Kate. She was still gazing out the window, but now she was slumped a bit, and at the mention of the name Buddy she sighed audibly. I wondered if the burst of energy she'd summoned to meet me had worn her out. I looked back at Cora and shook my head.

"Well, when I was a little girl, all I wanted was a puppy. You know, something to hug and love and take care of. But my daddy said no. He was a strict man. He said it was all he could do to keep the farm going, and he always said we didn't have the money for another mouth to feed that didn't earn its keep."

I realized my hands had torn a bit of chocolate bread off the piece that Cora had put on my plate. The moment it touched my lips, I felt a wave of warmth wash over my entire body. It was that good.

Cora paused and gave me an expectant look.

I nodded. "I'm listening!"

"Well, one morning my mother took me to town with her. Oh, I must have been about nine or ten years old. We stopped by the hardware store to pick up a case of jelly jars, and they had a basket of guinea eggs sitting by the woodstove — a nickel each! And they came with instructions for hatching, too. Well, lo and behold, my mother bought me one of those eggs, and I kept it cupped in my hot little hands the whole way home.

"For weeks I hovered over that darn egg like its own mama, making sure it didn't get too cold or too hot, keeping the air around it all nice and moist with a little misting bottle, and talking a blue streak to it. I even sang hymns to it on Sunday morning! My daddy just shook his head. He said it would never work and it was a waste of a good nickel, and he said the poor thing would just die in its shell without a real hen to hatch it proper.

"Well, Dixie, guess what? My daddy was dead wrong. That little guinea grew up to be big as a watermelon, and she followed me everywhere, pecking at my shoelaces and hopping up on my shoulder. Oh, my goodness, I loved that little bird. And she ate ticks and fleas in the yard and laid eggs, too, so my daddy couldn't say Buddy didn't earn her keep."

She slid her cup toward me and I filled it from the teakettle. I looked down at my plate and my piece of chocolate bread was completely gone. There was nothing left but a few crumbs, which I picked up with the tip of my finger like a bird pecking at seed on the ground.

Cora was watching me. I said, "Okay, then what happened?"

"One day I came home from school, and Buddy was nowhere to be found. I looked everywhere. She especially liked to roost in one of the apple trees we had out behind the house, but she wasn't there, so finally I found my poor mother upstairs. She was in bed with all her clothes on, taking a nap in the middle of the day, and I can tell you nothing like that had ever happened before. Right off the bat, I knew something was wrong."

Her eyes turned misty. "Turned out my daddy had killed poor Buddy. Wrung her neck. And not only that, but he was expecting my mother to make guinea stew for supper. He told me he was sorry, but that it was high time I learned a lesson, and that lesson was: don't ever get too attached to anything, and that way you can't ever get hurt."

She gave me a little nod and then popped a bite of chocolate bread in her mouth with a little wink.

I was staring at her with my jaw hanging open and my eyes wide as saucers. I said, "That's it?"

She nodded. "That's all she wrote."

I looked over at Kate, who appeared to have dozed off in the middle of the story, her teacup perched precariously on her lap. I said, "Cora, that is hands down the most depressing story I have ever heard in my entire life."

Her eyes sparkled as a tiny smile played across her lips.

"I know it."

29

Halfway down the driveway, I thought I saw fireflies flickering in the leaves and branches deep in the woods, but as I pulled the Bronco into the carport next to Paco's truck, I realized what I'd seen was the tiki torches around the perimeter of the courtyard. The big table in the middle was crowded with glassware and china, and Michael and Paco were buzzing around inside their kitchen. I raised both my hands over my head and did a little victory dance in the car before I got out, then I bounced up the steps to my apartment two at a time. As soon as I got inside, I threw off all my clothes and collapsed on the bed.

I hadn't been lying there five seconds when I heard a tiny plaintive, *"Meep?"*

Ella Fitzgerald's not allowed outside by herself. She won't run away — she's just as much a homebody as I am — but it's way too dangerous out here for a cat. Being an island, the Key is safe from the occasional panther or alligator our landlocked neighbors may have to contend with, but there's a whole cadre of predators up above: owls, eagles, falcons, ospreys, and red-tailed hawks. They patrol the sky like fur-seeking drones in search of four-legged critters, so Ella's only allowed outside when there's human supervision.

I sat up, thinking maybe Michael had brought her over so she wouldn't slip out the kitchen door while they were setting the table, but then I looked up to see her big tawny eyes staring down at me from the window that runs along the top of my bedroom wall. She was sitting on the sill outside. I slid the screen open and she hopped down onto the bed and stretched herself into a fluffy Halloween cat.

"Ella, who said you could go outside this time of night by yourself?"

She said, *"Thrrrrr,"* as I sat down next to her, and then she gave the back of my hand a sandpapery kiss and purred like a tiny jackhammer as she crawled into my lap. That's the thing about cats. It's hard to be in a bad mood around them. You can feel as cold and lonely as a piece of dry toast, but the minute you hear that soft purring, something opens up inside you and makes the world seem like a nice place to be after all.

There were clumps of wet sand between her toes, which meant she'd probably been down on the beach hunting for crabs and minnows. I took her into the bathroom and rinsed her paws under the tap, which she did not appreciate one bit but didn't put up too much of a fight, and then I dried her off with a spare towel. I was about to put her down when I caught the scent of something delicious wafting up from downstairs. I looked at Ella. She was cradled in my arms, her nose and whiskers quivering.

I said, "You hear it, too? Is that Michael calling us down for dinner? Okay, let's go see."

She twisted out of my arms and ran ahead into the closet, where she licked her damp paws with a vaguely accusing look in her eye while I put on a yellow V-neck tee and a pair of soft faded jeans, the cuffs of which I rolled up over my calves — I was already thinking I might take a nice quiet walk along the beach before dinner. Then we both scampered out and down the steps.

There was a cornflower-blue cloth laid over the table on the deck, with the silver candelabra that's usually on our grandmother's piano holding court over an artful arrangement of china and wineglasses, all reflecting the dancing flames of the tiki torches. There was a long white platter heaped with Paco's white bean and radish salad, topped with paper-thin slices of red onion, chunks of fresh mango, capers, and chopped parsley.

I couldn't resist. I picked a piece of mango out and popped it in my mouth, at which point I think I actually moaned out loud.

"Dixie!"

Michael was standing behind me watching me lick my fingers like Ella cleaning her paws. I must have jumped a foot in the air.

He frowned. "Funny, I don't remember announcing dinner."

"I know, but Michael, I'm totally starving."

He had a ceramic bowl the size of a satellite dish balanced in one hand and a bottle of white wine in the other. He said, "Good for you. Now I want you to back away from the table, and if you know what's good for you, you'll stay away until I say it's ready."

I glanced longingly at the bowl he was holding. There was a mound of pencil-thin asparagus stalks, all lined up with their tips pointed at me and glistening with melted butter, resting on a bed of baby greens sprinkled with toasted pine nuts. Next to that was a heap of crispy sweet-potato fries, sprinkled with ground pepper and freshly grated parmesan cheese. For a brief moment I estimated the size and weight of the bowl, trying to figure out how far I could run with it before he caught me.

I sighed. "Okay, fine. I'll just sit here and suffer."

I reached out for another piece of mango and Michael slapped my hand away. I folded my arms over my chest.

"Ugh! How much longer?"

"What are you, five years old?"

I was about to ball my hands up in fists and stamp my feet in response, but suddenly there were tears in my eyes. I tried to laugh it off. "Well, apparently yes."

"Wait, what's the matter?"

"Nothing, nothing, I'm fine. You just wouldn't believe the day I've had. It's been one hundred percent crazy."

He frowned and looked me up and down as he handed me the bottle of wine. "Okay, first pour yourself a glass of this, and then tell me what happened. How's your head?"

I picked up one of the glasses. "It's fine. Still a little tender, but the swelling's almost completely gone."

"Well, that's good, at least."

While I was filling my glass, he pulled

another chair over to the table and then looked at his watch.

I said, "So . . . I don't even know where to begin."

He nodded absentmindedly. "Crab cakes."

I said, "Huh?"

He raised his eyebrows, and I immediately knew he wasn't even listening to me. He said, "What?"

Michael and I have been through a lot together. I think I can safely say nobody knows me better, and normally I can read him like a compass. I guess I'd been so caught up in my own day that it was taking me a little longer than usual. He was nervously straightening the silverware around the table.

I said, "Where's Paco?"

"He's inside. We're eating a little early tonight."

I said, "Okay," and then we both fell quiet.

When you live with an undercover agent, especially somebody like Paco, who's often involved in high-stakes criminal investigations, you learn to speak in code. It's practically a foreign language. All the words are in English — they just have double meanings.

For example, I didn't need to ask where Paco was. I could see him standing over the griddle in the kitchen. What I'd meant was more along the lines of, *You seem nervous.* And what Michael meant by saying we were eating a little early was that Paco was working tonight, and probably leaving shortly after dinner.

Ultimately, what it all meant was that Michael and I would be walking around on pins and needles until Paco got back home, which might be hours or it might be days, you never know. Michael's shift at the firehouse started in the morning — he works two days on and one day off — so that meant he'd get to throw himself into his work, but for me, I figured I'd better enjoy having some big strong men around the house while I could.

It was then that I noticed the table was set for four. I said, "Hey," and pointed at the chair Michael had just dragged over to the table. That was code as well. It meant, *Hey,* but with a subtle reference to Ethan.

Michael nodded as he headed back to the kitchen. "Yeah, he's having dinner with us."

"Oh, I wasn't aware."

He cocked his head to the side, and I could tell he knew that already. "Yeah, he said you wouldn't return his calls . . ."

He left me standing there staring at the table, but then he poked his head out again and said, "Umm," and tipped his chin toward the beach.

I looked out at the ocean to see the silhouette of a man standing at the water's edge, illuminated by the moon. I said, "Is that . . . ?"

He'd already gone back inside and was standing at the griddle next to Paco with one arm hung over his shoulder. I let out a deep sigh as I looked down at my feet, where Ella was gazing up at me with an expectant look on her face. I held my hand out like a cop stopping traffic and said, "Stay." Then I guzzled the rest of my wine and walked down the path to the beach. At one point I looked back, and Ella was following along right at my heels.

Ethan was standing in his bare feet, his pants rolled up over his ankles like mine, and he was gazing quietly out at the water. When he heard me he turned and said, "Hey, there," and reached his hand out.

I folded my fingers in his and leaned into him. "Hey, I didn't know you were here."

"Surprised?"

"No. Michael told me."

He nodded. "I went for a walk and ended up here. That okay?"

"Of course . . . and I'm sorry I never

called you back. I had a really ridiculous day."

He studied my face for a moment, and then he said, "Let's walk."

We took off down the beach, following the line of foam the waves had left along the sand while Ella ran ahead, skittering back and forth, occasionally pouncing on something either real or imaginary, I couldn't quite tell. The sand was still warm from baking in the sun all day, but the cool water felt good rolling over my feet.

Finally, I couldn't take the silence anymore. I said, "So, I guess this is where we talk about kids and the future and all that icky stuff."

He squeezed my hand. "Ha. Only if you want to."

"Honestly?"

He stopped and turned to me with a solemn nod.

I thought for a second. "I kind of don't."

The moon had been momentarily hidden in a bank of clouds, but as we came to a stop they began to part, gradually painting the sky and the dunes all around us in a wash of silvery violet. Ethan turned and looked back up the beach in the direction of the house.

I said, "You think it's a deal-breaker?"

He said, "Huh. I wasn't expecting to hear the words *deal-breaker* tonight."

"I know. I'm just trying to figure out where you are."

He paused for a moment. "I don't know. I don't know where I am."

"So . . . you're saying you're not sure."

We both just stood there, each of us facing in slightly different directions, long enough that it began to feel awkward. Finally, he turned and took me in his arms. He kissed the nape of my neck and then nuzzled his face into the crook of my shoulder, and I felt goose bumps glide all the way down my sides and across the backs of my legs.

He whispered, "I just want to be here for now."

I could feel his heartbeat against my chest, as fast as a drum. "Okay."

He said, "Let's go back."

I nodded and took his hand again, but somewhere in the back of my mind I heard a tiny voice, just barely audible over the sound of the waves lapping up on the beach, the sound that's been the underlying sound track to my entire life.

It said, *We can't.*

30

The next morning, my radio alarm went off bright and early, like it always does, except this time it felt particularly jarring. It may have been that I'd been up late talking to Ethan, or rather, not talking to Ethan, but lying on my side in the dark and staring at the back of his head while he slept. It might also have been the song that was playing on the radio. It was some sort of heavy metal tune, although *tune* seems a bit generous since there didn't seem to be any kind of melody involved — just a cacophony of what sounded like a hundred drum sets, accompanied by a chorus of unintelligible screams and high-pitched wails, all submerged in a cavernous echo chamber of doom. I slapped my hand across the clock's snooze button to knock some sense into it, and then rolled over to see if Ethan was still asleep.

He wasn't there.

While I got dressed, I wondered if he hadn't gone out for an early morning jog, but by the time I backed the Bronco out of the carport there was still no sign of him. I left a note on the kitchen counter, but I was seriously beginning to think he'd gotten up in the middle of the night and gone home. The note just said, *Hey, where'd you go?*

Rolling down the driveway, I flipped the headlights on and a river of fog appeared before me, rolling across the road and into the dark brush in a slow, billowing wave, and just as I was getting the strongest feeling of déjà vu, there was a fluttering of parakeets in the treetops overhead. I was beginning to realize why Detective McKenzie had asked me to meet her so early in the morning.

She had already arrived when I pulled up in front of Mona's trailer and switched off my headlights. Her unmarked car was parallel to the crime-scene tape, next to the police cruiser that was still on duty, and she was standing in the road just beyond it. If I hadn't known better I'd have sworn she was wearing the same clothes she'd had on the last time I saw her: a knee-length skirt the same pencil-eraser-red as her hair, a drab beige blouse with small brown buttons down the front, and a wispy gray scarf tied loosely around her neck. But then I thought, who am I to judge? I've practically been wearing the same exact thing for five years straight.

As I made my way along the dewy grass in Mona's yard, I hoped it was early enough that McKenzie hadn't had any coffee yet. That way her mind wouldn't be in full, spinning-out-of-control, manic-hamster-on-a-wheel mode. But as I got closer, I saw she was holding not one, but two large cups of Starbucks coffee.

She smiled and handed me one. "They open at five, which is why I suggested we meet at 5:15."

"Ha. Thanks, that was smart." I took it from her and nodded.

"Shall we?"

I took one rut in the road and McKenzie took the other, and we walked through the stand of pines toward Levi's trailer. The crickets in the brush fell quiet as we approached, only starting up again once we were well past them, and the palest hint of dusky yellow was beginning to break through the trees to the east — almost exactly the way it had looked that morning Levi had been killed. There was a chill in the air, either from the fog or the place, and I was happy to have a hot cup of coffee to wrap my hands around.

As we got to the edge of the weedy yard, McKenzie slowed to a stop. "So, your friend Mona . . . have you learned anything else from her?"

Right away I knew the deputy outside Levi's place must have told her he'd seen me at the Duffys' trailer the day before. I said, "Yeah, about that . . . I was only visiting. Mona wanted me to help tell her grandmother the truth about her engagement to Levi, and I had a hard time saying no. She was really afraid to do it by herself."

There was a pause, and then she said, "Dixie, I'm sure you're aware that talking to anybody involved in this case only makes things more difficult. I really don't need you to do my job for me."

I gulped. "Detective McKenzie, that's not why I was there. Honestly, I told you, Mona came to me on her own. She just showed up at the diner. She's had a really tough life, and she seems to think I understand her, like I have some kind of special insight or something, and that I'm the only person who can help her."

She nodded. "Not to worry. I just think it's important that we all stick to our roles, yes? And anyway, I'm not so sure she's wrong. Let's have a look at Levi's car."

She turned and walked away, leaving me standing there at the edge of the yard. I wanted to take off one of my Keds and throw it at the back of her head, but luckily I managed to control myself. And anyway . . . she was right. When Mona had asked for my help, I should probably have said no, but it's not like I've never meddled in a criminal investigation before. Believe me, if I had a nickel for every time I've poked my nose in some place it shouldn't be, I could buy a guinea egg for every single person on the planet.

I joined McKenzie where she was standing behind Levi's LeSabre, which was still parked at an angle, its front bumper nearly touching the steps to the trailer. We were about the same distance from the car as I'd been that morning outside my driveway.

McKenzie pulled on a pair of rubber gloves and walked over to open the driver's-side door. Moments later the motor started up and the headlights came on, illuminating the trailer and filling the whole yard around it with a shimmering halo of white mist.

Just then, two glowing clouds of amber red lit up on either side of the rear bumper. McKenzie must have weighted the brake pedal down with something, because the lights stayed on as she walked back over to join me.

I was pressing the rim of my coffee cup to my lips, holding on to it with both hands like a baby bottle. Now I knew for certain why I was here. I remembered McKenzie saying if they could confirm it was Levi outside my driveway that morning it might help confirm the time of death. She must have known we were going to have another foggy morning, and it was those floating fields of red light she was pointing at now.

"This is about how far you were?"

I nodded. "Yeah, I think so."

"It's a 1990 Buick LeSabre. We ran a search, and you could almost count on one hand the number of cars like this in a two-hundred-mile radius, which probably wouldn't mean much otherwise, except for the taillights. They're quite distinct, as you can see. They're almost like two long dashes on the back bumper."

I stared at the blurry red squares floating in the mist, trying my best to compare their shape with my memory of the lights I'd seen that morning, but it was almost impossible.

I shook my head. "It might be the same color and everything, but I can't say for certain it's the same shape. I mean, I just remember two blobs of red light . . . and then it all happened so fast." I turned to her. "I wish I could tell you if it was Levi outside my driveway or not, but I really can't."

Even in the low light and fog, I could tell she wasn't looking me straight in the eye, but at a point just over my left shoulder. She said, "Oh, we know it wasn't Levi."

I felt my breath catch in my throat. "Huh?"

"We know it wasn't Levi. The coroner's examination all but confirms it. And anyway his blood alcohol level was so high he'd have had trouble walking, much less driving. By the time you arrived on the scene, Levi had already been dead for quite some time. In fact, we think he died around two a.m. That's why I wanted you to see his car in a similar light. If there was in fact someone else driving it that morning, there'd be a lot more unanswered questions."

I said, "But that's impossible. I mean, he started his paper route —"

She shook her head. "No. He never showed up for work. I talked to the delivery manager at the *Herald-Tribune.* He couldn't get ahold of Levi, so he delivered the papers himself. He said it took longer than usual because of course he wasn't familiar with the route. He said he had to stop and check the delivery list a number of times along the way. More than likely it was Levi's manager who was parked outside your driveway that morning."

I think my mouth was hanging wide open the whole time she was talking. I said, "So . . ."

She said, "So, what I'm saying is that Levi came home the night before, but I'm relatively certain he never left this trailer again."

I could feel my heart beginning to beat harder in my chest. I said, "Detective, I'm sure you already thought of this, but Mona told me there was a woman with him that night. She said Levi was drunk, and there was a woman with him that she'd never seen before."

She nodded. "Yes. Although Mona didn't tell me herself. One of the neighbors saw a woman in a white sports car, a BMW, with local plates."

My mind was spinning. "Then that's it, right? You need to find that woman. If she —"

McKenzie smiled wanly. "Thanks, but we already did. It was a rental car leased under the name Cohen. It only took a few phone calls to trace it to her."

"Who is she?"

"A tourist. She's renting a condo here for

the summer. She met Levi in a bar. They were drinking, and apparently he could be quite charming when he wanted to be. She came home with him, and . . ."

For the first time, I sensed a crack in McKenzie's confidence. She always struck me as the type of person who held herself at a distance, keeping her cards close and never letting her guard down, but there was something she wasn't telling me.

I said, "And . . . ?"

She sighed. "I could certainly understand why a man might single Miss Cohen out in a bar. She's quite beautiful, and I imagine it happens to her all the time, but . . . she appears to have been in a fight, and were it not for Levi's past record, I don't know if I would have believed her . . ."

"What do you mean, Levi's past record?"

". . . and her fingerprints are all over the trailer, so there's no doubt she was here, but . . ."

"Detective McKenzie, what past record?"

"Dixie, it would appear that Levi may have tried to rape her."

My jaw dropped open. "No. There's no way."

She tilted her head to the side and narrowed her eyes. "Why do you say that?"

"I don't know. I mean, I admit I don't

know much about his personal life, but I can tell you without a doubt . . . I mean, I went to school with him. He's lived here his whole life . . ." My voice trailed away. I could tell by the look on McKenzie's face I was getting nowhere.

She folded her arms across her chest, almost like she was hugging herself. "Assault and battery. Two counts. And six counts of sexual assault, all within the past four years. Dixie, I'm afraid Levi may not have been the person you thought he was."

I stepped back. "That's not possible . . ."

"It's true. In every case, his accuser dropped the charges, but you know as well as I do a woman could have any number of reasons for changing her mind that have nothing to do with the innocence of her attacker. Miss Cohen told me Levi was extremely drunk, so she managed to fight him off, and she has the scratches and bruises to prove it."

I just stood there, shaking my head back and forth mutely.

McKenzie said, "They were seen at Hoppie's Bar the night before. We'll know more after we see the security video from the parking lot of the condo where she's staying. She says she was home just after midnight, which, if the coroner's evaluation is correct, would be hours before Levi was stabbed."

I cringed.

The amount of blood in Levi's trailer should have been enough to clue me in, but I think I'd been doing my best not to think about how he had actually died. This whole time, I'd just assumed he'd been shot, which for some stupid reason seemed less . . . I don't know . . . less *horrible.* The idea that he'd actually been stabbed made me feel a little light-headed, and for a moment I felt like I might faint right there in front of McKenzie. She may have noticed, because she changed the subject immediately.

"Dixie, I asked you here because I wanted you to look at Levi's car, but it wasn't the only reason. Frankly, it's not something I think we could've discussed over the phone . . ."

I just stared at her and nodded.

She cleared her throat. "Normally, this would be way out of line on my part, but I think in this particular case it's warranted, and you seem to have established a certain . . . that is, it seems you know how . . ." She put her hands on her hips and looked down at the ground. "Oh, screw it. You know how to talk to people. And Mona trusts you. I'm afraid she sees me as the enemy, and I'm afraid she's not telling me everything she knows. In fact, I'm certain of it. I'm wondering if you might be willing to talk to her again."

I could feel my eyebrows slowly creeping up my forehead. I said, "So . . . basically, you're asking me to do your job."

She tilted her head to one side and the corners of her mouth rose slightly.

"Yes, Dixie. I suppose that's exactly what I'm asking."

31

When I opened the door at Tom Hale's condo, I heard Billy Elliot's toenails skittering on the parquet floor as he raced down the hall, and then once I got inside he pranced around in a circle, jumping up and lavishing me with kisses. There was a time when I would never have tolerated such behavior. He would have been required to sit quietly while I put my stuff down, and then when I was ready he'd be allowed to greet me, and with all four paws on the floor like a gentleman. But we've been friends for so long. We cut each other some slack now and then.

I found Tom out on the balcony overlooking the Gulf, sitting in his wheelchair with a book and a cup of coffee.

He said, "Billy wants me to tell you you're late."

I smiled. "Sorry, I had an early-morning meeting."

"How's your head?"

"It's all better, at least on the surface."

"That's progress. Did you ever solve your earth goddess mystery?"

I leaned against the doorway and folded my arms over my chest. "Yeah. I did. The whole thing was a dream."

He frowned. "A dream?"

I nodded. "Yep. The attack, the curtains, the whole kit and caboodle. Honestly, I think what happened is, after I fainted, my brain just decided to come up with a more entertaining explanation."

Tom turned in his chair. "What?"

I shrugged. "Believe me, I don't like it one bit. I was hoping if Mrs. Keller had started a collection of those figurines it might mean I hadn't imagined the whole thing, but no such luck. As it turns out, if she's collecting anything, it's old jars of cornmeal."

He slipped his glasses down his nose and peered up at me over the rims.

I waved my hand in the air. "I know. Don't even ask. I'm done trying to figure it out."

"Dixie, if I recall correctly, you told me you slipped on an orange peel."

Billy Elliot raised his head off the floor and looked up at me, his ears pointing out like two radio towers.

I gulped. "I did?"

"Yeah, you did."

"Oops. Sorry. I was probably afraid you'd think I'd lost my mind."

"Well, it's a little late for that." He swung his chair around to face me. "Dixie, I saw something in the paper about a string of robberies in the area . . ."

I crouched down and rubbed the scruff of Billy's neck. "Yeah, I heard about that, too, but trust me, this wasn't one of them. The cops came and checked everything out. There was no break-in, nothing missing. It was all my imagination. I even saw two candles burning in the living room, and I dreamed the guy who hit me was wearing one of Mrs. Keller's masks — a big scary thing with gnashing teeth and weasel eyes, like this . . ."

I made a face, trying my best to imitate Dick Cheney's menacing grimace, but Tom was just staring at me blankly.

I said, "What?"

"Well . . . I don't want to get you all riled up again, but it's funny you say . . ."

I waited. Billy looked up and wagged his tail. "Funny I say *what*? Come on, Tom, this dog needs some exercise."

He closed his book and slowly laid it down on the table. Then he released the locks from his wheelchair and without saying a word rolled right past me. Billy offered a low-pitched, *"Wuff!"* as if to say, *Let's go!* and then followed him in, leaving me standing there on the balcony all by myself.

I looked out at the Gulf. There was a huge white cruise ship making its way south, probably to Key West, and I imagined everyone on board lolling around by the pool half naked with nothing but the sun and the sea to distract them from their daiquiris and margaritas and lobster rolls. I thought about swimming out to them, but instead I went inside.

Tom was at his desk, scrolling through a list of articles on his computer.

"Dixie, I think you better look at this. As soon as you said . . ." He clicked a couple of keys and a picture appeared, and then he pointed at the screen like he was shooting it with an imaginary gun.

It was a beautiful painting of a wizened old woman, with glowing cheekbones and a strong jaw, her gray hair blowing around her tanned face like a wispy halo of ghosts, her blue eyes wise and knowing. There were ghostly ears of corn floating in the air all around her.

With a note of triumph in his voice, he said, "That's Pachamama."

I leaned forward. "Wow. She looks awesome."

"She is. That's one way she's depicted, but she can also look like this . . ."

He clicked a couple of keys and another picture appeared — a small female figure carved out of white stone, bald and big-eared, with soft rounded shoulders and big voluminous breasts.

I said, "Yeah, Tom. I know. You printed that out for me already."

He cast me a sidelong glance and raised one eyebrow. "Okay, except Pachamama is still worshipped today in a number of cultures with all kinds of rituals and ceremonial prayers, and guess what's often sprinkled around her as a devotional offering . . ."

I said, "No . . ."

He said, "Yes."

My eyes must have grown ten times bigger. "Cornmeal?"

He nodded.

I leaned forward to get a closer look, and a shudder trickled down my body. The figurine's face was crudely carved, with very little detail — just two half-moons for eyes, mounded cheeks, and thin Mona Lisa lips — but the overall effect was stunning. It was a combination of raw, terrible power . . .

tempered with peaceful, unadulterated bliss.

"Her devotees use cornmeal as an offering, like a gift, or a show of respect. Usually they'll light a couple of candles and say a prayer, and then they sprinkle it on the ground, like in a garden."

I was speechless. Tom looked at me and said, "You heard me say candles, right?"

I nodded. He closed the picture and opened another article, the title of which was *Pachamama and Modern Culture.*

He said, "Pachamama's actually a very interesting lady. It seems no matter what happens to her, she never gives up. She just keeps on going like the force of nature she is. And believe it or not, the people who worship her today? They're mostly Catholic. They believe Pachamama is actually the Virgin Mary, only hiding her face . . . behind a disguise."

I felt my jaw slide forward as my eyeballs tried to jump out of their sockets. I said, "You mean, like she's wearing a mask?"

He looked up at me. "That's exactly what I mean."

It felt like time had slowed to a crawl. I said, "Tom, these people, the ones that worship Pachamama, where do they live?"

He said, "Mostly in the Andes."

I nodded, fairly certain I already knew the

answer to my next question.

"And Tom . . . where is Peru?"

I was standing next to the Bronco, just around the corner from the Sea Breeze's front entrance, with my cell phone pressed up against my ear. I was still out of breath. I don't think poor Billy Elliot ever had a shorter, more disappointing walk in his entire life, and I'm sure as we were riding back up in the elevator he wondered what the hell he was paying me for, but I promised I'd make it up to him next time with an extra-long walk.

My head was swimming. Those lit candles on the coffee table, the yellow powder sprinkled in the garden, the mask, the statue, Daniela's cross . . . and then I remembered Mr. Paxton saying he'd been out of town on a buying trip in the Andes. There were just too many coincidences. That sculpture I'd seen . . . it had to be real.

It just *had* to.

After the phone rang about six times, there was a quick beep on the line so I perked up, and then, miraculously, I heard the familiar sound of Mrs. Keller's voice.

"Hello, this is Linda Keller. Thanks for calling, but Buster and I are indisposed this week.

Please leave a message and we'll get back to you just as soon as we can."

I took a deep breath, thinking when she heard what I had to say she might never speak to me again. After the beep, I said, "Mrs. Keller, it's Dixie. Listen, I may have some bad news. Could you please call me right away? Everything's totally fine with Barney Feldman. He's doing great and Lizette has been a big help too, but . . ."

I hesitated. I didn't want to say anything that might get Mrs. Keller in trouble with her husband, but he'd have to find out sooner or later and I didn't think I had a choice.

"Mrs. Keller, I know about the urn of cornmeal you bought. I'm really sorry, but I had to open that box — it's a long story, but I needed to know what was inside it. The thing is . . . did you also buy an ancient figurine? Because I think somebody may have attacked me with it in your house, and now I think it's gone. I'm calling the police now, but I need you to call me as soon as you get this."

I hung up and dialed the sheriff's office. It probably would have been smarter and faster to just dial 911, but I knew it would've been next to impossible to explain the whole thing to an emergency operator. I needed to speak to Deputy Morgan directly.

As it was ringing, I heard a soft crunching, which at first I thought was static on the line, but then I realized it wasn't coming from the phone at all. It was behind me. There was someone walking by, and just as their shadow passed, I heard a loud *crack*! — like the sound of a baseball bat hitting a long ball right out of the park.

And then everything went dark.

32

I woke up to a pulsing red blur in the corner of my eyes, fading in and out to the rhythm of my heart. My head throbbed, and my whole body felt like mush, as if it had taken a spin in a blender set to pulverize. I heard a voice in my head whisper, *You're dead . . .* but somehow, in my loopy state of mind, the fact that my ears were ringing seemed proof enough that the voice was wrong.

I could smell bleach and something else, like fresh dirt or clay. I took a few deep breaths to slow my heart down a little, and then the ringing in my ears subsided enough that I could hear muffled voices coming from somewhere nearby. There were men, at least two of them, arguing, and then I heard a woman's voice.

She said, "And then what? Leave her here?"

I had no idea where "here" was. All I knew was that it was dark and really, really cramped. I was enclosed in some kind of box. My knees were folded up against my chest with my shoulders scrunched up around my ears, and my hands were lying limply on top of my knees. All around me were faint circles of light, like blurry stars coming out at dusk. At first I thought I was just seeing things, but then I reached up with one finger and carefully touched one of the stars. It was a hole, about the size of a penny, and the sides of whatever I was locked in were rigid, not cardboard, but metal or hard plastic.

Of course, my first instinct was to scream like a banshee, but I figured whoever it was that had put me here wouldn't be too happy if I started making a bunch of noise, so I kept quiet. I figured as long as they thought I was unconscious — or dead — I had an advantage. It wasn't much, but it was something.

My arms and legs were stone-cold, and as I wiggled my fingers and toes to try to get the blood flowing again, pain shot through my body. I didn't mind, though. It was just further proof that I was in fact alive.

As slowly as possible, I maneuvered my left shoulder out of the way so I could lean my face closer to one of the holes. It wasn't easy, but by pushing my shoulder down and craning my neck to one side I was able to get a view to what was beyond my little cell.

About ten feet away was a cinder-block wall, lined floor-to-ceiling with stacks of dusty cardboard boxes and old cans of paint. I moved my eye to another hole and saw a rolling bucket with a mop sticking out of it, and next to that was a big black duffel bag, about six feet long. In the middle of the wall right in front of me was a wide metal door with a frosted square window in the middle, which I realized was where the light was coming from. I could see the silhouette of someone pacing back and forth beyond it.

Just then the wide metal door swung open and I froze.

Two men walked in. I couldn't see much above their waists, but one was wide and bowlegged, with black loafers and faded jeans pulled halfway over his belly, held up with a braided black belt. The other was taller and thin, in a dark pin-striped suit. He stepped up and knocked the front of my enclosure with the tip of his shoe two times. I smelled something acrid, like kerosene or motor oil.

He said, "Hey . . ."

I held perfectly still, praying with all my

might for the loud pounding of my heart to stop.

He knocked again, this time louder. "Hey!"

It might have been the blood churning past my eardrums or perhaps a fan in the other room, but in the few moments that followed I thought I could hear the steady thrum of passing cars in the distance.

The voice said, "Okay. She's still out."

"Now what?"

"Now we search the Kellers' house." The man's voice was low and growly, with a slight British accent. "But first things first."

There was a pause, and then I heard a light tapping just over my head.

"Our little cat sitter here. I think perhaps she's hiding something. If Paxton was telling the truth and really didn't know where that statue is, it might be worth our while to search Miss Hemingway's home."

The bowlegged man said, "But Mr. Fiori, what if she don't live alone?"

"You'll think of something. The more important problem is we have no idea where she lives."

A woman's voice said, "Yes, we do."

It came from the other room, and then I heard the tapping of heels on the floor. The whole time the two men had been talking,

I'd had my eyes shut and my jaw slack just in case one of them happened to squat down and look through one of the holes, but now I squinted one eye open and peered out.

The woman was slim, in a dark skirt and high-heeled boots, and as she walked up to the taller man I heard a rustle of paper. "Her address is on Levi's newspaper delivery list. Right here — Dixie Hemingway, Midnight Pass Road."

"Brilliant. That bloody list is worth something after all. You stay here and wait. If she wakes up, try to convince her to tell you where it is. And if we find it, we'll call you."

The woman said, "Mr. Fiori, then what?"

There was a brief silence. "We'll load her in the van with Paxton and dump them both in the bay tonight. That's the only way out of this mess. And if we still haven't found that statue, we'll have to schedule a little homecoming party for the Kellers."

The two men walked out, leaving the woman standing next to me in silence, and then I heard a door slam shut. The woman just stood there, not moving, but in a few seconds there was the sound of an engine starting and then a car rolled by outside.

The woman hurried into the other room.

Now I had a clear view of her through the open doorway. I wasn't sure at first, but I thought I recognized the long dark hair tied back in a ponytail. Then she turned toward me and I saw her black horn-rimmed glasses . . .

It was Daniela. I was sure of it. She was wearing the same kind of elegant clothing she'd worn in the elevator at Tom Hale's and the Paxton gallery: a long-sleeved silk blouse with a narrow skirt and knee-high boots. She knelt down and pulled a pair of jeans, black sneakers, and a T-shirt out of a bag — the same leather bag she'd had at the gallery — and then pulled off her boots one by one and stepped out of her skirt.

Even at this distance, I could see long red lines running up and down her legs, almost as if a manic child had attacked her with a felt-tipped marker. She pulled on the jeans and then took her blouse off, and there were the same angry red lines on her forearms. I can't say exactly how long it took me to add it all up, but by the time she'd changed her clothes completely, something clicked.

Barney Feldman . . .

Just then, as if to confirm what I was thinking, she reached into her bag and pulled out something about the size of a softball, wrapped in a dark red cloth, like velvet, and tied with what looked like a braided rope of long straplike leaves. I already knew what it was, but still, when she gently pulled the rope away and unfolded the cloth, my eyes opened wide as saucers.

It was Pachamama.

And not just any Pachamama. She was made of white stone, her head as smooth as an egg, her plump legs folded one over the other, her exaggerated bosom completely out of proportion with her tiny feet, which were painted a bright crimson red . . .

I had to hold my hands over my mouth to stop whatever noise my throat was trying to make, and the pressure made my ears pop. It felt like they'd both been loaded with tiny firecrackers, and my eyes filled with water from the pain of it.

Daniela gazed at Pachamama with such calm that I was reminded of a young mother looking into the eyes of a newborn child. She whispered something that sounded like a prayer, holding it out in front of her with both hands as if offering it up to the sky. After a moment, she folded it back together and secreted it back down in her bag. Before she zipped it closed, she crossed herself, and then hoisted it over her shoulder.

She walked back into the room, and then

I heard the sound of a number being dialed on a cell phone. After a pause, she said, "It's me. Fiori left to search the cat sitter's place."

I could hear a man's frantic voice come over the line as Daniela crossed to the big duffel bag and then back to me. She said, "It doesn't matter. Paxton will never know I was working for Fiori . . . because he's dead."

The voice rose on the phone. "What?"

"Fiori got to the gallery right after the cat sitter left. Mr. Paxton had already opened up the box, and when he showed me there was nothing inside but a jar of cornmeal, I pretended to be just as shocked as he was. But when Fiori found out, he was furious. Mr. Paxton pleaded with him, saying there must have been a misunderstanding, that Mrs. Keller must have accidentally sent the wrong box."

She knelt down, her face inches from mine.

"But Fiori wasn't buying it. He said, 'I know a rat when I see one,' and then he pulled a pistol out of his vest. Mr. Paxton tried to get away but it was too late. He shot him. And when Fiori figures out who the real rat is, he'll try to kill me, too."

There was a pause, and then she whispered, "But by then I'll be home. And soon Pachamama will be back where she belongs . . . with her true people."

I heard the sound of something metal, like a high-pitched shimmering, and instinctively my eyes shot open. She was still crouched next to me, and through the holes I could see she was holding a long gleaming knife. She grasped its base with both hands, and then there was a ripping sound, like tearing flesh. It started down near my left foot and flew all the way up past my head.

I gasped, but whatever sound the knife made must have covered it, because then there was the clattering of metal as it slid across the floor away from me, and then nothing but the sound of Daniela's footsteps receding into the other room.

My heart was racing, and I wondered if now was the time to start screaming. If this woman was about to kill me, my only hope was there might be someone nearby . . . but then I heard the door in the other room slam shut again, and then the sound of a car starting. In a moment, it rolled past and disappeared in the distance.

I waited, counting to ten over and over again and praying I was actually alone. I knew I needed to act fast, but I wasn't sure what my options were. Finally, when I didn't think I could wait any longer, I pressed my legs against the wall in front of me, and to my utter surprise it swung away with ease.

I rolled out in a heap on the hard concrete floor and looked back.

I'd been inside a small refrigerator. It was riddled with what I now recognized were bullet holes. There were three thick stripes running around the exterior, one at the bottom, one at the top, and one in the middle, and as my eyes adjusted to the dim light I realized with a shudder they were bands of gray duct tape. Whoever had put me in that refrigerator . . . they hadn't planned on ever taking me out again. The tape was wrapped layer upon layer all the way around, except where Daniela had sliced it open along the door's edge.

I felt completely paralyzed, but I knew there was no time to waste. It took practically every ounce of willpower I had to crawl toward the door, but as the blood started flowing through my body I started feeling a little stronger and pushed myself up on wobbly legs.

The other room was empty except for an old metal desk against one wall, with piles of bills and newspapers littering the floor around it, and there was an old water-damaged calendar on the wall with a bikini-clad girl firing a big machine gun and flashing a toothy smile at the camera.

Right underneath her, flung up against the wall next to the desk, was my backpack. I practically lunged for it, and then I looked down to find my cell phone and my car keys sitting in the middle of the desk, right on top of a short stack of wrinkled computer printouts. Right next to that was the picture of Pachamama I'd had in my back pocket.

I picked the whole pile up and went to the door, which was just beyond the desk in the far corner. It was painted shiny black, with three commercial-sized dead bolts down the right side. In quick succession, I flipped all three bolts open, hoping with all my might there weren't other locks on the outside, and also that Daniela or some goon wasn't standing guard somewhere, waiting for me to show myself.

With a deep breath, I whispered a silent prayer. If ever I needed a guardian angel on my side — somebody up there in the clouds watching over me — this was it.

I closed my eyes, grabbed the doorknob with both hands, and pulled.

33

The door swung open, and right in front of it, facing me in a blaze of blinding sunlight, was my Bronco.

If there'd been a choir of angels singing I wouldn't have been a bit surprised — I don't think I've ever been more excited by the sight of a car in my life. I didn't even stop to see where I was or if anybody else was there. I just stumbled out into the hot light, guiding myself with one arm along the hood as I made my way around to the driver's side, and then once I was in, I started it up and backed away from the door.

Only then did I realize I was in the middle of some kind of storage compound. There were long cinder-block buildings on either side, stretching almost as far as the eye could see in both directions, with low-slung roofs painted bright brick-red and black metal doors spaced every twenty feet or so.

Each of the doors was painted with a big number in bright yellow. I glanced at the door of the cell I'd been locked in, and as I threw the car in gear, I whispered to myself, "Remember that number."

Then I drove like a bat out of hell.

It didn't take me long to find the exit. It was around the corner at the end of one of the buildings, blocked with a tall chain-link gate, and just as I was thinking I might have to crash right through it, there was a high-pitched whine as the gate automatically rolled open.

Beyond that was a busy four-lane thoroughfare. I pulled to a stop and slowly shook my head back and forth. I think I'd just assumed my kidnappers would have taken me to some creepy remote hideout in the middle of nowhere, but as soon as I saw the hodgepodge collection of fruit stands and thrift stores on the other side of the street, I immediately knew where I was.

It was Tamiami Trail, the main road through the middle of Sarasota, and I was standing at the entrance to Happy Time Self Storage, not five minutes past Grand Pelican Commons.

As soon as I merged into traffic, I had to consciously will myself not to slam the gas pedal through the floor. I wanted to get as far away as possible before anybody saw me, but I didn't want to kill myself or somebody else in the process. At that point I realized I'd been operating on pure adrenaline, because the moment it dawned on me that I was going to be okay, every cell in my body exploded. My muscles must have been in a state of atrophy after being crammed in that refrigerator for God knows how long, and the blood pushing its way back into all the nooks and crannies felt like a thousand stinging needles.

I ignored it, concentrating instead on the road in front of me. My instinct had been to head home, but I knew I couldn't do that, so I headed south out of town. Once I felt it was safe, I pulled into a parking lot off the road and cut the engine. My backpack and the computer printouts I'd taken were sitting on the passenger seat next to my cell phone. I reached over and flipped it open.

It was off, of course. They'd shut it down so it couldn't be tracked, so while I waited for it to power up, I tried to organize the jumble of thoughts and images that were swimming around in my head.

The first thing I saw, looming over me with those intense aquamarine eyes, was Barney Feldman . . . and then I saw the long red scratches on Daniela's arms and legs. Mr. Fiori and his goon may not have known it yet, but she was clearly double-crossing them. Of course, that didn't mean she wasn't fully capable of murder, but for whatever reason, she had decided to cut me loose from that refrigerator. I couldn't say for sure if she'd felt so generous after she'd knocked me unconscious in the Kellers' laundry room, or what her plans had been for me as I lay there on the floor after, but I knew who it was that had stopped her.

It was Barney Feldman.

He had attacked her. He must have sensed I was in danger and put those sharp claws to good use — It was entirely possible that Barney Feldman had saved my life that morning.

I also had a very strong feeling that Daniela was the woman McKenzie had talked to, the woman who'd gone home with Levi the night he died. She'd tricked him into taking her home, and then she'd probably gotten him drunk so she could get her hands on that delivery list. And since she couldn't very well tell the truth about where she'd gotten those scratches, she'd lied and said Levi had tried to rape her — knowing full well he wasn't around to defend himself.

I reached over and picked up one of the

computer printouts and read the heading across the top of it. "*Sarasota Herald-Tribune* — Siesta Key." It was Levi's delivery list, with the names and addresses of his entire route. There were about fifteen names that had been marked with a yellow highlighter, and at the end of each one was a notation: "Stop Delivery."

That list was what Daniela had been after.

There'd be plenty of time to figure out the details later, but for now, it was slowly dawning on me that Levi must have been selling his delivery lists to criminals, who were then targeting any house whose paper had been stopped temporarily because they were on vacation . . . which meant their houses would be vacant and ripe for picking. That would explain the string of burglaries in the area that Paco and Tom had mentioned.

And I couldn't prove it yet, but I now knew it was either Fiori or his goon or Daniela who had stabbed Levi, maybe even with the knife Daniela had used to cut me free. They had murdered him for the same reason they'd murdered poor Mr. Paxton: so he wouldn't talk.

I remembered Mona telling me she knew Levi had been hanging out with some rather shady characters, one of them a "Mexican," and that he drove a motorcycle. I had a feeling I knew exactly who that particular shady character was. He answered on the first ring.

"Dixie?"

I said, "Paco, I know you said this number was only for emergencies, but I'm pretty sure this qualifies."

"What's going on?"

"It's a long story but we need to hurry. When I was leaving Tom Hale's place today, somebody jumped me. They hit me over the head and took me to a self-storage unit south of town, and then they locked me up in a refrigerator."

He said slowly, "A self-storage unit . . ."

As soon as I heard the tone of his voice, I knew my instincts were right. If there happened to be a local ring of thieves selling stolen artifacts on the black market, it was a pretty sure bet that Paco and the Special Investigations unit would be on the case.

I said, "Yeah. There were three of them. Two men and a woman. The woman let me go. I'm driving down Tamiami . . ." I paused, trying to figure out the best way to phrase what I needed to tell him. Being a secret agent, Paco has to deal with crap most people never even dream of, like, for example, the fact that at any given moment somebody might be listening in on his phone conversations.

I said, "Paco, the thing is, Ella needs you."

"Ella?"

"Yeah. She's got company on the way right now . . . and they're dangerous."

I could almost hear his mind working over the phone. He said, "Uh-huh. How do they know where she lives?"

"She's on their list."

"Their list?"

I said, "Yeah . . . their delivery list."

There was a long pause, and then he spoke quickly. "Okay, listen. Call the cops right now and tell them everything. Are you someplace safe?"

"Yeah, I'm fine."

"Okay. Don't go anywhere until you hear from me."

I said, "Paco, be careful."

"Don't worry."

I hung up and dialed Detective McKenzie's number without even thinking. She answered with a short, "McKenzie here."

I took a deep breath. "Detective, it's Dixie. There's no time to explain everything now, but I know who killed Levi. It's a man named Fiori. He was trying to track down an ancient statue called Pachamama that Mrs. Keller bought. I think it was stolen from a museum or a church in the Andes and sold on the black market, and I think it's probably worth way more than she paid for it . . . like millions."

I paused to take a breath and McKenzie said, "How do you know all this?"

"They kidnapped me, and I heard them talking."

She took a quick breath. "All right, where are you?"

I said, "I escaped. I'm in my car, but they think I'm still locked in a storage unit. And detective, there's a body there. It's Wilfred Paxton. He's the owner of the Paxton gallery downtown. They thought he was double-crossing them, but really it was his assistant, Daniela. She's on her way to the airport with that figurine right now. She's trying to take it back home where it belongs."

"What storage unit?"

"It's called Happy Time. It's on Tamiami Trail just south of Sarasota. It's unit number nine. There's a big duffel bag, and his body's inside it."

She said, "Dixie, are you sure?"

"Unfortunately, yeah, I'm positive."

"Okay, I'm sending a unit there now and I'll alert airport security. Where are you?"

I shook my head. "There's one more

thing. Fiori and his henchman . . . they're headed to my house, in fact they may already be there. And I think if you check with the SIB, you'll find they've already sent a team there."

There was a long pause. "Dixie, why are they going to your house?"

"They think I took Pachamama. I was supposed to deliver it to them, but Daniela got to it first and replaced it with a jar of cornmeal."

"A what . . . ?"

"Yeah. It was Daniela that attacked me at the Kellers' house. And those candles I saw? She was performing a ritual to Pachamama. There's even some cornmeal sprinkled in Mrs. Keller's garden outside — that's why those doors were open — but Barney Feldman interrupted her."

"Dixie, I have no idea what . . . I mean, I don't know why . . ."

I nodded. "I can explain everything later."

She sighed. "Okay, where are you now?"

"I'm in my car, a few miles south of Happy Time."

"Where specifically?"

I looked out the window at the sign over the store in front of me. "I'm in the parking lot of Henderson's Liquors."

"Okay, I want you to stay where you are.

I'm sending a deputy straight there. I don't want you on the road alone, do you understand?"

I nodded. "Okay. I'll wait here."

She hung up, and I dropped the phone down in the cup holder and took a deep breath. There was a steady stream of cars rolling by, and it suddenly occurred to me that if Fiori and his henchman came back anytime soon and discovered Daniela had let me go, they'd probably be cruising up and down this very road searching for me.

I started up the car and drove around behind the liquor store, where I pulled in next to a line of old metal garbage cans. Just then, my phone rang. The caller ID read *Sara Mem Ho,* and if I'd been thinking clearly I would have let it go to voice mail, but instead I flipped it open and said, "Yeah?"

The voice on the line said, "Uh, Dixie? This is Dr. Dunlop at Sarasota Memorial Hospital."

I said, "Oh, Dr. Dunlop, I'm sort of in the middle of something, is it urgent?"

He said, "To be honest, yes. It's about Mona. I thought you should probably know."

I frowned. "Know . . . what?"

He said, "I examined her yesterday,

and . . . there's a problem."

"Yeah, Dr. Dunlop, I should have warned you. She's a bit unhinged. I was hoping maybe you'd be able to refer her to a psychologist or something?"

"I already have. She's seeing an associate of mine today, but the reason I'm calling is . . . I don't know if you're aware of the cigarette burns."

"I am. That's why I sent her to you, and I was worried about infection."

He cleared his throat. "Okay, yeah. I mean, I'm not so worried about infection at this point . . . I'm more worried about her situation at home."

I said, "Oh, gosh. I know it's a little hard to believe, but she's actually doing that to herself."

He said, "No."

I blinked. "Yes."

"No. Those burns are not self-inflicted. That's why I'm calling. They're not just on her chest, but across her back as well."

"Oh." I thought for a moment. "Maybe she's reaching around with —"

He stopped me. "No. That's what she said, too . . . but the burns on her back, they're not random. They're arranged in letters. Dixie, I think the police need to be notified. They spell out a name."

I was staring at the line of garbage cans along the back of the liquor store, and the lid on the can closest to me was slightly ajar. Just then, almost as if on cue, something moved, and then a brown rat poked its little head out from under the lid and blinked in the bright sunlight.

I closed my eyes and said, "Dr. Dunlop. What name?"

He said, "Levi."

34

As I drove down the main drag of Grand Pelican Commons and made my way slowly toward Mona's trailer, the sun was already spilling long shadows across the road to the east, so I pulled the sun visor over to the left to shade my eyes.

The street was empty except for a few cars parked here and there, and at the end of the road, just beyond Mona's place, the police tape was still strung up blocking the road to Levi's trailer, but the deputy who had been on guard there the past few days was gone.

Mona's car wasn't in front, and I couldn't see signs of Ricky anywhere except for his pogo stick lying in the lush grass just outside the porch. I noticed it had little red reflective streamers hanging from the handlebars.

Just as I started up the steps to the porch, I had the strangest feeling I was being watched. I looked up to find a great white heron, easily three feet tall, balanced on one spindly leg at the edge of the roof, with his long sharp beak turned to the right, glaring down at me with one hypnotic yellow eye. I got the impression he was trying to tell me to turn around and go home, and then, as if to make his point a little clearer, he turned his beak to the left and glared at me with his other eye.

I opened the screen door and knocked lightly, but there was no answer. I knew it was crazy, but at this point I didn't care. I needed to talk to her. I turned the handle and the door opened with a whisper, and as I closed it behind me, I said, "Mona?"

There was no answer.

I looked around the living room. None of the lamps were on, just the late afternoon light filtering through the windows. The snowmen were all lined up on the sofa watching me silently, and all the tinsel and glass ornaments were perfectly still.

I tiptoed into the kitchen, but there was no one there, and then I moved down the hallway, trying to be as quiet as possible. Mona hadn't yet cleaned up the mud stains off the carpet, and as I made my way to Mrs. Duffy's bedroom I tried not to step on any of them. The door was standing open, and in the dim light inside I could see she was sitting propped up against her pillows, her eyes closed and her mouth slightly agape.

I stepped around to the side of the bed and looked down at her.

Her long white hair appeared to have been recently combed. It fell perfectly straight across her frail shoulders and came to rest at her hands, which were folded together in her lap. The bones of her fingers were almost visible, as if they had been enveloped in a translucent layer of parchment.

I thought about the story she'd told me, how she'd taken that doll to Mona on Christmas morning. I thought about how hard it must have been for her . . . to report her own daughter to child welfare . . . to know she'd brought a child into the world who was capable of such unspeakable abuse.

I could only think that if I'd been in her shoes, I'd have done anything I could to make sure Mona never went through that kind of pain again. *Anything.* I glanced at the closet door next to the bed, and my mind went back to that morning in the diner when Mona had asked for my help. She'd told me all about her grandmother's illness, and how she was getting worse and didn't have much longer to live, and how she could barely get out of bed now, and how, when she did, she needed a walker.

I thought about that morning I found Levi, when I was sitting on his front steps and Mona was passed out in front of me. I had my arm locked in place to keep her from falling down, and I looked up to see that group of children. They'd been playing in the street, but after the ambulance arrived they stood in a quiet huddle at the end of the road, watching. Just beyond them was Ricky, Mona's little boy. He was standing on his tiptoes, straining to see, as if he couldn't go farther, as if he wasn't allowed beyond the edge of his own front yard.

And then I knew . . . Ricky hadn't played with his pogo stick inside the house.

I turned to look at Mrs. Duffy. My hand rose to my mouth as if it had a mind of its own. Her gaunt face became clearer and clearer, and everything around her blended into the background. It was then that I realized her eyes were open, and she was watching me.

She whispered, "Hello, child."

I said, "Mrs. Duffy, I'm so sorry. I didn't mean to disturb you."

She smiled slightly. "You can't disturb me."

"I was just . . . I mean, I came by to see Mona, but . . ."

"She ain't here. She went to talk to a doctor, somebody that can help her. I guess we got you to thank for that."

I said, "Oh, good. I'm glad. She needs help, but then . . . I guess you already knew that."

The smile faded from her lips, and then finally she nodded.

I said, "Mrs. Duffy . . . Ricky's not allowed to leave the front yard, is he?"

Her eyes turned steely, and for a moment we just stared at each other.

I said, "I'm just asking because he seems like such a good boy, and I don't know how he managed to track all this dirt through the house . . . when your lawn is so perfect."

Mrs. Duffy looked down at her hands and stared at them for a long time. When she finally spoke, her breathing was labored, as if every word was an effort.

She said, "The closer I come to leavin' this world, the more I think about my daughter, and the more I wonder. I think what kind of person she was . . . how she could lock up her own child, her own flesh and blood. Lock her up in a cage. Starve her. Beat her. I try to think what I done wrong . . . to make her like that."

Tears began streaming down her cheeks.

She said, "God tried to tell me. He gave me this cross to bear . . . this sickness. He wanted to warn me, to show me I was no good, and that I shouldn't have no children to carry my bloodline on. But I was too proud . . . I wouldn't listen. That's why I know I'm goin' to hell, and I know one day I'll see my daughter there, too. But Mona . . . Mona's different. She's a good girl. She deserves a good life."

Her voice had fallen to barely a whisper, and I found myself holding my breath and leaning in toward her. I said, "Mrs. Duffy . . . when did you know?"

She frowned slightly and turned to me.

"When did you know what Levi was doing to her?"

She took a long breath, and I thought I heard a distant rattling in her chest.

"She come out of the shower. I washed her robe and folded it up with some of her things, and it was there on the dresser. She thought I was asleep, and she come in to get it. That's when I saw . . . that's when I saw that boy's name . . . but I didn't say nothin'."

Her voice trailed away. She looked down and stared at her hands, and for a moment I had the strangest feeling that time had come to a stop. It was almost as if I could see myself in her, and it made me think of my own little girl, and how I was never given the chance to save her. Then something else flashed in my mind . . . it was an image of myself as a little girl, outside Mrs. White's history class with Levi, my eyes wide open as he kissed me.

He didn't even ask. He just took it.

Mrs. Duffy whispered, "I'm tired now. It pulled out all the strength I got left." She closed her eyes. "You go do what you gotta do."

I nodded silently, resisting the urge to touch the top of her hands with mine. Instead, I reached out and carefully slid the door of her closet open. There, inside, was an aluminum walker, folded flat and leaning against a stack of shoe boxes next to an old vinyl suitcase.

The plastic handles of the walker were worn and stained with use, and as my eyes followed the curving metal down to the carpet, I felt the hairs on the back of my neck stand up. Each of the walker's four legs were capped with a white rubber tip, and there was a ring of mud crusted around their edges. It was the same dark clay color as the spots of mud leading around the bed and down the hall . . . the same color, in fact, as the dirt road to Levi's trailer.

Without looking back at Mrs. Duffy, I slid the door closed as quietly as possible, and then walked down the hall and out the front door.

The sky had turned a pale orange, like the creamy glow of a frozen dreamsicle, and the great white heron that had greeted me from the roof had flown down to the yard. He was standing perfectly still now, one leg planted firmly, the other poised in the air, scanning the lush grass for earthworms and grasshoppers.

I had been sitting in the car outside Mona's trailer for who knows how long when my phone rang. It was Detective McKenzie. I let it ring a few more times while I considered letting it go to voice mail, but right at the last moment I flipped it open.

She said, "Dixie. I have a deputy in the parking lot at Henderson's Liquors. He says you're not there."

I said, "Oh. Yeah, sorry. I couldn't wait."

"Okay. Where are you?"

I thought for a moment. "I'm at the beach."

"You're at the beach . . ."

"Yeah," I lied. "I just . . . I felt like everything was closing in on me. I just needed something . . . something big to look at it."

There was a moment of silence, and then she said, "Okay, I understand. I just wanted you to know, Mr. Fiori and another gentleman were caught lurking outside your house by a team of SIB agents. They've been arrested for the murder of Levi Radcliff."

I held my breath.

"Also, I'm at Happy Time Self Storage now, and just as you said, it was indeed Wilfred Paxton in the duffel bag, but you were wrong about one thing. He was indeed shot. He was also gagged, and his arms and legs were wrapped in duct tape, but he wasn't dead. In fact, he's very much alive, thanks to you. We got him to the hospital just in time, and on the way there he confessed to being connected to a worldwide ring of stolen antiquities dealers."

My jaw fell wide open. "You have got to be kidding me."

"I'm not. He told us a very interesting story about Mr. Fiori, the man who kidnapped you. At his direction, that figurine you saw was stolen from a church in a remote village in the mountains of Peru, but the man he paid to steal it decided to sell it himself, and Mr. Fiori has been after it ever since. Paxton was helping him, as was his assistant, Daniela, who not surprisingly has disappeared."

I nodded, imagining Daniela returning Pachamama to her true home in Peru, and I imagined all of Pachamama's worshippers gathered around her, crossing themselves and bowing in prayer.

McKenzie said, "Hello?"

"Sorry, I'm here — I'm just trying to process everything."

"Dixie, do you think you'd be able to identify the two men that kidnapped you?"

I gulped, knowing exactly what she was going to ask next. "Yeah, I can identify them. Where do you want me?"

"Let's meet at my office. I should be there within the next twenty minutes. All right?"

"Yes, of course."

"And after the crime technicians give the clear, I'll need to walk through this storage room with you. I'll need to know everything you saw, every detail, no matter how small."

I looked over at Mrs. Duffy's yard to see if my heron friend was still there, but he'd flown away.

I said, "Sure. I'll tell you everything."

35

Sometimes when I wake up in the morning I open my eyes and I see Christy. She's on the bed next to me. Her head on the pillow, her eyes wide open. They're big and clear blue. She's watching me, her face still and quiet, searching my face for answers the way a child does.

When it happens, I know what I'm seeing is more like a memory than a dream, because it feels real. The day Christy died might as well have been a million years ago, but at the same time, it feels like right now, like all those years are rolled into a tiny ball that I carry like a lump in the breast pocket of one of my sleeveless T-shirts, no bigger than a pebble but as heavy as the world.

In the beginning, when I'd wake and see her on the pillow next to me, her reassuring smile, her wise eyes, I'd cry. But now I just smile back, reveling in the miracle of her face as the edges blend and blur with the sounds of the gulls and the waves rolling in on the beach down below. She usually vanishes after a few moments, and then there comes a moment of gratitude, grief, clarity, silence, guilt . . . guilt that I couldn't give her any of the answers she was looking for.

It breaks my heart a little, and sometimes I spend the rest of the day rebuilding it.

Lately, though, I wonder if maybe I've been reading it wrong this whole time. Lately I wonder if perhaps she's not so much looking for answers as giving them — giving me a little advantage in the world, sending me little clues the way a cat's whiskers send tiny electronic signals to its brain. Like magic.

Like providence.

I was lying in bed, and when I opened my eyes, it wasn't morning at all, and it wasn't Christy there next to me, but Ethan. At first I thought he was sound asleep, his dark lashes still, his lips slightly parted, but then he opened his eyes and smiled sleepily at me.

He said, "Hi."

I smiled back and then his eyes closed and he was almost instantly asleep again, his breathing deep and heavy. I raised my head off the pillow to find Ella curled up in a ball on his chest, one paw stretched out daintily across his neck.

The coroner had examined the knife that Daniela had used to free me from the refrigerator in the storage room. He didn't rule it out completely, but he'd been unable to definitively connect it to Levi's stabbing. Of course, that didn't mean it wasn't still considered evidence, especially since Daniela's fingerprints had been all over Levi's trailer. As it turned out, I'd been right — she was the woman who'd come home with Levi that night.

And now I knew why: She wanted to get her hands on Pachamama before Paxton could hand it over to Fiori, who had probably paid off the owner of the shop outside Tampa for information on who he'd sold it to. Mrs. Keller had told them she'd have her cat sitter return it because she was out of town, but she'd refused to give them her home address.

Daniela must have thought she'd find Mrs. Keller's address on Levi's delivery list, but she hadn't considered the possibility that the Kellers didn't take the morning paper . . . but we've had the paper delivered for as long as I can remember. All it took was a quick look in the yellow pages under "Pet Sitting" to get my name, and she knew

I'd lead her straight to Pachamama.

It hadn't been Levi outside my driveway that morning at all. It was Daniela. And as for the security monitor outside the Sea Breeze, the video files had mysteriously disappeared, so whether Daniela had lied about what time she got home that night was still a complete unkown.

As it stands now, she's wanted for the murder of Levi Radcliff. They still haven't found her, and I doubt they ever will.

Mrs. Duffy passed away quietly in her sleep about a week later. There was a small service, attended by Mona and a handful of neighbors, including Tanisha and her sister. Mona didn't say a word, but I think she was grateful I was there. We never spoke of Levi or Mrs. Duffy again.

The air was warm, and the night-blooming cereus was sending out its sweet, magical scent, transporting me back to my youth, when I'd sneak out of bed in the middle of the night and go out to the courtyard. I'd lie on my back in one of the chaise lounges and stare at the stars. Sometimes I'd wake up to the birds announcing the sunrise, and there'd be a blanket on top of me and I'd have no idea how it got there.

But it wasn't the cereus that had woken

me up now. I realized it was the dream I was having. It's a dream I've had before: Christy is running on the beach. She's wearing a blue one-piece bathing suit under a Disney World T-shirt that I've had since I was a teenager, and she's throwing chunks of bread high in the air and laughing as seagulls swoop in to catch them. Her hair is almost white in the sunshine, white as the seagulls' wings, white as the flashes of light bouncing like diamonds off the rolling waves in the sea.

In the dream, I'm watching her, and I'm thinking in a little while I should make her come back into the shade so she won't get burned.

ABOUT THE AUTHOR

John Clement is the son of **Blaize Clement** (1932–2011), who originated the Dixie Hemingway mystery series and collaborated with her son on the plots and characters for forthcoming novels. Blaize is the author of *Curiosity Killed the Cat Sitter, Duplicity Dogged the Dachshund, Even Cat Sitters Get the Blues, Cat Sitter on a Hot Tin Roof, Raining Cat Sitters and Dogs, Cat Sitter Among the Pigeons,* and *The Cat Sitter's Pajamas.*

The employees of Thorndike Press hope you have enjoyed this Large Print book. All our Thorndike, Wheeler, and Kennebec Large Print titles are designed for easy reading, and all our books are made to last. Other Thorndike Press Large Print books are available at your library, through selected bookstores, or directly from us.

For information about titles, please call:
  (800) 223-1244

or visit our Web site at:
  http://gale.cengage.com/thorndike

To share your comments, please write:
  Publisher
  Thorndike Press
  10 Water St., Suite 310
  Waterville, ME 04901